The Man Who Broke into St Peter's

Chick Yuill

First published in Great Britain in 2018

Instant Apostle
The Barn
1 Watford House Lane
Watford
Herts
WD17 1BJ

Service order taken from the Church of England website
https://www.churchofengland.org/prayer-and-
worship/worship-texts-and-resources/common-worship/holy-
communion#na (accessed 8th May 2018)

Quotations from *The Pilgrim's Progress*, John Bunyan (1628-1688),
available at http://www.ccel.org/ccel/bunyan/pilgrim.html:
public domain.

Quotations from *Alice in Wonderland*, Lewis Carroll: public
domain.

Quotation from *Macbeth*, William Shakespeare: act 5, scene 1.

British Library Cataloguing-in-Publication Data

A catalogue record for this book is available from the British
Library

This book and all other Instant Apostle books are available from
Instant Apostle:

Website: www.instantapostle.com

E-mail: info@instantapostle.com

ISBN 978-1-909728-87-5

Printed in Great Britain

For Marg –
a fiftieth wedding anniversary present

Contents

Prologue

The town of Penford never expects visitors and seldom seems to receive any. Not that it's particularly remote or out of the way. It's less than ten minutes' drive from the motorway and no more than a dozen miles from Manchester on one side and twenty miles from Liverpool in the other direction. But, as folk in that part of the world often say, Penford is the kind of place that isn't really on the way to anywhere, so you'd only go there if you really needed to. And since most folk don't really need to, they simply don't go there. Occasionally some of the bargees from the narrowboats meandering along the canal that skirts the edge of the town will stop off for a drink at a canal-side pub or call in at a shop to pick up some supplies. But nobody thinks of them as visitors. Just passing strangers who might offer a cheery greeting to while away the time before getting on their way again as quickly as they can.

It's not as if there's nothing to see in Penford. For the serious student of history who's willing to look for them, there are reminders aplenty of the town's industrial heritage. Though most of the present-day inhabitants probably wouldn't be aware of the significance of their surroundings when in their cups, they can and do still quench their thirst in the local hostelry where, back in the seventeenth and eighteenth centuries, their ancestors used to bring the rough fustian cloth they had woven in their cottages to be collected by the merchants and middlemen from Manchester. And when it comes to closing time and elderly men and women, having drunk their fill, step unsteadily out of the Penford Arms and into the cool night air to stumble home, they might look up at the imposing five-storey brick building with its impressive stone quoins and distinctive sixteen-paned windows looming over the street. Some years ago it was converted to 'the perfect retail factory outlet' by an enterprising local businessman, but those senior citizens remember being told as children that this was the old mill where cotton and silk were woven until the first couple of decades of the twentieth century. And even the youths who hang around the fast-food restaurants in the evenings will have learned from their parents and grandparents that the rolling stretch of grass at the far end of what is now the shopping precinct was landscaped to absorb the black heap that was disgorged from the old Penford Mine until it was closed in the mid-1970s.

Perhaps that history has helped to forge the peculiar character of the town. For if few visitors make their way to Penford, even fewer locals want to leave it. Why go anywhere else when mills can be built, mines can be sunk and money can be made right where you live? So for more than 300 years a mindset has been so firmly established and a pattern so tightly woven into the fabric of life that only those with eccentric personalities or exceptional abilities have either the strength of will or the breadth of imagination to resist it. *People who are born in Penford stay in Penford*. They grow up there, get married there, raise their children there, grow old there and are buried there. Thus has it been for generations.

Of course, many of them board trains or drive on to the motorway every weekday and commute to Manchester or Liverpool for work. But that's merely a necessary excursion, an unavoidable concession to the hard realities of earning a living in the twenty-first century. By six or seven o'clock they'll be back in Penford, sitting down to their evening meal with their own family in front of their own television in their own front room – back in the familiar and comfortable surroundings of the town they call home. Even when they travel further afield for their summer holidays, their pleasure in enjoying sun and sea in warmer climes is quickly overtaken by their delight in returning to more familiar scenes. 'It was very nice, and great for a couple of weeks' break,' they'll often say, 'but I wouldn't want to live there.'

None of this is to suggest that the forty-odd thousand Penfordians are any more unfriendly or narrow-minded than the majority of their countrymen and women. It would be quite unfair to describe them as *selfish* or even *self-centred*. They have a sense of community that finds expression in the kinds of clubs and organisations you'll come across in most towns of a similar size, and they have an awareness of the needs of the wider world that manifests itself in giving to good causes and even to worthy charities that work far beyond the boundaries of their town. They read their newspapers, watch the news on television and spend as much time online in front of their computers as people in any other place. No, this is neither a particularly *selfish* nor an unusually *self-centred* place. But it is *self-contained*. This is where life happens for most of its inhabitants. Momentous events on the national and international stage are of passing interest, but they form only the backdrop to what really matters – the everyday goings-on in Penford. A dispute between neighbours over where to erect a boundary fence is of greater concern than a major conflict on the other side of the world, and the manoeuvring for power and position in the local council chamber or on the board of the Penford Rugby League Club figures far larger in their consciousness than the intrigues in Westminster or Washington.

It could be argued that in recent times the world has come to Penford. Or, to be more precise, as in many of the surrounding communities, there has been an influx of immigrants to the town, mainly from the Indian subcontinent. And that is true, of course. For the most part, after some initial teething problems, the town has welcomed or at least assimilated these newcomers. They remain a minority within the population and their distinctive customs and devotion to their Muslim faith set them apart somewhat. But they too have very quickly become Penfordians, seeing this place as their home, putting down roots, taking their place in the life of the town, and thinking to themselves that this is where they and their families will settle for the long term. Penford has a way of doing that to people. Most folk hurry past en route to somewhere else, seeing nothing that would cause them to pause, and they go quickly on their way without giving so much as a thought to what it must be like to live there.

But those who do come to Penford usually stay for a lifetime, happy to live out their ordinary lives in a place that's as comfortable as a favourite armchair by a warm fireside on a winter's evening.

All of this Pippa Sheppard learned very quickly on her arrival in Penford some two years before our story begins. Pippa, it must be understood, was definitely not a visitor. The *Reverend* Pippa Sheppard, to acknowledge her clerical status, had been eagerly appointed by the bishop and, at first, grudgingly accepted by her flock as the vicar of St Peter's. Their initial misgivings were aroused only partly by the fact that she was the first woman incumbent since the parish had been established in the middle of the nineteenth century. Much more disconcerting to the lifelong members of the congregation were her comparative youth when she arrived – she was in her mid-thirties – and the fact that she was a southerner. It was even whispered before her induction by the bishop that she was from east London, and the prospect of a cockney occupying the pulpit in St Peter's was more than some of the older parishioners could bear. They might even have transferred their allegiance to another church, had not the rumour turned out to be unfounded. The new vicar, it was learned, had been born and raised in Basingstoke, a town which few folk from Penford had ever visited, but which seemed an unobjectionable place of birth to even the most fastidious of northerners.

The bishop's eagerness to install the new incumbent arose from his assessment that Pippa was a natural pastor, a more than acceptable preacher, and that her relatively tender years would be a happy contrast to those of her predecessor who had passed retirement age and had, in the prelate's view, rather run out of steam in the latter stages of his tenure of office. And so it had turned out. Despite the demands of being a wife and mother to two primary-school-aged children, Pippa had brought an energy and enthusiasm to the task that had quickly endeared her to even the most critical of the worshippers who looked up at her from the pews on a Sunday morning. The contrast with her predecessor went beyond her age and gender. Whereas he had been tall and balding and had carried out his duties with a dignified solemnity, she was no more than five foot four, had shoulder-length dark brown hair, and did everything with a vigour that left some of her flock breathless. Her husband, Joe, was a teacher and was readily snapped up by the maths department at Penford Grammar School, and eight-year-old Harry and six-year-old Zoe soon picked up the accent of the children around them and merged into the life of St Peter's Church School without any difficulty. The Sheppard family and St Peter's were indeed, just as the bishop had predicted, a good fit.

Before she even realised what was happening, Pippa found herself drawn into the close-knit life of the town. She took her place in the Penford Churches Together group that met monthly, assumed the chair of a working party that was focused on developing closer links between different faith communities in the area, became a governor of the adjoining church school, was co-opted on to half a dozen local committees, and generally made it her business to get beyond the walls of the church and engage with local community leaders and anyone else who was involved in working to improve things for their fellow residents. When all of this was set alongside her parish responsibilities, her family duties and the preparation needed by the regular – sometimes she even described it as relentless – rhythm of two or three services every Sunday, there wasn't much time or energy for other interests or pursuits. Monday would have been the obvious day to take off each week, had not Joe and the kids been in school. And though they were all at home on a Saturday, her mind was usually occupied by thoughts of what the following day would demand from her. So often their free time consisted of a couple of hours of playing games with the kids in the nearby park – what Joe called, with a slight raising of his eyebrows and a pained expression, 'family fun time'.

But none of this detracted from their happiness in any way. Pippa and Joe would often remark on the blessings of their life together – two salaries which allowed them to live more comfortably than many people in the town, a house provided by the church which freed them from the worry of mortgage payments, meaningful and satisfying jobs and, most of all, a happy marriage and two healthy children. What's more, there was an unexpected bonus: they had wondered if it might prove difficult to adjust to life in a Lancashire town, but to their mutual surprise they had quickly come to love life in this part of the world. Penford had an unpretentious character that they found surprisingly endearing.

'This place,' Joe would sometimes comment, to his wife's approval, 'doesn't have ideas above its station. It's a solid northern community and it doesn't try to be anything else.'

And for Pippa, there was something about parish life within a self-contained medium-sized town that helped to set manageable parameters to the challenges of her ministry and engendered a sense of hope that it might be possible to make a significant impact. They could understand why her predecessor had remained in post for such a long time and even wondered, although this was her very first time as priest-in-charge, if they might stay long enough for Harry and Zoe to complete their schooling.

And so life in Penford might have continued for the Sheppard family, but for an unexpected visitation just after their second Christmas in the town...

The Intruder

One

An Unexpected Visitation

It was gone eight o'clock on the Saturday morning just two days after Christmas, but the Sheppard family were all still fast asleep. Pippa had gone to bed early, declaring herself to be 'absolutely pooped' after all the additional services and extra demands of the Advent season. Joe was weary from the combination of end-of-term activities at school, generally supporting his wife, looking after the children and taking over the running of the house since the beginning of December. And Harry and Zoe were exhausted after having been allowed to stay up well past their normal bedtimes for several nights in a row.

The doorbell must have rung half a dozen times without the residents of the vicarage waking up, and before any of them could rouse themselves from their well-earned slumbers, whoever was standing outside had begun pounding loudly on the door with their fists. Joe hurried to reassure the startled children, and Pippa threw on her dressing gown. By the time she'd stumbled halfway down the stairs, the bell-ringing and door-knocking had given way to loud shouting.

'Vicar, ye're wanted in the church. I think we've got a problem an' I'm no' sure whit to dae aboot it.'

Pippa's heart sank as she recognised the unmistakable rasping hoarseness of the man on the other side of the still-locked door. There was only one member of her flock with a voice like that – Billy Ross, the church caretaker. Billy's life had followed a tortuous route from a poverty-stricken childhood in a run-down housing estate on the outskirts of Glasgow, through some scrapes with the law in his teenage years, on to a decade of relative affluence and stability when he'd made decent money playing for a succession of middle- and lower-league football teams in Scotland and England, followed by the downward spiral of a dozen years when he'd lost everything to alcoholism and depression. It had been a long uphill struggle to reach the level of recovery and sobriety he now managed to maintain, albeit with a constant struggle and the occasional lapse when he would fall off the wagon and land heavily in a quagmire of regret and self-recrimination.

Quite how the journey had brought him to Penford, neither he himself nor anyone else had any idea. But Billy had made a habit of ending up in places most folk would never dream of visiting, and shortly after the Sheppards' arrival in the town, he'd turned up at the vicarage one day looking for help. Pippa had provided him with a meal, got him into a local rehab unit, found him temporary lodgings with a sympathetic parishioner, linked him up to the Alcoholics Anonymous group that met in the church hall on Thursday evenings, and eventually helped him to settle into his own flat in a social housing project near the church.

Billy, for his part, had discovered in the congregation of St Peter's a family to replace the one he'd lost, and found a role for himself in the life of the church. It had taken all of Pippa's negotiating skills to persuade the more cautious members of the Parochial Church Council, who were aware of his history, to employ him as the caretaker. In the end they'd agreed with some reluctance and, apart from a couple of regrettable episodes which Pippa had conveniently forgotten to mention to the PCC, Billy had proven himself to be reliably painstaking – some said even mildly obsessive – in carrying out his duties.

When she eventually managed to open the door, one look at the man standing in front of her was enough to alert Pippa to the fact that something much more serious than the things that usually irritated their conscientious custodian – litter left in the pews or coffee spilled on a carpet – must have aroused his ire. His face was ashen and his hands were trembling, and her first thought was that he must have succumbed to the temptations of the festive season. But Billy was only a couple of feet away from her and, despite the torrent of words that was tumbling from his mouth, there wasn't the merest whiff of alcohol on his breath. Even in everyday conversations she sometimes had difficulty understanding Billy's strong Glaswegian accent. But trying to follow him in this agitated state was almost impossible. She took hold of him by the shoulders, looked directly into his eyes and said as firmly as she could, 'Slow down, Billy. Just take a breath and tell me what's happened.'

'We've been burgled, Vicar,' Billy blurted the words out. 'The side door intae the porch has been forced open wi' a crowbar. It's lyin' beside the door. An' he's still in the church...'

Pippa's heart began to beat faster as she contemplated the prospect of having to deal with an intruder who'd been disturbed before he could escape with whatever he'd hoped to find, and whose anger would only be compounded by his inevitable realisation that St Peter's had little in the way of church treasures with a resale value on the black market. But that was followed by an immediate sense of relief as it occurred to her that any burglar practised in his felonious arts would surely have made his escape as soon as his presence was discovered.

'Well, let's take a look,' she said, making a conscious effort to sound more confident than she felt. 'But he's probably well gone by now. You'll have scared him away.'

Billy clearly found her line of reasoning entirely unconvincing.

'Naah, Vicar. See, that's the thing. He didnae move when he seen me. He's no tryin' to hide or get away. In fact, he's kneelin' at the communion rail, like he's prayin'. An' I don't think he could hurry anywhere if he tried. I mean ... he's auld, *really auld*. Got to be gettin' on for seventy if he's a day. An' he's just kneelin' there, bletherin' away to hisel'...'

Billy's voice trailed away and Pippa felt a wave of confusion and annoyance come over her. What on earth was going on? And why was Billy so worked up about an elderly vagrant who somehow or other had managed to get into the church for no other reason than that he had an urge to pray? It was a pity, she thought ruefully, that there weren't more folk as keen as that to come to church.

Doubtless, the whole thing had an entirely innocent and mundane explanation. More than likely somebody had forgotten to lock the building properly and The Intruder had just wandered in. And there was in all likelihood some perfectly innocent explanation for the crowbar. Probably left there by an absent-minded workman when they'd had some repairs done recently.

To be honest, her explanation didn't sound terribly plausible, but it was the best she could come up with at this time of the morning when she was half asleep and hoping that it'd still be possible to get back into bed for another hour. She was brought back to the moment by the sound of Billy's voice picking up where he'd left off.

'An' there's somethin' else, Vicar. I don't quite know how to say this withoot it soundin' really weird...'

Again, he left his sentence unfinished. His earlier state of high anxiety had subsided a little, only to be replaced by what seemed to Pippa to be a mixture of embarrassment at what he was about to say and fear of how the words would actually sound if he were to speak them out loud. Something about his expression made her feel just a little nervous. What had begun as a mildly irritating early morning interruption was threatening to become something much more nerve-racking.

But before Billy could finish his sentence he was interrupted by the sound of Joe's footsteps coming down the stairs. He'd obviously been able to hear most of their conversation from the landing.

'I've just phoned Lizzie,' he said, referring to one of their elderly parishioners who lived just along the street and had become their unofficial and unpaid childminder. 'She's coming straight over to keep an eye on the kids. This doesn't sound like a matter for the police, so as soon as she gets here we'll head over to the church and see what's what.'

As they all stood waiting together, Pippa looked at Billy, expecting him to pick up where he'd left off. But Billy just shook his head. Whatever had been on his mind, he'd obviously thought better of it and decided to say nothing more for the time being.

Lizzie arrived in less than a minute, still in her slippers and apron, more than happy at the opportunity to look after Harry and Zoe, who'd become her surrogate grandchildren in the last eighteen months.

With the children safely taken care of, the trio quickly made their way across the stone pathway that cut across the lawn separating the church from the vicarage. Pippa was surprised just how relieved she was that Joe had joined them and was taking charge of the situation. She'd become used to dealing with all kinds of odd characters, but whatever it was that Billy wasn't saying was having an unusually disturbing effect on her. It occurred to her that if anyone had been watching, the three of them must have made an odd sight in the grey morning light – Billy wearing shorts and a black T-shirt, his usual attire when cleaning the church whatever the temperature and whatever the time of the year, and she and Joe still in their pyjamas and dressing gowns. It was, she thought to herself, like a scene from a black comedy about the coming of the Magi in which three odd figures, who looked neither wise nor kingly, were processing towards an epiphany they would gladly have avoided if they could.

Pippa had often tried to dismiss the thought, but as they approached the door to the porch she realised again how much she instinctively disliked the forbidding edifice that loomed over them. The building had been consecrated in 1850 and, while its stern neo-Gothic architecture gave an undeniable impression of solidity and authority, it certainly did not project an air of welcome. With its hammered sandstone walls, its bold ashlar dressings and its tall castellated tower it demanded a considerable degree of courage and determination of anyone who entered through its doors for the first time. Its construction had been the outcome of a series of events which had long since been forgotten by all but a few eager amateur historians with a particular interest in the origins of the parish, and Pippa had learned its history only when flicking through some long-neglected dusty parish records she'd come across by accident in the bottom of a cupboard.

St Peter's, she discovered, had originally been part of a larger parish until a combination of personal tragedy and subsequent unyielding authoritarianism had led to a redistribution of the boundaries and the erection of a new church building. On Christmas Eve 1839 a shocked housekeeper discovered the body of the parson, William Boniface, who was still only in his early forties, lying where he had fallen, face down in a pool of blood at the bottom of the vicarage stairs. The Reverend Boniface, an unmarried man who had devoted himself single-mindedly to the work of the parish for almost twenty years, had by all accounts been greatly loved, particularly by his less-affluent parishioners, many of whom had benefited from his unsung but frequent acts of generous charity. His death had given rise to an outpouring of grief and his funeral had brought Penford to a standstill.

His successor, however, turned out to be of a very different ilk. The Reverend Andrew McIntyre had been appointed at the instigation of Lord Penford, the local aristocrat whose family held the patronage of the parish. Andrew McIntyre was a dour Ulsterman whose autocratic cast of mind manifested itself in his refusal to baptise, confirm, marry or bury any parishioners whom he judged to be irregular in their attendance or, worse still in his view, sympathetic to nonconformist ideas. His devotion to church order and his dogmatism in matters of doctrine far outweighed any slight disposition to be charitable to those of straitened means or limited education, and by 1845 a petition deploring 'the deprivation of the rights of the parishioners by their clergyman' had been raised with the aim of removing him from office, or at least restricting his powers.

The strength of feeling was such that some contemporary accounts estimated the completed petition to be more than 150 feet long. Whether or not that was an exaggeration, quite clearly his predominantly working-class parishioners were unanimous in their antagonism towards the unbending incumbent. A meeting was convened under the chairmanship of a local mill owner, a compromise was reached and a resolution was passed that a new parish should be created and a new church should be erected, over which the Reverend Andrew McIntyre could have no jurisdiction whatsoever.

And so it was, Pippa had discovered, that the Parish of St Peter's had been birthed after a lengthy and difficult labour. Little wonder, she thought to herself as she shivered in the chill morning air, that the vulnerable infant congregation in the middle of the nineteenth century, feeling like an ill-treated stepchild, bereaved of its much-loved pastor and bullied by his ill-chosen successor, had seen fit to find security in a building that looked more like a protective fortress than a quiet place of sanctuary.

When they reached the church, Joe stooped just in front of her to pick up the shattered pieces of wood that had been jemmied from the door and handed them to Billy, who placed them neatly on top of the crowbar that was lying to the side of the steps. It felt to Pippa a singularly appropriate act in the bizarre ritual they were enacting, a symbolic representation of the truth that no fortification was strong enough to keep out a determined intruder. With growing trepidation she followed her husband and Billy through the door and into the porch, wondering again what kind of person would go to such trouble to force an entry into a church if they had neither intention to steal what they could nor any desire to make good their escape before they could be caught.

They made their way without speaking through the porch and into the refurbished reception area at the back of the church. This was one of Pippa's recent improvements: she'd persuaded the Parochial Church Council to spend money fitting it out as an informal welcome and café area – a deliberate strategy to make the interior of the building more people-friendly than the severe exterior. She'd even managed to convince them to move the painting of the face of Jesus that had hung on the wall facing everyone who came in through the porch. It had been explained to her that it had hung there ever since it was painted nearly fifty years ago by a long-deceased member of the congregation who had been head of the art department at the school where Joe now taught. And it was, some assured her, not merely of sentimental value but also of considerable artistic merit. An original work of art unique to St Peter's, they would tell her with no little pride.

Pippa, who readily confessed her lack of expertise on the subject of the visual arts, had no objection to it on aesthetic grounds. What disturbed her was the expression on the face of Christ, a look of such deep hurt and utter perplexity that, once glimpsed, would leave her feeling troubled and unsettled for the rest of the day. Conversations with newcomers left her in no doubt that it had a similar effect on them. She reluctantly acknowledged that the painting did have a place in the church but she remained gently insistent that it should not be the first thing visitors would see as they entered. In the end, a compromise had been reached and it had been agreed that it should be relocated to the little side chapel where a small group of elderly parishioners met for the early morning traditional communion service every Sunday. It had been placed in temporary storage at the vicarage until it could be rehung in its new setting at a simple service of dedication on the first Sunday of the New Year.

Even those who had been initially resistant agreed that the relocation of the painting and the refurbishment work had made the reception area a much more welcoming environment. The issue, much to Pippa's relief, had been satisfactorily resolved.

At this time on a cold and gloomy December morning, however, it was impossible for Pippa to imagine a less convivial setting. She had a sudden urge to turn back and leave it to the two men. But Joe was already gently sliding open the door in the glass partition that separated them from the main body of the church and ushering her through. They walked quietly up through the nave – Pippa at the head of their odd procession, Joe just behind her, and an increasingly nervous Billy bringing up the rear.

They reached the lone form bowed at the communion rail. He was wearing hiking gear and heavy brown walking boots whose worn soles suggested that he might well have travelled a considerable distance on foot. Pippa moved slightly to the side to get a better view of The Intruder, and from this position she could see that his hands were clasped in prayer. His hair was unkempt, as if it hadn't been combed in many days, and his face was covered in a heavy grey stubble. They stood for a moment or two, Pippa to the side and the other two just behind the kneeling figure, half-expecting him to react in some way to their presence. But there was no sound from him other than the merest hint of a whisper as he mouthed his prayer.

It was Pippa who broke the silence, reasoning that a woman's voice would be less threatening to The Intruder than that of either of her male companions. She spoke very gently, for fear of startling a man of whose mental and emotional state they could not be certain.

'Excuse me, sir. Are you alright?'

Her voice sounded small and thin in the empty building and, as soon as she'd uttered the words, they struck her as ridiculously banal and inappropriately formal. She had wanted to say something more sensitive that might elicit a response. But the visitor neither spoke nor moved. There was no sound other than the flapping of some heavy-duty plastic sheets that Billy had attached to the upper windows a few weeks earlier to minimise the winter draughts that blew through the church on a windy day.

The three of them remained still for almost a minute, unsure what to do or say next, until Pippa gestured to Billy to remove a section of the communion rail to allow her to step through the gap and into the chancel, from where she could turn and face the stranger. She stooped down in front of him, stretched out her hands, just as she would when offering the bread and wine to a row of waiting communicants, and spoke very softly.

'You're welcome in this place. I'm sorry that the church wasn't open and you had to force your way in. My name is Pippa Sheppard and I'm the vicar here.'

Her words were followed by a long, heavy stillness and she felt a surge of panic. What if he wouldn't or couldn't respond? What if he refused to speak or move? The prospect of having to remove him forcibly from the church was something she definitely didn't relish. But then, very slowly and deliberately, he raised his head, looked into her face and, to her utter surprise, smiled at her. She could see that this was a man certainly of advanced years and possibly of failing health. Nonetheless, his strong, well-defined features suggested that he would have been considered handsome in his younger days, even if the sadness in his piercing blue eyes suggested only years of pain and disappointment. But it was his smile more than anything else that made an immediate impact on Pippa, reminding her instantly of the time when she'd sat up through a long night with Harry when he'd been sick and feverish. It was one of those childhood illnesses that had come with such suddenness and severity that it made her fearful for the child's life. And then, around three o'clock in the morning, the fever had broken and he'd opened his eyes and smiled, still weak and not quite sure what was happening, but realising that he was safe, with someone he trusted and in a place where he was loved. It was a moment and a memory that moved her at a depth she did not quite understand. And she felt a tear trickling down her cheek.

Billy and Joe, who were still standing on the other side of the communion rail, had seen only the lifting of The Intruder's head and were puzzled by Pippa's emotional reaction. Joe was about to ask his wife if she was alright, when The Intruder responded to her greeting.

'Thank you,' he said. His voice seemed to come from somewhere deep in his being and sounded desperately weary. 'I'm sorry, too, for breaking in. But there's something important I have to do, and not much time left, I fear. In fact, I might be too late. I might have missed it. I thought I'd better pray about it.' He paused, as if struggling to remember what he wanted to say next, and then added, 'And, if you're willing, I would really like to receive communion.'

This man, Pippa thought, was very different from the sad procession of petty thieves, opportunist burglars and mentally disturbed trespassers who typically break into churches up and down the land. He spoke quietly, and there was something about his fluid vowel sounds that betrayed his origins in this part of the country, but his words were delivered with a quiet precision that suggested he had travelled far and had learned to converse with people well beyond the boundaries of his birthplace.

She wondered what he meant by his remark that there wasn't much time left for what he needed to do and that he might be too late. But she was relieved that this wasn't the demented outburst that she'd feared and half-expected. She began to reply, still unsure what she was going to say. It felt to her as if the words that were forming in her mouth were dictating her thoughts and her course of action rather than communicating a conscious decision made by her mind.

'It would be a privilege to celebrate communion with you. Just allow me a couple of minutes to prepare. That's my husband, Joe, standing on your right, and Billy Ross, our church caretaker, on your left. They'll stay with you while I go to the vestry and get ready. But can I ask you your name?'

She had a moment of anxiety that she might have been unwise to ask that question, fearing that it might provoke a hostile reaction. The Intruder seemed to sense her nervousness.

'You've no need to be afraid of me. I promise you that I mean you no harm. I can't remember my name right now. But I know I had to come here. It's very important. Please don't turn me away.'

He lifted his head as he spoke, and this time there was no smile; just a steady and sorrowful gaze that Pippa found impossible to ignore or avoid. That was when she realised the reason for Billy's agitation when he'd arrived at the door of the vicarage ten minutes earlier. The face she was staring into was older – much older, maybe even half a century older – for this, she guessed, was a man in his late sixties. But, despite the passage of time and the ravages of the years, she recognised it as the same face, with the same troubled expression, that had disturbed her so often when entering the church. *It was the face in the painting that was due be hung in the side chapel in just a few days' time.* She glanced towards Billy and she could see immediately from the look in his eyes that he had noticed the same startling likeness. She saw too from Joe's perplexed expression that he sensed that something was passing between them, but could only wonder what was happening.

Pippa struggled to remain calm, though her heart was beating quickly. And, even in the cold morning air, she felt her palms beginning to sweat. She wanted to say something in response to The Intruder's cryptic words, but, unable to think of an appropriate reply, she turned and walked into the vestry. St Peter's was definitely of the 'low church' variety. 'We don't do bells and smells,' she would tell people new to the congregation who wondered what kind of churchmanship to expect. Consequently, she rarely wore any ecclesiastical garb more elaborate than the obligatory dog collar. This morning, however, the thought of celebrating communion in her night clothes seemed a little too casual even for her relaxed approach. So she quickly pulled on her cassock and surplice, poured the wine, placed the bread and the chalice on a silver tray, walked back into the church and set the tray on the altar.

Joe and Billy were still standing on either side of the kneeling figure at the communion rail. Sensing their uncertainty as to what they should do next, she quietly suggested that they too should kneel as she led them in a simple, informal communion liturgy. She recited a prayer of confession and read the passage from Luke's Gospel in which Jesus shares the Last Supper with His disciples, offering up the bread and the chalice at the appropriate points in the reading as she'd done so often. Her hands trembled slightly. Presiding at the celebration of the Eucharist had always been a solemn responsibility for her, but never had she felt quite so inadequate for the task as she did at that moment. The mystery of the whole thing threatened to overwhelm her and flooded her mind with questions. Why did this simple ceremony of bread and wine have such power to move people across the centuries? Who was she to assume this priestly role? And who was this stranger, The Intruder, whose very features were in themselves a powerful image of the One who had first shared the cup and the loaf and commanded His followers to do the same thing?

As she pronounced the invitation, she looked at the men kneeling in front of her – one, an elderly vagrant who'd forced his way into the church and whose name she didn't even know; another, a recovering alcoholic who was more worried about the compromised security of the building than any encounter with the divine; and the third, her husband, who would rather have been still asleep and who was there primarily out of concern for her safety – and she could not escape the unintended irony of the summons she was delivering:

Draw near with faith.
Receive the body of our Lord Jesus Christ

which he gave for you,
and his blood which he shed for you …

It was a congregation of only three people, seemingly thrown together more by the vagaries of fortune than by any pursuit of faith, and Pippa wondered if a more unlikely company with such mixed motives had ever gathered together anywhere in the history of the church.

Now, as she leaned forward, saying quietly, 'The body of Christ, broken for you', all three held out their cupped hands in anticipation. For some reason that she couldn't fully fathom, she decided to take the sacrament first to Joe on one side and then to Billy on the other before coming to their unexpected visitor in the middle. Perhaps it was a desire for a kind of symmetry, a sense that the other two should simply be the supporting cast and that the mysterious stranger who bore an uncanny resemblance to the painting of Christ should be the central character in the drama being played out that morning in St Peter's. Whatever it was, she was totally unprepared for what she saw as she stooped to place the piece of broken bread into the cupped hands of The Intruder. For there, clearly visible in the palm of each hand, was a wound, the like of which she'd never seen in any living person, but only in works of art depicting the crucifixion of Jesus Christ.

Pippa felt herself swaying and she was afraid she might faint completely. For a moment or two everything around her seemed to fade into the distance. Somehow she managed to pull herself together, place the remains of the bread on the altar table and bring the chalice to each of her communicants. She had spoken the words, 'The blood of Christ, shed for you', hundreds of times, to the point where she had sometimes reproached herself for repeating them automatically and unthinkingly. Now, however, they seemed to echo round the empty church. It was as if she was hearing herself saying them for the very first time. As she approached The Intruder she forced herself to look again at his hands, half-hoping that the image imprinted on her mind was nothing more than a trick of the morning light, or a bizarre illusion, merely the result of tiredness. But as he stretched out his hands to take the chalice from her she could see the broken flesh even more clearly than before: a small, raw wound in the palm of each hand.

She might still have managed to conclude the impromptu communion service with a simple benediction and a modicum of dignity had not Billy glanced across just as The Intruder handed the cup back to the anxious celebrant. Had he been raised on the other side of the sectarian divide in the West of Scotland, what he saw might have prompted him to genuflect or to make the sign of the cross. But Billy's spirituality, such as it was, had been forged in the crucible of a narrow brand of Protestantism in which visual representations of the passion of Christ were taboo – 'papish paintings and statues', his father had called them – to be dismissed as nothing more than superstitious idols. Now it was as if one of those heretical icons had sprung to life before his eyes.

The uncanny resemblance of the man kneeling beside him to the painting that had hung in the entrance porch had been difficult enough for Billy to cope with. The sight of the wound-prints in his hands pushed him to breaking point. He let out a low curse, leaned his weight on the communion rail and levered himself up from his knees.

'This isnae right. I'm no stayin' here,' he shouted, hurrying to the back of the church. And before either Pippa or Joe could act to calm the situation or find the words to call him back, the building echoed with a resounding thud as the door of the porch slammed shut behind him.

Joe, who still had not seen what had so disturbed Billy, looked up at his wife with a puzzled and questioning expression. Pippa was struggling to know what to say or do, when The Intruder spoke again: 'I'm sorry.' He looked down at his hands and let out a low sigh. 'I understand what's troubling you. I'm a little confused, to be honest, but if you can help me up, please, I'll try to explain as much as I can.'

And so, after the elements of the communion service had been cleared away, Pippa and Joe helped The Intruder to his feet. They were walking slowly through the church, supporting him on either side, when he suddenly stopped, an expression of relief and amazement on his face. 'The stones!' he gasped. 'The stones, they've gone! Thank God, they've gone!'

He wept very softly, and the tears that trickled down his face left two clean lines. It was something that Pippa had only ever seen on the faces of her children, and instinctively she reached out her hand and gently wiped each cheek as they began to walk again.

Neither she nor Joe asked him what he meant by those words. It was just one more mystery in a morning unlike anything they had ever known, and neither of them had any idea how this strange and unexpected turn of events would be resolved.

Two

Meet the Press

A stranger in Penford with a more than passing interest in classic cars would immediately have recognised that the opalescent light-blue car pulling into one of the parking spaces in front of St Peter's vicarage just after six o'clock on the Saturday evening was a 1960s Jaguar Mark II saloon in immaculate condition. And they might reasonably have deduced that the driver of such a vehicle would be a well-groomed individual of both style and substance with a passion for the good things in life and a level of sartorial elegance to match his vehicle.

They would, however, have been taken aback when an obese man standing no taller than five foot six and weighing more than twenty stone struggled out of the plush grey leather driver's seat by pushing himself up with one hand on the walnut veneer fascia while pulling with the other on the half-opened door. Their surprise would have been all the greater at the sight of his crumpled navy-blue pinstriped suit, unpolished brown shoes, grubby white shirt and food-stained tie. To the stranger, the motorist and the motor car would have seemed a curious mismatch.

A native of the town, however, would instantly have known that driver and vehicle belonged together and would have recognised the man emerging from the car as Eddie Shaw – owner, editor, sometime reporter and general factotum of *The Gazette*, Penford's weekly newspaper. *The Gazette* had been a typical locally owned daily paper until circulation began to decline sharply in the second half of the twentieth century under the challenge of television and local radio. For a time it was taken over by a media conglomerate who owned a dozen or so small-town tabloids and turned it into a weekly, but the new owners had no real interest in life in Penford and sales plummeted to the point where the accountants and number-crunchers in their London office deemed that it was no longer a viable business proposition.

It was set to go the way of so many similar publications across the country until Eddie Shaw stepped in back in the sixties. Quite how Eddie, who was still in his twenties at that time, who seemed to have no regular employment and who was the nearest thing Penford had to a playboy, managed to marshal the funds for such an acquisition no one was quite sure. His teenage years had been spent at an expensive fee-paying school in the south of England, but on his return to the town he seemed to have neither professional qualifications nor gainful employment. There were those who speculated that, as a young man with a weakness for gambling, he'd had a winning streak at the roulette table in a Manchester casino. Others suggested that he'd come into an unexpectedly large legacy from his parents who'd recently died. But the majority opinion was that the previous owners had been so relieved to get *The*

Gazette off their hands that they'd sold it for a song and that Eddie was the only person foolhardy enough to take it on.

Whatever the truth behind the transaction, what could not be denied was that Eddie had changed *The Gazette* and *The Gazette* had changed Eddie. From being a tired and predictable local rag with no semblance of an identity, he'd turned it into a witty and provocative weekly that cast a revealing spotlight on every aspect of Penford life, combining objective reporting with an irreverent slant designed to puncture pomposity and challenge hypocrisy. As a concession to the digital revolution he'd set up a small team only a few years earlier to launch an online version of the paper while he kept control of the print edition, which, in Eddie's opinion, was 'the real newspaper'. The circulation figures rose to a very respectable eight and a half thousand with a readership estimated at around 25,000. Whenever there was an issue of local concern, it was common for Penford folk to ask, 'What's *The Gazette* got say about it?'

In the process, Eddie had become a different man. Running the paper took up all his time and absorbed his full attention. His previous predilection for smart clothes and the company of a procession of attractive young women became a thing of the past. He married a local girl he'd known from childhood and settled down to a life of apparent domestic contentment until she died in 2000. There were no children from their marriage to check on how their father looked, and since his wife's death his lack of attention to his personal appearance had descended into a comfortable scruffiness as he threw himself ever more single-mindedly into his work. The thought of cooking for himself or employing a housekeeper to look after him never crossed his mind. Eating out, either on the run at fast-food outlets or with prominent local figures at more expensive establishments, became a way of life. It was a standing joke in the town that every time there was an upsurge in *The Gazette*'s circulation it was matched by an equivalent increase in Eddie's girth.

The only thing that remained unchanged from his earlier life was his beloved light-blue Jaguar Mark II. He'd owned the car from new and had lavished significant sums of money on it to maintain it in pristine condition across the years. Few people in Penford had ever seen Eddie using public transport to get around the town, and fewer still had seen him walk more than a couple of hundred yards. The car was intrinsic to his identity, an expression of his personality, a defiant statement that, despite the undeniable changes of the passing years, the overweight man in his seventies with the pelican chin and the bags under his eyes, the man who wheezed and coughed when he was forced to walk up the slightest incline, was one and the same as the youthful dandy who'd turned heads when he'd sauntered down the street half a century earlier.

Pippa and Joe watched his arrival from an upstairs window in the vicarage with growing trepidation. When Billy had run out of the church that morning they'd guessed that it wouldn't take long for news of their unexpected visitor to get around Penford. And, knowing that the period between Christmas and New Year was always a slow news week, they'd been anticipating some contact from *The Gazette*. Their fears had been confirmed by a phone call in the afternoon saying that, although there was only a skeleton staff because of the holiday, someone from the paper would like to call that evening. They had, however, hoped that it would involve nothing more than a brief, ten-minute conversation with one of the two junior reporters who scoured the district each day to find sufficient items of interest to fill a column or two in the weekend's paper. But, as everyone knew, no one had a nose for a story like the editor of *The Gazette* himself. So when Eddie turned up, rather than a member of his staff, it was a clear indication that he considered he'd come upon something of more than usual interest. Husband and wife looked at each other, took a shared deep breath and headed downstairs to meet their second uninvited caller of the day.

Joe opened the door and ushered Eddie into the study-cum-office, the one completely child-free area in the house where visitors could avoid the risk of tripping over children's discarded shoes or toys. Pippa greeted their guest with a handshake and invited him to take the armchair while she and Joe sat on the couch opposite. She was always on her guard with anyone from the press and was trying to look more relaxed than she felt.

For a few minutes they made small talk, reminding each other of the occasions when they'd met before at various functions in the town. But Eddie, she could see, was impatient to get down to business. He cleared his throat and gave a wheezy cough. 'I'm sure you're trying to get some downtime after all the demands of the last few weeks. And I know tomorrow's another full Sunday for you, so I won't take up too much of your evening. But I've heard you had an unusual visitor to St Peter's this morning...'

He delivered the last sentence slowly and allowed his words to hang in the air for a second or two as he took a pen and a small leather-bound notebook from the inside pocket of his jacket. He looked at his hosts quizzically, willing one of them to speak.

'Well,' Pippa responded with a raise of her eyebrows and the half-smile of someone making their first move in a chess game, 'why don't *you* tell *me* what you've heard and we can go from there?'

Eddie laughed good-naturedly and put his notebook and pen on the arm of the chair.

'Ah, you're obviously used to dealing with the press, Vicar. Honestly, I'm not trying to catch you out in any way. But one of my staff ran into Billy Ross this morning. In quite a state, by all accounts. Gave some garbled account about someone who looked like that picture of Jesus that you've just got rid of breaking into the church and demanding that you put on a whole service just for him. I just had a feeling there might be something more to it than that...'

Again Eddie left his sentence unfinished, and Pippa had a strong suspicion that he knew more than he was letting on. But she ignored it and tried to give the impression that she was taking his words at their face value.

'Well, I'm not getting rid of the picture you're talking about, as you should know from the article your paper ran on it a month ago,' she said, wondering again which disgruntled member of the congregation had taken the story to *The Gazette*. 'Like I told your reporter then, we've just agreed to reposition it somewhere more appropriate. And Billy Ross is safely tucked up in his flat with strict instructions from me not to talk to anybody. We managed to find him this afternoon in the George and Dragon. He'd fallen off the wagon, as we suspected, but Joe got to him before he'd had time to drink himself to oblivion. One of the men in the congregation is staying with him overnight just to make sure he stays put and doesn't go wandering off.'

Eddie smiled in recognition of her spirited response. It was turning into the kind of lively encounter that he thoroughly enjoyed and that kept him on his toes. He was formulating a suitable response in his mind when Pippa spoke again.

'But with regard to our early morning visitor, that's pretty well it, really. Though he didn't "demand a whole service", as you put it. He just asked for communion, and I was happy to do that for him.'

Pippa felt she'd seized the initiative in the conversation and decided to press home her advantage.

'I'd really appreciate it if you didn't print anything in your paper for the time being. We brought our unusual visitor, as you call him, back here to the vicarage and called a doctor. Despite the fact that he'd broken into the church, he didn't give the impression of being violent or aggressive in any way. It was just that something seemed to be telling him that he needed to get into St Peter's. He appears to be reasonably physically fit for his age, though he's obviously exhausted and confused, but he couldn't tell us his name and seems to have some kind of memory loss. They've given him an emergency bed at the Infirmary while they check him out. There's really nothing more to tell you.'

Joe, who was finding it difficult to play a passive role in this meeting, stretched across and patted his wife's hand. Perhaps, he thought to himself, he could at least bring things to a conclusion.

'I guess it's all in a day's work for a vicar. I don't know how she does it. We get all sorts of people turning up. She takes it all in her stride. Takes me all my time coping with a room full of teenagers.'

Eddie nodded again. He pulled the kind of face intended to convey the impression that he fully understood that this was just another incident of the kind that occurs every other day for clergy and began to put his pen and notebook back in his pocket. But he was too old in the tooth to be sidetracked so easily. It was time for one of his favourite ploys. He paused, notebook in one hand and pen in the other, as if he'd just remembered something. Pippa recognised the sinking feeling she always had when something she thought she'd fixed suddenly began to unravel. She guessed what was coming next.

'There's just one thing that's troubling me,' he said, pretending to think aloud and watching carefully the effect his words were having on his hearers. 'Billy's imagination could've been working overtime, of course. I know I've spoken to hundreds of people over the years who thought they'd seen things that turned out not to be real. But when my reporter spoke to him earlier today, he seemed quite convinced, not just that your burglar bore a strong resemblance to the face in the picture, but that he also had some kind of cuts in the palms of his hands, like the nail prints in the hands of Jesus. Now, I'm not a particularly religious man, and you'll know much more about this sort of thing than me. It's called stigmata, isn't it? The marks of Christ's passion…'

Eddie did what he always did when he felt he'd got an evasive interviewee where he wanted them. He pushed his pen and notebook into his jacket pocket, put his hands on his knees, closed his lips tightly and breathed noisily through his nose for a few seconds before summing up his case.

'Now if that was true,' he said, looking straight at Pippa, 'this would be anything but an everyday story of life in the vicarage. My reporter thinks he managed to persuade Billy not to talk to anyone else about this, but you can't keep a watch on him 24/7, and you can't be sure that he'll be able to keep it to himself for long. You can just imagine what the national tabloids will do if they get hold of this. So why don't you trust me and tell me the whole story?'

Pippa knew that had this been a chess game, they had reached the point at which her opponent would have called checkmate. But this was no game, and she realised that she needed the man sitting opposite her to be an ally rather than an opponent if they were to prevent the story getting out of hand and degenerating into the kind of tabloid trivia in which cheap sensationalism sweeps away any semblance of objective reporting. She knew right then that she had to trust Eddie Shaw, take him into her confidence and give him a full account of what had happened that morning. Five minutes earlier she had been hoping that their guest would be gone quickly and let them have the evening to themselves. Now she and Joe were busying themselves checking that the children were safely asleep, making coffee, putting out the remains of the

Christmas cake and inviting Eddie into the kitchen – the place where, in Pippa's experience, the most productive meetings always took place.

As soon as the coffee was poured and the three of them had settled themselves around the old, well-marked oak table, the atmosphere began to ease. What had been a tense confrontation gradually became a more relaxed conversation in which first names replaced formal titles.

'Before we go any further, can we agree on a couple of things, Eddie?' Pippa asked. 'Can we agree that we both want to find out the truth and then share it with the town in a way that doesn't expose a vulnerable man to the wrong kind of scrutiny and doesn't pander to an appetite for lurid headlines?'

Eddie tapped his fingers on the table as he spoke, to emphasise his words.

'Pippa, I've made my reputation in this town by being honest and fair in what I publish, and I'm not about to throw that away at this stage of my life. So you have my word that whatever we print will be just that – honest and fair.'

For the next twenty minutes he listened attentively while Pippa, with occasional interjections from Joe, narrated the sequence of the day's events. Most of what had happened in the church that morning was already known to him, since his reporter had quizzed Billy Ross closely and succeeded in constructing a fairly accurate record of events from his somewhat rambling account. But it was when they reached the subsequent events of the day that his interest was really piqued and he began to make copious notes.

After Billy had fled from the church, Pippa explained, she and Joe slowly led The Intruder across the path to the vicarage. He was clearly exhausted and they laid him gently and carefully on the couch in the large front room. Within moments he had fallen into a deep sleep, leaving them to try to work out what they should do. The obvious person to call, they immediately agreed, was Katie Morgan, a regular member of the congregation at St Peter's and a consultant in geriatric medicine at Penford Hospital. Katie was driving to visit a friend in Yorkshire when they called but, on hearing about the morning's events and sensing the concern in Pippa's voice, she turned the car around and headed straight back to Penford.

By the time she reached the vicarage it was around eleven o'clock and the man on the couch was beginning to show signs of rousing from his slumber. Pippa and Joe still hadn't eaten that morning, so, while they sorted out breakfast for themselves and their guests, Katie knelt on the floor in front of the couch and gently quizzed her unscheduled patient for the next twenty minutes. He was neither averse to conversing with her nor aggressive in any way, though it was plain to her that he was troubled and confused. He was unable to tell her his name or where he'd come from and didn't appear to have any identification documents with him. Despite his confusion, however, he was adamant about two things: St Peter's was exactly where he wanted to be – 'I *know* I had to come here,' he insisted; and he was equally sure that he was very hungry and needed to eat something.

Katie knew that she'd solicited as much information as she could at that time from The Intruder, so Joe took him into the kitchen and sat him at the table, where he quickly devoured the toast and scrambled eggs that were set in front of him before asking for more. While Joe served him with a second helping, the two women took the opportunity to have a whispered conversation. Katie agreed that the man who'd broken into the church was probably in his mid-to-late sixties and, notwithstanding his present muddled mental state, in reasonably sound health for a man of his age. She quickly scribbled down some notes as she spoke and, from the tone of her voice, Pippa could discern that she was both fascinated and perplexed by his condition.

'I'm not a psychiatrist, so I'd want to get another opinion,' Katie said thoughtfully, 'but my best guess is that he's suffering from some form of what's known as dissociative amnesia. It's a temporary memory loss brought on by shock or trauma. It can last for just a few hours, a few days or even weeks, but not usually longer than that. And it often results in the sufferer wandering from home, even sometimes travelling considerable distances. We need to get him into hospital for a general check-up and to get a proper diagnosis of his mental condition.'

Pippa was grateful to have at least a partial explanation for the unexpected arrival of The Intruder that morning, even if it left the bigger questions unanswered.

'That still doesn't account for him forcing his way into the church. And it certainly doesn't shed any light on his startling likeness to the painting of the Christ. Or, what troubles me most, the presence of what appear to be nail prints in the palms of his hands. I can't get my head round that.'

Had she been an Anglo-Catholic rather than the low-Church evangelical she was, Pippa might have had a spirituality and a theological framework that would have gone some way to accommodating something as strange and apparently mystical as the appearance of bodily marks corresponding to the wounds of the crucified Christ. She knew from her reading of the lives of the saints that the phenomenon had first been observed in St Francis of Assisi in the thirteenth century, and she had a vague recollection that there had been a number of subsequent occurrences up to the present day, usually in members of Roman Catholic religious orders and often treated with some scepticism by senior clergy. She'd always considered herself to be open-minded on the authenticity or otherwise of such manifestations, though it wasn't something to which she'd ever given more than a passing thought. But never in her wildest dreams had she imagined such a thing occurring at an ordinary Anglican church in an ordinary town in the north of England.

Katie had no answers to the questions about the reason for the break-in or the likeness to the painting, but she did have something to say on the matter of the apparent stigmata.

'Well, ironically,' she said with a faint smile, 'that might just be the easiest bit of this mystery to clear up. I don't think this is a case of classic Catholic mysticism. It's unlikely that our man is a stigmatic in the usual sense of that term. In fact, I think there's a far more prosaic medical explanation. When I asked him about the injuries, he produced these from his pocket...'

She held out two hand-forged rosehead nails – the kind used in reproduction antique furniture, each about three inches long – and passed them to Pippa.

'It wasn't easy to follow everything he said,' Katie explained, 'but when I asked him about the scars on his palms he produced these from his pocket and said, "I did it. These are mine." I have a sense that he's carried these with him for a long time and that he's been self-harming for much of his life. Something's been troubling him for years and, from what he's told me, I think that whenever the emotions associated with whatever it is become too much for him he self-harms by digging these into his palms.'

Pippa sat quietly, holding the nails in her hands and giving an involuntary shudder as she tried to imagine what level of distress would drive someone to inflict such hurt on themselves. She was relieved when Katie stretched across and took the nails from her.

'Let me take care of those,' she said, wrapping them in a tissue. 'He was reluctant to let me keep them and I had to assure him that I'd look after them for him. Now I need to make a phone call and get him into hospital so he can be checked over properly. And we need to call the police, too, and put them in the picture. It'll certainly be interesting to find out more about our mysterious visitor. But whatever the truth behind all this is, he's convinced that it has something to do with this church.'

Katie was on the point of leaving when she remembered something she hadn't mentioned.

'I'm not sure if I caught his words properly, but I think he was mumbling something about stones. Do you know what that's all about?'

'Did he say that to you, too?' Pippa asked. 'He seems to have lost some stones. Or he's got rid of them. He seemed relieved not to have them any longer. Just another part of this mystery, I guess.'

Pippa had reached the end of her account of the oddest day of her life. She turned to Joe, who nodded in confirmation, and then to Eddie, who hadn't stopped scribbling furiously in his notebook all the time she'd been speaking.

'That's it, really,' she said with a shrug. 'We got him into hospital, the police called, and I made a statement. Now you know as much as I do.'

Eddie made no reply. But Pippa noticed that his eyes narrowed a little and there was the faintest of smiles on his lips. It was the kind of expression that made her wonder whether the man from *The Gazette* did, in fact, know more than she did, more than he was letting on at that moment.

'What are you thinking, Eddie?' she asked. 'You've got an interesting look on your face.'

Eddie didn't respond straight away. When he did eventually speak, he did so carefully and thoughtfully.

'Hmm… I'm not sure what I'm thinking. Or at least, I'm not sure enough to say it out loud. But you've given me a lot to chew over. And you've stirred some vague memories. I've got some work to do.'

He put his notebook and pen back in his pocket and then began to push himself up from his chair – not something he ever managed to do quickly or easily.

'But the first thing I need to do,' he said, as he struggled for breath, 'is to find out if any of the national dailies have got hold of the story and what they're intending to do with it. I'll do my best to get them to hold back on it, but it might well be too late to stop them. You know what those guys are like.'

'And I need to spend what's left of the day,' Pippa replied with a rueful laugh, 'trying to get ready for tomorrow's services while my head's still buzzing with all this stuff.'

Pippa and Joe walked to the door with Eddie and watched him as he slowly lowered himself into his car. He turned on the ignition and rolled down the window. His face was a mixture of genuine concern for the couple standing in the doorway and barely concealed anticipation at the prospect of uncovering a story that he suspected might prove a lot more challenging and interesting for a newspaper man than the usual routine fare of life in a northern town.

'Just be ready,' he called out. 'This could turn out to be a bigger story than I first thought. But don't forget – we're on the same side on this one. You do your bit by speaking to your Boss up there.' He pointed skywards, and his wheezy laugh gave way to a chesty cough. 'And we'll see what an old sinner like me can do to make it a story with some kind of happy ending!'

And with that he drove off, leaving Pippa and Joe uncertain as to whether they should feel comforted or concerned by his words.

Three

The First Sunday of Christmas

Pippa always felt mildly irritated by the fact that the Church calendar designates the Sunday immediately following the 25th December as the First Sunday of Christmas.

It never felt like that to her. More a kind of anticlimax after all the festivities than a day of new beginnings. By the time it came round each year she was just relieved that Christmas had come and gone and was looking forward to life beginning to get back to normal. Combining motherhood and ministry was demanding enough throughout the rest of the year. When carol services, school concerts and 1,001 other events were added to the mix it brought her to a point where she just wanted a break.

'It's not the first Sunday of anything,' she'd complain to Joe, who would listen patiently to a recitation he knew by heart. 'It's the last Sunday of the year – the day when you never know who's going to be in church or whether the folk who are there are paying any kind of attention. The adults would just appreciate a lazy day and the kids would rather be at home playing with their toys. First Sunday of

Christmas – I don't think! Must have been a man who thought that one up.'

Her feelings about the day meant that normally she'd struggle to put together the homily. However, she'd never anticipated a First Sunday of Christmas like this one, and by the time she got to bed around midnight she'd managed to type out almost word for word what she wanted to deliver to the congregation.

Throughout the service that morning she was aware of a very different atmosphere from anything she'd ever experienced before on what she considered to be the most inappropriately named Sunday of the year. And when she climbed into the pulpit at a quarter past eleven she could sense a much higher attention level from the sea of faces in front of her than in past years. Word of Saturday's visitor had obviously got around the congregation, thanks in large measure to Billy Ross' loose tongue, and they were anxious to hear more. Pippa took a slow sip from the glass of water in front of her and gave a knowing smile to Joe, who was sitting in the front row, as she began to speak.

'My husband will tell you that this isn't my favourite Sunday of the year. I hope you won't be too shocked to hear your vicar confess that it's a day when normally I'd rather be relaxing at home with a cup of coffee and quietly listening to some music while the kids are safely up in their rooms playing with their Christmas presents...'

Some of the older congregants seemed a little uncertain as to how they should deal with this personal revelation, but there was a reassuring buzz of agreement from the younger parents in the pews.

'However, today is rather different. I know from the snippets of conversation I was hearing before the service that most of you are aware that yesterday morning we had a rather unusual visitor to St Peter's. Somebody so keen to get to church that he couldn't wait for Sunday or even for the building to be opened. I don't mind admitting that it was initially a bit of a shock to discover someone in our church on a day and a time when I'd have preferred to be tucked up in bed for another hour or so.'

Pippa noticed that one or two regulars who weren't normally particularly attentive were leaning forward in the pews and listening closely. She suspected this had more to do with what Joe described as 'good old-fashioned northern nosiness' than a deepened interest in her preaching, but she quickly dismissed that distracting thought and continued with her sermon.

'I'm sure there have been numerous stories and rumours sweeping round the town, and I understand that everyone is naturally curious about what happened. So this morning I want to take just ten minutes to share three things with you.'

Her voice faltered and her confidence wavered a little as it occurred to her that she'd never known the congregation to be so quiet on a Sunday morning. Of course, the children had gone out to their age-appropriate classes, which always reduced the noise level. This, however, was a silence quite unlike any she'd known at St Peter's, and it unnerved her a little. She held on to the sides of the pulpit and forced herself to continue.

'Of course, you're probably thinking that preachers always seem to deal in threes, but this is just a little different from how I normally speak to you from the pulpit on a Sunday morning. I want to give you a promise, I want to ask for your help, and I want to share with you what I think God might want to say to us this morning through the events of yesterday.'

She began to step down from the pulpit and walk towards the communion rail as she asked, 'Is everyone OK with that?'

Her predecessor having been firmly of the opinion that preaching should be strictly in the form of a monologue and should be delivered from a pulpit standing safely six feet above contradiction, it had taken the congregation some time to get used to Pippa's habit of seeking a response from them or coming towards them at various points of her sermon. Some of her more staid parishioners were still less than fully comfortable with any request for their active participation. This morning, however, a combination of sympathy awakened by what they had already heard of the church's unexpected visitor and curiosity aroused by a desire to find out more brought a collective nod of approval from almost everyone present.

Encouraged by the positive reaction to her question, Pippa drew a deep breath, placed her notes carefully on the movable lectern that she'd set in place precisely for this purpose before the service began, and went on.

'Let's start with my promise. In fact, it's really a double promise. First of all, I promise you that we will try to do everything we can to make sure our uninvited guest yesterday morning is made as welcome in this church as anyone else would be and that we'll try to respect his privacy, just as I know you'd want the church to do for everybody who comes into the building. That's why we will postpone the service of dedication that had been planned for next Sunday when we had intended to rehang the painting, *A Portrait of Pain*, in the side chapel. I'm sure you will understand from the rumours that have circulated in the last couple of days that such an event would be inappropriate and unhelpful just at this time.'

There were some murmurs of 'Hear, hear' from around the congregation and a man sitting on the back row, much to the surprise of those seated on either side of him, even shouted a loud 'Amen'. This was going better than she had dared hope. She glanced down at her carefully prepared notes. She wanted to make sure she got the next bit right.

'And the second part of my promise is simply this: knowing that this has already aroused a lot of interest in the town and that people are likely to ask you what you know, I promise to share with you what I can in a way that allows me to honour my first promise about our care for our guest. And that's where I need to ask for your help. We know this might well be picked up by the national tabloid newspapers and our concern is that the whole thing might get sensationalised and that a vulnerable elderly man might be exposed to insensitive, ill-informed and unhelpful publicity. Of course, we can't control that fully, but it will help enormously if we're all careful in our conversations with our neighbours and folk at work. And above all, everyone here this morning can help by making this whole business a feature of their prayers this coming week.'

Pippa glanced at Joe who mouthed to her, 'You nailed it. Keep going.' She was grateful for his reassurance, and having got through what she had imagined would be the most difficult part of her talk, she was relieved to turn her attention to the reading from the Gospels that morning – St Luke's account of the angels' announcement of the birth of Jesus and the visit of the shepherds to Bethlehem, where they found the baby lying in a manger. That was where she'd found the inspiration for the challenge she wanted to leave with her congregation.

'Could there be a more significant time of year for this church to have an unexpected and unusual visitor? Isn't Christmas the season when we remember and celebrate the coming of another unexpected and unusual visitor who was not made particularly welcome on His arrival? In fact, you could sum up the world's reaction to Him across the centuries in two little one-syllable words – *no room*. Even the Church has often struggled to find room for Him. And there's another passage in the New Testament that I'm thinking about this morning, one that's found in the last book of the Bible. It's a message to the church in the ancient city of Laodicea – a church that had forgotten that its first responsibility was to be loving and welcoming – a message in the form of a poignant word picture in which Jesus Himself stands outside the church, seeking to be allowed in. You might remember the words…'

Pippa walked back across the chancel and climbed the steps to the pulpit. She stood long enough to make sure she had everyone's full attention before she began to recite the words from Revelation slowly and clearly:

Here I am! I stand at the door and knock. If anyone hears my voice and opens the door, I will

come in and eat with that person, and they with
me.

Then she paused again, raised her hands in a sign of
blessing, and delivered her benediction:

This morning – this *First Sunday of Christmas* – we
thank God for unexpected visitors.
May he grant us the charity to love the strangers
in our midst
and the humility to learn all they may have to
teach us.
Amen.

Some of the faithful in the pews were a little bemused,
wondering what had happened to the customary closing
hymn. But the sight of their vicar leaving the pulpit,
making her way through the nave and then standing at the
back of the church to greet them left them in no doubt that
the service was at an end. Pippa, who was herself a little
uncertain as to how her words and the somewhat abrupt
ending to the service might have been received, was
relieved at the response she received from the departing
congregation. Those who were less than comfortable with
what had happened contented themselves with a
handshake and a polite 'Thank you, Vicar', while those
who had found the message from the pulpit significant and
challenging were quick to express their appreciation.

By the time she got back to the vicarage after the service,
Harry and Zoe were already sitting at the table and Joe was
wearing an apron and waiting to serve up lunch,
something he did most Sundays and something that

always made her smile. In the early years of their marriage, Pippa had followed the pattern she'd seen in her parents' relationship and assumed most of the household duties, but following her ordination they had come to share their roles in the home much more. Engaging in such domestic tasks wasn't something that came as second nature to Joe, and he hadn't ever managed to shake off his natural clumsiness and irritating untidiness in the kitchen. It served only to make her all the more grateful for his willingness to try his hand at things that didn't come easily to him, and today she was doubly grateful for his support both in church and in the kitchen.

It wasn't until the children had gone off to their rooms that the couple had time to chat as they cleared the table and put the last of the plates in the dishwasher.

'You done great this morning,' Joe said in the voice he always used when he wanted to do an impression of a football pundit. 'Pippa United 2 – Penford Gossips nil.'

'Well, thank you,' Pippa responded, going along with the joke. 'Yeah, but it's only one game. We ain't won nothin' yet and there's a long way to go. Winning the league is a marathon, not a sprint.'

'Seriously,' Joe said, reverting to his normal voice. 'I thought you handled that well. Most of this morning's congregation trust you and respect what you had to say. With a bit of luck, we might just be able to keep a lid on this. But you're right. We're not at the end of this yet.'

He beckoned his wife towards him and hugged her tightly to him. Pippa always found it comforting to hear the rise and fall of his breathing and feel the rhythm of his heart beating.

'Don't know how I'd do it without you,' she whispered. 'You didn't know when you married me that you'd end up having a vicar for a wife. Thanks for not running away.'

'Oh, don't you worry. I'm going nowhere. Certainly not while we're in the middle of this one,' he said as he laughed and released his wife from his arms. 'I mean, you couldn't make this up. I want to see how it all turns out. And now you've got Eddie Shaw and *The Gazette* on our side, who knows what we might find out in the next few days. I half-wondered if he might even turn up in church this morning just to hear what you had to say and see how the congregation would react.'

In fact, it was an idea that the editor of *The Gazette* had himself considered, albeit briefly, when he struggled out of bed that morning. It was a struggle that resulted from his general physical condition and the after-effects of the extra-large nightcap that he'd taken to induce sleep at one o'clock in the morning. Churchgoing definitely wasn't his thing, though he turned up in places of worship occasionally in the line of duty when there was a civic function or a service that he considered to be of unusual interest. By the time he'd showered and shaved and drunk his first cup of strong black coffee, however, he'd decided that his time would be better spent in the office. There would be no one else around on what he deemed the deadest Sunday of the year in terms of newsworthy stories, and this would give him ample opportunity to check through the archives without any interruptions.

So just as Pippa was climbing into the pulpit to deliver her sermon, Eddie was climbing the stairs that led to the first floor of the offices of *The Gazette*. Since his wife had died he'd made a point of not spending any more time at home on his own than was absolutely necessary. It held too many memories of what had turned out to be a far happier marriage than he'd expected. But this morning his relief at getting away from the confines of the house was overtaken by the surge of adrenaline he felt at the prospect of finding the key that might unlock the mystery of The Intruder at St Peter's Church. There was something lurking at the back of his mind, something he felt he should remember but couldn't quite bring into focus, and he knew the best place to start. It was where he often went when he needed to submerge his own painful sense of loss in the broader history of the town he knew so well and to which he'd devoted his adult life.

Before becoming the headquarters for *The Gazette* back in the 1950s, the building, which was more than 200 years old, had initially served as a flour mill and subsequently gone through a number of changes of use. Although it had been refurbished and updated several times since being adapted for its present purpose, it still retained something of its original character. Eddie had resisted all suggestions that the exposed brick walls should be plastered over or that the wooden floorboards should be replaced by some kind of modern laminate. The juxtaposition of twenty-first-century digital technology and solid eighteenth-century construction pandered to his conviction that a local newspaper office should be a place where past and present meet, a place where objective commentary on the happenings of today is firmly rooted in a sense of continuity with yesterday. It was a place that had become his life, the place he loved more than anywhere else on earth

The wooden floorboards groaned under his heavy footsteps as he walked past the bank of state-of-the-art computers which had been installed just a few months before and headed straight to the old microfilm reader that sat on a desk in a dark corner of the room. It was a machine that had been purchased back in the 1960s, which, in the eyes of the younger members of *The Gazette* staff, qualified it as an antique. For Eddie, however, it was his favourite piece of equipment in the office, and getting it ready to use had become an almost mystical ritual that linked him with the past in a way that a computer screen could never do.

He carried out each step, repeating the instructions to himself as he did so with all the reverence of a holy man reciting an ancient sacred text. First, he reached over to the filing cabinet on his left, opened a drawer marked '1955–1960', picked up a box and, after wiping his hands on his handkerchief, carefully removed a roll of microfilm, which he placed gently in front of him. Then, without needing to look at what he was doing, he felt along the underside of the machine until his right hand found the rocker-switch that brought it to life with a satisfying hum. He eased the tray out from underneath the lens and placed the film on the spindle on his left, remembering to make sure it would roll clockwise. Next, he placed the end of the film under the rollers and on to the take-up reel on the right-hand side, winding the reel precisely three and a half times to ensure it was fully engaged, and then briefly touched the red fast-forward button to reach the start of the reel. Finally, he pushed the tray back under the microscope to reveal the first image on the screen in front of him.

Everything was set, but for one thing. Just as he always did at this point in the ritual, Eddie got up and went to the windowless back room that served as a kitchen-cum-staff lunch area, where he made himself a mug of instant black coffee with three large sugars and took two chocolate biscuits from the tin in the cupboard above the sink. Only when he'd carried these back and settled himself comfortably in his chair was he ready to begin. He unwrapped one of the biscuits, placed it beside the mug and sat for a full minute, his elbows on the desk and his hands clasped as if in prayer, just to clear his mind. With the added stimulus of coffee and sugar, he was now ready to address the task in hand.

Ever since his reporter had told him the previous day of Billy Ross' mention of the resemblance between the face of The Intruder and the painting of Christ, Eddie had been trying to recall the details of an article he'd read when pouring over the archives of *The Gazette* some years earlier, something he did from time to time which largely accounted for his almost encyclopaedic knowledge of the history of Penford over the last fifty or sixty years. It related to an event that had taken place before he took over the paper, and though he couldn't quite recall what it was about the story, he remembered that there was something that had puzzled him when he read it. He scrolled through to 1957, finding only some brief references to church services that a junior reporter would have filed. A quick search through the following year was no more rewarding.

When he reached 1959, however, he found what he was looking for. It was the front-page story from the edition of *The Gazette* dated Saturday 28th March of that year, and underneath the banner headline, 'NEW WORK BY LOCAL ARTIST STIRS CONTROVERSY IN THE PEWS', was a black and white photograph of the painting that had hung in the entrance porch of St Peter's for the next half-century. Eddie pushed his coffee mug to one side and began to read the article to himself.

There was dissent among the faithful yesterday at the conclusion of the Good Friday morning service at St Peter's Church, when an oil painting of the face of Christ with the crown of thorns on his head was unveiled by the vicar, the Revd Simon Peabody. The painting, which is entitled *A Portrait of Pain*, is the work of distinguished local artist Herbert Donnington, who has presented it to the church as a gift.

Mr Donnington, who is also the head of the art department at Penford Grammar School, has a growing reputation nationally and specialises in a style of painting which art critics have characterised as a fascinating cross between the contemporary realism of Stanley Spencer and the raw and sometimes violently distorted figures featured in the paintings of Francis Bacon.

It remains to be seen what the aficionados and experts of the art world who rate his work so highly will make of Mr Donnington's latest offering, but anyone who was present at yesterday's unveiling could be in no doubt that the parishioners of St Peter's gave it a decidedly mixed response.

There were some who felt that, given the subject matter and the significance of the day in the Christian calendar, the artist had perfectly captured the pain and suffering of the events of Good Friday. But a significant number of others seemed to find the painting, particularly the expression on the face of Christ, unpleasant and even deeply disturbing. 'Unnerving' and 'unsettling' were the words most frequently used by irate churchgoers after the painting was revealed for the first time.

Sam and Norma Arbuckle, lifelong members of the congregation who were married in St Peter's sixty years ago, felt they were speaking for the majority of those present when they said, 'We understand that Good Friday is a day to contemplate the pain of the cross. But this painting goes beyond what's acceptable. You just don't want to look at it. It certainly doesn't do anything to strengthen faith. And we think it could put a lot of people off coming into the church. It might be alright in an art gallery. It's definitely not alright in a place of worship.'

There had been rumours prior to the unveiling that it was unlikely to be universally popular, but no one, it seems, was quite prepared for the strength of the reaction. The Parochial Church Council is determined to keep the newly acquired painting where everyone can see it. In a statement to *The Gazette,* the Revd Peabody said, 'We understand that not everyone finds it entirely to their taste. However, we believe it to be a work of considerable artistic merit that speaks to us about something that lies at the heart of the Christian faith. We believe that over time people will come to appreciate its value, and we are deeply grateful to Mr Donnington for this generous gift of an original work of art. In keeping with his request, we have agreed to display it where it will be seen by everyone who enters the church as a constant reminder of the suffering of Jesus Christ on behalf of us all.'

The artist, currently on holiday in the Swiss Alps with a group of students from Penford Grammar School, was unavailable for comment. But this controversy is a long way from being over.

By the time he was halfway through the article, Eddie remembered what had puzzled him on his first reading. To a national newspaper the unrest among the congregation at St Peter's over a religious painting by a local artist would have been nothing more than a local spat, hardly even worthy of half a column somewhere in the inside pages. But in a small town, this was the stuff that makes headlines, a story that could run for months with enough powerful emotions to fuel a bitter dispute that could smoulder for decades.

And that was precisely the problem as he saw it. Despite the strong feelings aroused by the painting on its unveiling, the spark of controversy seemed to have been extinguished before it really took flame. He had searched in vain through subsequent weeks and months to find some further reference to the story. There was nothing. And this wasn't at all like life in Penford. There had to be something more. He could understand how over the course of years people would eventually just get used to the painting being there and wouldn't even notice it. What he couldn't understand was why it had all died down so quickly and why a local newspaper, always desperately looking for anything of interest that would help boost circulation, had allowed the story to disappear seemingly without trace.

Eddie was about to turn off the microfilm reader when he decided to scroll through the weeks following 28th March one last time, just to double-check if he'd missed anything that might be relevant to his search. That was when he noticed a brief report tucked away on page 5 of the 11th April edition of *The Gazette*. It was only a paragraph but it was enough to raise questions in his mind.

ST PETER'S REPAIR WORK TO GO AHEAD IMMEDIATELY
The much-needed repairs to the roof of St Peter's Church, which have been delayed for eighteen months because of lack of funds, are to go ahead in the next few weeks. At an extraordinary general meeting of the Parochial Church Council on Wednesday evening 8th April, members were informed of a substantial donation which will cover the work in its entirety. Mr Ernest Higginbotham, secretary to the PCC, said on behalf of the members, 'We are enormously grateful to Mr Herbert Donnington, who has already shown his generosity to St Peter's by the gift of his painting *A Portrait of Pain*. Now he has further demonstrated his kindness by making this donation which will enable us to proceed with the necessary work immediately.'

Could there be a link between this apparently big-hearted act and the surprisingly quick acceptance of a painting that had threatened to divide the congregation? And what, if anything, did all this have to do with the man who broke into St Peter's yesterday? Evidently, the answers to those questions couldn't be found in the archives of *The Gazette*. But Eddie was already thinking about where to begin his enquiries.

Four

Comings and Goings

Pippa was in a state of high anxiety. The last thing she needed on the Monday morning after Christmas – especially after the weekend they'd just come through – was a visit from the bishop at very short notice. The phone call from his secretary had been brief and to the point. Word of Saturday's break-in had reached Bishop Gerald (as most things that happened in the parish seemed to do) and, since he'd be passing on the motorway en route to another engagement, 'he'd like to pop in for twenty minutes and just catch up with what's been happening'. He was already on his way and would be with them in less than half an hour.

'You've met Bishop Gerald,' Pippa complained to her husband as she scurried round making sure the study was tidy enough to receive their unexpected guest. 'He's not the "popping in" type. He's always very formal and correct, makes appointments months in advance. He never turns up at a moment's notice unless there's a problem. And he lives in a palace, for goodness' sake. I'll bet there's never a speck of dust to be found. And he doesn't have kids like ours to leave a trail of destruction through the house.

It's at times like this I wish you'd persuaded me that becoming a vicar was a very bad idea.'

'Well, it's too late for that now,' Joe laughed as he tried to relieve the stress Pippa was feeling. 'And the bishop's not that bad. Yeah, he's very proper and a bit stiff and starchy, but he's always kind enough from what I've seen of him. And he seems to think highly of you. Probably just wants you to know you've got his support and...'

The doorbell rang before he could finish his sentence, and Pippa quickly tucked the duster she was holding behind the cushion on the armchair while Joe hurried to the door to greet their distinguished visitor. He led him into the study and was about to excuse himself when Bishop Gerald beckoned to him not to go.

'No, please stay, Joe,' he said. 'I want to talk to both of you. Let's sit down.'

He spoke very precisely in the public-school accent that always made Pippa a little nervous. But here in their home she noticed that he seemed more at ease than he did in public settings, and there was a genuine note of concern in his voice that lifted some of the tension she was feeling.

'I'm sure you could do without a visit from me today,' he said with a smile. 'But my secretary got one of those phone calls that come to us from time to time. Someone with a garbled version of what happened on Saturday. All I want is for you to fill me in as succinctly as you can on what really took place and to let you know that I'll do all I can to support you. I know how draining these unusual events can be – on both of you – on top of everything else. So, I'm all ears.'

Pippa told the story of the weekend's events while the bishop listened intently. When she'd finished, he nodded thoughtfully.

'Hmm... I can see this could turn out to be a tricky situation. I'm glad you've got Eddie Shaw on board. I've met him once or twice in the past. Always had the feeling there's something troubling him deep down. For all that, there's something I can't help liking about him. Keep him on side. If the national tabloids get hold of this, particularly the stigmata, who knows what they might do with the story. Eddie will help you deal with that. And our PR person at the diocesan offices will be there if you need her. Just keep us in the picture. And now I need to be going.'

Before he left, he stood with Pippa and Joe for a moment. He took them both by the hand, told them again of his sense that this might well be a difficult time for them, and offered a prayer for wisdom and protection. Joe, who couldn't recall ever having his hand held or being prayed for by a bishop before, felt slightly awkward, but grateful nonetheless for the concern of the man he usually described to Pippa as 'your boss, the bish'.

It wasn't until they were saying goodbye at the front door that Bishop Gerald took a piece of paper from his inside pocket, folded it over and handed it to Pippa.

'I'm going on sabbatical later this week. Spending some time in Africa and visiting the diocese there that we partner with. That's really why I wanted to call in today. But I'm leaving you this. It's the details of how to contact an old friend of mine. He's getting well on in years and he's a little frail these days. He's different from anyone you'll ever have met, a bit scary until you get to know him, to be honest. If you need someone with insight and wisdom, he's definitely the man to call. There's nobody I'd rather have around or that I'd trust more in a crisis. So if you think things are getting a bit too hot to handle, just call him. Tell him I told you to get in touch. And don't forget, you'll both be in my thoughts and prayers.'

As he drove off, Pippa unfolded the paper. On it was a Manchester phone number, an email address and the name 'Sam Andrews' in block capitals. It wasn't a name she recognised. She folded it over again and placed it under the paperweight she kept on top of the pile of papers on her desk that never seemed to go down. Once again, just as when Eddie Shaw had left on Saturday evening, she was unsure whether to be comforted or concerned by the words of a departing guest. And that thought was enough to set her wondering where Eddie was, when they might hear from him again and whether he had found out anything since he'd left them with his cryptic comments.

The truth was that she would have been surprised had she known the precise whereabouts of the editor of *The Gazette* at that moment. Pippa had been at St Peter's only a few weeks when someone told her that it was a standing joke among the townsfolk that Eddie was so devoted to his work and so determined not to miss anything that might happen in Penford that he hadn't left the town in years. It might have been said in jest, but it was nearer the truth than those who told the tale realised. Apart from the occasional and unavoidable business trip to Manchester or Liverpool, Eddie hadn't ventured beyond the boundaries of the town since his wife had died. He took no pleasure in travel for its own sake, and the thought of heading off anywhere on holiday brought back too many memories of times they'd enjoyed together. It was easier just to bury such memories and throw himself into his work.

This morning, however, Eddie was travelling north, far beyond the confines of Penford, and by ten o'clock he was driving his blue Jaguar Mark II by the side of Coniston Water. It was a bitterly cold but bright morning, the kind of day when anyone else might have wrapped themselves up and got out of their car to drink in the bracing air and marvel at the beauty of the Lake District. But Eddie had more pressing matters in mind than admiring the scenery, however impressive it might be.

He continued on for a mile or so, past the sparkling water of the lake on his left, before turning right off the road and onto a dirt track that led to a two-storey whitewashed cottage set behind a dry-stone wall and surrounded by an overgrown garden. When the track narrowed to the point at which it was impossible to drive any further without risking damage to the paintwork of his beloved car, he parked the vehicle and began to walk the remaining 100 or so yards.

Had he been one of the many hikers in the area that morning rather than an unfit, overweight man in entirely unsuitable clothes for such exercise, he might have stridden past without so much as a second glance and assumed that the neglected-looking house was deserted. Eddie knew better. It wasn't simply the fact that the wisp of smoke rising lazily from the chimney in the still air betrayed the fact that someone was in residence. Although they hadn't met for more than a decade, he was certain that the occupant of this out-of-the-way dwelling was unlikely to be anywhere other than at home. Just like himself, though for very different reasons, this was a man who rarely strayed far from the place where he lived and worked.

Eddie walked up the uneven stone path, picking his steps carefully to avoid tripping, and knocked loudly on the door. He waited for more than a minute without anyone answering. But, having travelled the best part of ninety miles and driven his immaculately clean car up a stony and muddy track, he wasn't about to turn and leave. Besides which, he was sure that the individual he needed to speak to would respond to his knocking eventually. His persistence was rewarded after another two or three minutes when the door was opened by a man who, despite the coldness of the day, was dressed in khaki shorts and a paint-stained T-shirt that had once been white. He was more than six feet in height, and his wiry and muscular build was in sharp contrast to that of his visitor. It took him a moment or two to recognise the person standing on his doorstep.

'Good grief, it's Eddie Shaw!' He half-shouted the words. 'What have I done to deserve this? I came up here to get away from folk like you. If only I'd known you were coming I'd have gone away for the day.'

His tone was brusque, but there was something about his manner that suggested he wasn't quite as annoyed as he wanted his hearer to think. He took a long look at the man standing in front of him.

'What the ...?' He hesitated just long enough to hold back the expletive that was on the tip of his tongue. Then he shook his head and laughed. 'What have you been doing to yourself? You look as if you've eaten all the pies, stuck glue on your body and run through a really bad second-hand clothes shop. You'd better come in. You're making the place look untidy.'

Spoken to anyone else and in any other context, his humour would have sounded ill-chosen and hurtful. To Eddie, however, his comments merely served to confirm that his journey hadn't been wasted and that he'd found the person he'd driven all this way to see on one of his better days. He stepped through the door and straight into a room that was unfurnished except for a scratched and worn table in the far corner that was covered in tubes of paint and countless brushes of different shapes and sizes, and one uncomfortable-looking metal chair. There was, however, a wood-burning stove in the corner of the room that Eddie was grateful to see after standing on the doorstep for so long, and the bareness of the room was alleviated by the dozens of canvasses of different sizes and in various stages of completion that were propped several deep against the bare walls. The daylight that flooded through the curtainless window to the right of the door served to illuminate an almost-completed landscape in oils standing on an artist's easel that Eddie took to be a painting of Coniston Water.

The two men had first met a decade earlier when *The Gazette* had run a six-week feature on sons and daughters of Penford who were making their mark on the wider world. It had taken some research before the name of Frank Cassidy had come up, simply because he'd left the town as a teenager shortly after his mother had died and hadn't had any subsequent contact with anyone in the area.

Initially after they'd managed to track him down he'd been reluctant to give an interview, but he'd relented when Eddie had promised him that they'd publish the article only when he'd approved it in full. He wouldn't speak about growing up in Penford beyond confirming the basic facts, and had refused point-blank to discuss the reasons for his apparently sudden departure. The difficulties of interviewing someone as taciturn as Frank Cassidy meant that Eddie had never been satisfied that he'd either captured the essence of his subject or got to the truth of his relationship with his place of birth. He'd always considered it to be the weakest article in the series.

There were, however, two things about their previous encounter that had stuck in Eddie's memory. There was the interviewee's reaction to his description of him as a 'landscape artist'. Frank Cassidy had responded with a grunt of annoyance and said he'd rather call himself a '*land-escape* artist'. And when he was pushed to elaborate a little on what he meant by that term, he'd come back with a few short sentences which Eddie had quoted verbatim and around which he'd tried to construct the rest of the article.

'Well, what's *not* in my paintings is as important to me as what *is* there. There are never any people. Not even a house or a shed or a bit of machinery. Nothing that would remind me of people. When I paint I want to *focus* – focus on the natural world. But I also want to *forget* – forget all about people. It's a way of being on my own, with my own thoughts, in my own place.'

The other thing that Eddie had remembered – the thing that had prompted him to drive to the Lake District on a cold December day – was that in the course of that interview he'd learned that Frank Cassidy had first discovered his talent as a painter when he was a pupil in the art department at Penford Grammar School. If his calculations were correct, Frank would have been in the sixth form around the time of the presentation of Herbert Donnington's controversial *A Portrait of Pain* to St Peter's. And if he was to begin to solve the mystery surrounding the painting and to discover the identity of the man who'd broken into the church a few days earlier, he'd more than a hunch that this was as good a place to start as any.

Eddie knew that the man he'd come to see was not the kind of person to be smooth-talked into helping him with his quest. So when he'd sat down on the only chair and Frank Cassidy had perched himself on the edge of the table, he came straight to the point.

'I know you don't like unexpected visitors, so let me explain why I've turned up on your doorstep unannounced. Something's happened in Penford in the last few days and I think you just might be able to help me begin to get to the bottom of the matter. In fact, it all starts with another unexpected visitor…'

'I can't imagine what it's got to do with me,' Frank replied, with an expression of weary impatience on his face. 'But go on. I'll stop you straight away if I think it's just you trying to get another story. I've done my one interview for your paper.'

But he didn't stop his visitor or even interrupt him. The more he heard, the more intently he listened to Eddie's account of the break-in at St Peter's, the startling resemblance of The Intruder to the face of Christ, and his uneasiness at the way in which the controversy over the unveiling of the painting more than half a century ago seemed to have dissipated so quickly.

Over the years Eddie had mastered the art of telling a captivating story that would elicit an immediate response from his hearers. But when he'd finished speaking there was no reaction from this audience of one. The room was quiet apart from the crackling of the wood in the stove. He looked in vain at the face of the man opposite him, trying to gauge what he was thinking and whether or not he knew anything that would be relevant to his search.

He was beginning to think that his journey might turn out to have been pointless when Frank broke the silence. His blank expression morphed into a look of the deepest sadness and his words came slowly. The abrasive jocularity of his initial greeting had disappeared completely.

'I've tried not to think about Old Man Donnington since I left Penford. But he's always been there, lurking in my memory. I had a feeling that one day I'd need to deal with him again. But this won't be easy, so you'll have to give me some time. Let's have something to eat and then maybe I'll summon up enough courage to talk.'

The two men went into the kitchen, which was in stark contrast to the bare room that served as the studio. This was obviously where Frank spent his time when not painting. The cupboards and fittings were old but well maintained and everything was brightly painted and sparklingly clean. The walls were covered in original works by artists from schools of painting very different to the naturalistic landscapes that filled the front room of the cottage. And, to Eddie's relief, there were two reasonably comfortable solid wooden chairs on either side of a Formica-topped table.

As he watched his host set out the meal, it quickly became clear that while Frank Cassidy was something of a recluse, he was certainly not an ascetic when it came to food. Within ten minutes they were sitting down to a lunch of homemade soup and bread and cold meats with fresh salad and a variety of side dishes. Eddie declined the invitation to wash it all down with a pint of his host's home-brewed beer, making the excuse that he shouldn't drink knowing he would be driving home in an hour or two. He could have added, but didn't, that the offer of a glass of wine would have been much more of a temptation to a man who hadn't drunk beer since his student days.

Nothing was said beyond the normal small talk of a shared meal until they had finished eating and Frank had emptied his pint glass. He added nothing to what he'd said before lunch until he'd washed and dried the dishes from which they'd just eaten. He very carefully wiped the surfaces, making sure that everything was tidy. Then, still standing at the sink with his back to Eddie, he began to speak again. His words came in short sentences.

'Herbert Donnington was a gifted artist. An even better teacher. He was an inspiration to us boys. Gave us hours of his time. Must be four or five of us who've gone on to become professional painters. In that sense we owe him a lot.'

He stood very still, keeping every muscle under control, and his breathing became heavier and more audible. Eddie said nothing, sensing that what was about to follow would be as difficult for him to hear as it would be for Frank to speak it aloud.

'He was brilliant. Could be incredibly generous. But he was...' he struggled to find the words, 'he was ruthlessly demanding. Not just about art. Not just about you giving your best. *He wanted you to give yourself to him.* I mean, he literally wanted you – emotionally, physically. And in the end it left you with nothing worth keeping.'

He slumped over the sink and began to sob. It was like the crying of an abandoned and wretched child, a child who'd lost father and mother and brothers and sisters, a child who could see nothing to hope for, nothing to live for. And it seemed like it would never end.

Eddie got up from his chair, walked across the kitchen and stood beside him. He wanted to put his arm on his shoulder, say something that would comfort him, but he knew that any words would sound like mere platitudes, any gesture would be an insensitive intrusion into a profound anguish he could only begin to imagine. There was something terrible and disturbing in witnessing this tall, strong, elderly man in such distress, utterly overcome by grief. It was as if his dignity and self-worth were draining from him as tears, spit and snot ran down his face and over his mouth. There was nothing to do but to allow the torrent of sorrow to run its course.

Eventually the sobbing began to subside. Something that had been bottled up for years had been released. Frank slowly straightened up and looked out of the window at the bare winter landscape that mirrored the cold desolation of his heart. He let out a long sigh and leaned forward again until his head was almost touching the bottom of the sink. His right hand searched for the cold tap and turned it on full so that the water poured over his head, over his clothes and splashed over the floor.

Eddie did the only thing he could think of. He picked up a towel that was lying on one of the worktops and waited until this strange baptism was complete and the tap was turned off. As he handed the towel to Frank, he felt like an acolyte assisting at some primitive rite of cleansing. Something had happened that he did not understand and could not adequately explain. His years in journalism had not prepared him, had given him no frame of reference, for this. His ability to paint word pictures that offered his readers an insight into the meaning of events was unequal to the task of adequately describing a moment like this. The truth was that he felt totally out of his depth in the face of what he'd just witnessed.

It had never occurred to Eddie when he had left home that morning that by midday he'd be mopping a floor or making a pot of tea for a man he barely knew. Now it was a relief to be doing something useful while his host went upstairs to change out of his sopping wet clothes. But those simple actions gave him the opportunity to steel himself for what was about to be revealed. He'd seen and heard enough already to know that Frank's story would not be a pleasant one. What he didn't know was precisely what it would tell him about Herbert Donnington and his painting, or about the man who'd broken into St Peter's two days earlier.

The story that unfolded over the next couple of hours was a chronicle of control and abuse that was painful for an old man to tell and excruciating even for a hardened newspaper man to hear. The sharp, clear light of the late December day had given way to the lengthening shadows of a midwinter dusk by the time the story was complete.

'Do what you will with what I've told you,' Frank concluded. 'I should have spoken up years ago. But I couldn't. It's all been trapped inside me. A mixture of embarrassment and guilt, and the fear that nobody would believe me, or if they did they'd despise me. I don't know if I'd ever have said anything if you hadn't turned up today and told me about what's just happened in Penford. Maybe that'll be what changes things and helps me – helps all of us – begin to get free of this.'

He slumped back in his chair, exhausted physically and emotionally. It was obvious just how costly it had been for him to reveal what he'd buried and kept hidden for so long. The two men sat quietly together for almost half an hour until Frank suddenly stood up. He seemed to have regained his composure, and even the feistiness with which he'd greeted his guest that morning had returned.

'Come on, I don't need you cluttering up my place and stopping me from getting on with what I need to do. Time you got yourself back to Penford. You're getting nothing more out of me today.'

His expression softened and he added with an easy laugh, 'Leave me your number and I'll get in touch later in the week if I think of anything else you need to know.'

Eddie was reluctant to go, unsure if it was alright to leave a man in whom he'd stirred up such memories. But there was no doubting Frank's insistence that he was OK as he ushered his visitor towards the door. They shook hands and, just as he turned to walk to his car, Eddie thought he saw him mouth the words, 'Thanks for coming.' But it was too dark for him to be sure.

He reversed slowly and carefully until the track widened sufficiently for him to turn the car around and head back to the main road. And as he accelerated along the side of Coniston Water, he was aware of very mixed emotions. He'd got what he'd come for, found out even more than he'd expected, and that kind of result never failed to give him a sense of elation and satisfaction. It always delivered an adrenaline rush that made him feel awake and alert, however long and demanding the day had been. But what he'd heard had also produced in him a weariness, the like of which he'd seldom experienced. He felt something wet on his cheek and immediately assumed that he must have left the car window slightly open, allowing the rain to come in. Instinctively he reached out to wind the window up, only to discover that it was already tightly shut. It was only when his vision of the headlights of a car coming towards him seemed to flow and distort that he realised to his surprise that what he could feel on his cheek was a tear. He was beginning to cry and he couldn't stop it.

He managed to get as far as the first services on the motorway, where he pulled in and booked himself into the motel for the night. But before he showered and went to bed, he did two things. First, he emailed Pippa Sheppard to ask if they could meet at nine o'clock the following morning, saying nothing more than that he had 'picked up one or two bits of information that they should talk about'. Then he took his laptop and wrote up a full account of everything Frank had told him. Normally, he would have constantly checked his notebook to confirm that his recollection of any interview or conversation was accurate. Tonight, tired though he was, he could remember the story in every detail. In truth, he suspected he would never be able to erase any of those details from his memory.

Five

The Price of Truth

Eddie Shaw arrived at the vicarage just before nine o'clock the following morning to find Pippa and Joe sitting at the kitchen table poring over the newspapers for that day. They had quickly scanned the quality broadsheets and put them to one side. The attentions of their reporters had clearly been focused on weightier issues of national and international significance than the goings-on, however unusual, in an ordinary Anglican church in an ordinary northern town. The tabloids, however, were a different matter entirely. They'd all picked up on the story of the break-in at St Peter's on Saturday, although, to Pippa's relief, most of them had given it only a few column inches in the inside pages, confining their reports to the facts that The Intruder had requested that 'the vicar provide him with his own communion service', and had displayed a remarkable likeness to a painting of Christ that had hung in the church for many years.

Pippa wasn't surprised, however, to see that *The Dawn*, which had the well-deserved reputation of being the most popular as well as the most scurrilous of the national dailies in the north-west, had devoted a double page to the story, which it was claiming as an exclusive. The headline, running across both pages in white block capitals and framed on a black background, posed the question 'Is this the Messiah?' And just above the main text was a subheading, 'Or is he just a naughty boy?' There were several photographs – one of the church, one of Pippa they'd taken from St Peter's website, an old black-and-white image of the unveiling of Herbert Donnington's painting from fifty years ago, and – taking pride of place – a close-up of Billy Ross sitting in the George and Dragon with a half-finished pint of beer in front of him. It was obvious to Pippa that Billy had been the source of most of what was in the article. From the state he was in when they'd found him later on the Saturday, she suspected that he'd been paid for the information not in cash but in as much free alcohol as he could consume. She gritted her teeth as she read the article.

> The Lancashire town of Penford was awash with claims and counter-claims this weekend after an unusual break-in at St Peter's Anglican Church. The intruder appears to have stolen nothing but refused to leave the church when he was discovered early on Saturday morning by the church caretaker, Billy Ross, a former professional footballer who has struggled with alcoholism for years since retiring from the game.
>
> According to Billy, the intruder was an elderly man who, despite his age, bore a startling resemblance to the face of Christ depicted in a painting by a local artist that has hung in the church entrance for fifty years. The painting has recently

been the focus of a bitter dispute between the vicar and members of the congregation.

What has increased the level of interest almost to fever pitch in the local community is Billy's insistence that the man he found kneeling at the front of the church had what appeared to be wounds in the palm of each hand reminiscent of the nail prints made in the hands of Jesus when he was nailed to the cross.

Some devout members of the congregation at St Peter's are speculating that this is some kind of spiritual visitation akin to the miraculous appearances of Mary that have been claimed at sites like Lourdes in France. The majority of the townspeople are more sceptical, however, and are asking if the likeness of the visitor to the painting of Christ is nothing more than a coincidence, and if the claimed sighting of the wound prints in his hands is just a trick of the light or the product of an overactive alcohol-fuelled imagination. Some are even suggesting that Billy Ross might have been the victim of a deliberate deception by a clever con man who preys upon the devout.

The Reverend Pippa Sheppard, the Vicar of St Peter's, was unavailable for interview but has issued a statement through the Bishop's office saying only that an elderly man had been discovered in the church on Saturday and that he is now in Penford Infirmary undergoing tests. The Bishop, the Right Reverend Gerald Taylor-Smith, is on sabbatical somewhere in Africa at present but is rumoured to be about to fly home to deal with what many in

Penford feel has the potential to become a full-blown crisis.

Eric Jones, a local independent councillor and an active member of the Penford Atheist Association, said, 'We need a clear statement from the church on this matter. Penford is generally a tolerant town with far more agnostics, atheists and humanists than people who adhere to a religious faith. But if this is allowed to go unchecked it could lead to the kind of religious hysteria that may well have a detrimental effect particularly on people with mental health problems. Someone needs to look at this whole thing rationally so that we can learn what really happened.'

Pippa groaned and pushed the paper across the table for Eddie to see. 'That's nothing more than a collection of lies and half-truths. Mentioning Billy's problems with drinking isn't fair. The implication is that the whole thing's just some kind of alcohol-induced hallucination. And there's no bitter dispute between me and the congregation. And they've made up that bit about the Bishop cutting short his sabbatical. How can they write this stuff?'

Eddie, who'd read the article earlier, just shook his head. 'That's the tabloids for you, I'm afraid. By the time I managed to speak to someone at *The Dawn* it was too late to stop it. The problem is, truth is cheap for these people. If you just want to sell newspapers, then playing up the latest sensation gets results faster than the hard work of providing accurate information. Believe me, I've seen far worse than that.'

'Well, it'll all be fish 'n' chip paper by the end of the week,' Joe suggested, sitting back in his chair and putting his hands behind his head. 'Maybe the whole thing will be forgotten before the end of January.'

'If only,' Eddie responded with a raise of his eyebrows. 'I'm afraid we'll have to live with this for a bit longer. But there are some things I need to tell you.'

He stooped down and drew a buff-coloured folder out of the briefcase he'd brought with him.

'I'll email you electronic copies of this stuff later,' he said, as he opened his folder, 'but I didn't want you to get it before I could go through it with you. I went up to the Lake District yesterday to talk to a man I interviewed ten years or so ago for a series we were running in *The Gazette*. I had a feeling he might be able to shed some light on this business, and I wasn't wrong.'

He pushed his chair a few inches back from the table, put his hands on his knees, closed his lips tightly and breathed noisily through his nose. It was a sequence of actions that Pippa had noticed on his first visit and already she recognised it as a sure sign that Eddie had something significant to say to them.

'The man I went to see was Frank Cassidy, and he told me a story that answers quite a few of the questions that were in my mind. Raised a few more, to be honest, but let me read to you what I've written. I have to warn you that that it won't be easy or pleasant listening. It'll probably be best if you wait until I'm finished before you ask any questions.'

Pippa and Joe were happy just to listen, and Eddie pulled his chair nearer the table again. He cleared his throat and gave a wheezy cough. Another of his habits, Pippa noted to herself, whenever he felt he needed to take the initiative in a situation. He opened the buff file in front of him and began to read.

Frank Cassidy was a pupil at Penford Grammar School in the mid-to-late 1950s. He was a popular character who performed well both academically and on the sports field, captaining the rugby team and also representing both the school and the county at cricket. However, most notably, he was a particularly gifted young painter and his ability was quickly noticed by Herbert Donnington when he became the head of the art department.

Donnington, who was gaining a reputation nationally as a painter of exceptional talent, immediately took Frank under his wing, giving him individual tuition, exposing him to different styles of art and generally developing his talent. Frank was understandably flattered by this attention and became part of a group of boys that Donnington would take on trips to art galleries and even, on occasions, invite to his home, some five miles outside Penford.

Frank remembers him as being not only single-mindedly committed to painting but also being devoutly religious. This combination of piety and artistic talent initially made a great impact on the group of students he was gathering around him and whose talent he was nurturing. It also meant that their parents were happy to entrust their teenage children to the care of a man who was highly respected for his seeming religious devotion and his generosity with his time.

There was, however, a darker side to Herbert Donnington's personality and a far more unsavoury reason for his interest in his young protégés. From time to time he would have individual boys stay at his home overnight. The first couple of times this happened, Frank recalls, Donnington's wife and young daughter were present at the house and nothing untoward took place. There would be two or three hours of intensive practical teaching during which Donnington would not only work on the techniques of painting but also stress the importance of giving oneself entirely to the pursuit of excellence in art. He would speak at great length about artistic ability being a special gift from God and the exercise of that talent being in itself an expression of religious devotion. At the end of an evening session, his pupil would spend the night in an attic bedroom while Donnington and his wife would sleep in a room on the floor beneath.

Only when the trust of a boy and his parents had been gained would the darker motives of their mentor begin to emerge. The more often a boy visited the house overnight, the more likely it would be that Donnington's wife and daughter would not be present. He always accounted for their absence by explaining that they were visiting Mrs Donnington's elderly mother, whose health was frail.

Eddie lifted his eyes from the document in front of him and Pippa noticed that that he was hesitant about reading what followed. The easy confidence of the experienced journalist that he'd exuded on his previous visit to the vicarage seemed to have deserted him. Joe noticed it too and sprang to his feet to rescue the situation.

'Why don't we take a break?' he said, trying to sound as casual as he could. 'I'll make some coffee and then we can carry on. I could certainly do with a cup.'

The truth was that all three of them were grateful for the opportunity to steel themselves for what they were inevitably about to hear. They took a little more time over the coffee break than was absolutely necessary before Eddie began to read again.

> Frank believes that the first time he was alone with Donnington was on his third visit to his house. He remembers that at first the evening followed the usual pattern until it was time for him to retire for the night. He was just drifting off to sleep when Donnington entered the room and came across to sit on his bed. He suggested that it was time 'to take the teaching and learning to a deeper level', and said that from now on he wanted to pray privately with each of his 'special students'. He added that it would be better not to tell other people about this aspect of their relationship as 'not everyone would understand'. Donnington then got into the single bed, wrapped himself around the boy and began to touch him intimately. It was a deeply disturbing experience for the boy who instinctively knew this was wrong but who was in awe of his teacher.
>
> On subsequent overnight visits to Donnington's house, of which there were probably ten or a dozen, these sexual assaults progressed beyond

inappropriate touching to what can only be described as full-scale rape. A mixture of guilt, confusion, embarrassment and a lack of a suitable vocabulary to express what was happening meant that Frank was unable to tell his parents or anyone in authority. It was only after he left Penford Grammar School and went to art college at the age of seventeen that he managed to free himself from Donnington's attentions. The experience has scarred him for life. He has never married and has found it impossible to form mature adult relationships of any depth.

Once again Eddie stopped reading. He frowned and pursed his lips as he turned the folder over.

'Look, I'm not going to read through the next two or three paragraphs,' he said wearily. 'The details are all there and you can read them for yourselves. Like I said, they don't make pleasant reading. I can't begin to comprehend what it must have done to Frank all these years. I felt soiled just listening to the stuff. I didn't sleep well last night. Couldn't get it out of my mind.'

Joe got up, walked across the room and opened a window, allowing a cold draught to blow through the room.

'I just need to get some air… clear my head. I'll close it in a minute. But there are a couple of things I don't understand. Why did he open up to you after all these years of staying silent? After all, that was only the second time he'd met you. I can't imagine he's easily persuaded by newspaper reporters. And, most importantly, how does this help us to find out who our unexpected visitor is?'

'Well, if you'll close that window before I freeze to death and sit down,' Eddie came back at him, grateful for the opportunity to regain his composure, 'I'll tell you.'

Relieved to put the sordid details of Herbert Donnington's abusive behaviour aside for the moment, Eddie gave them a brief report of his search through the archives of *The Gazette* the previous Sunday and the questions that had prompted him to set off for Coniston the following morning.

'I knew that Herbert Donnington was the artist who painted *A Portrait of Pain*,' he explained, 'and I remembered from my interview ten years ago that Frank Cassidy had been one of his pupils. Now the only conclusion I could come to from the resemblance of our mysterious Intruder to the face in the painting was that he had to have been the model that Donnington used. And it seemed to me to be a reasonable assumption, given his age, that he, too, was probably one of his students.

'My mental arithmetic is still good enough for me to be able to work out that, if my assumptions were correct, there was every likelihood that his time at Penford Grammar School had overlapped with that of Frank. So I was hoping against hope that Frank would know something about the history of the painting and that he might just be able at least to give us a clue to the identity of the man who broke into the church.'

He paused, looking for a reaction that would confirm they were following his line of reasoning. 'Are you still with me?' he asked, with the expression of a lawyer presenting his case to a jury that was a little slow on the uptake.

'Yes, I think so,' Pippa answered, looking slightly puzzled. 'Go on.'

Joe nodded his agreement, and that was all the encouragement Eddie needed.

'Well, it turned out that Frank *did* know about the painting. In fact, that's the thing that got him talking. He recalls it as Donnington's all-consuming project at that time. As he put it, "That was the thing that brought together all of Donnington's obsessions – his art, his fixation on religion and his unhealthy interest in teenage boys."

'He'd chosen as the model for his work a pupil who was a contemporary of Frank's. Of course, that gave him the opportunity and the excuse to spend even more time alone with the boy without too many people asking awkward questions. Frank described the boy in question as being a tall, good-looking lad with piercing blue eyes. He was physically well developed and could have passed for being in his early twenties rather than what he was – just sixteen or so.

'It's hard for us, knowing what we now know about grooming and the whole subject of abuse, to comprehend why the authorities were not more alert to what was going on. But it was a long time ago. No doubt the headmaster and governors were seduced – no pun intended – by the increasing attention Donnington brought to the school. And they were understandably well disposed towards the handsome young man who was also exceptionally talented, not only in art but right across a range of subjects. Donnington, of course, wanted him to go on to art college. His teachers in other subjects, however, reckoned that he was Oxford or Cambridge material, particularly in Classics or English.

'Now here it starts to get even more interesting, though interesting isn't the right word,' Eddie went on with a shudder. 'There were three or four boys, of whom Frank was one, who were particularly the object of Donnington's unwanted attentions, and almost inevitably they gravitated towards each other. They said little to each other in specific terms about what was happening to them. But there was, Frank said, a kind of tacit understanding that they were the unwilling members of Donnington's chosen circle. Their common bond somehow helped them to function as a kind of support group for each other. It enabled them to compartmentalise things and, at least to an extent, to lock away the terrible things that were being done to them and carry on with the rest of their lives.

'But for the boy who'd been chosen to model for the painting, the burden was heavier. He was having to spend even more time in Donnington's company and became increasingly isolated from the rest of the group. Eventually and inevitably it began to take a toll on his work and on his mental and physical health. From being a star pupil with a bright personality and great career prospects he gradually became morose, shut in on himself, and lost all interest in his studies.'

Pippa shifted in her seat. She wanted to ask the name of the boy and whether he was one and the same as the man who'd broken into the church, but she guessed that there was more to come of the story Eddie was telling before he would be ready to reveal what she so much wanted to hear. He sensed her impatience and dismissed it with a slight shake of his head and a wave of his hand. 'Don't worry, I *will* tell you what I know you want to hear. Just let me go on with the story a little bit longer. Now where was I? Yes… As Frank recalls it, to everyone's surprise, the young man for whom his teachers had predicted such an outstanding future began to lose all interest in his studies and eventually ended up leaving the school and moving away from Penford all together. By that time, Donnington had lost interest in him. His masterpiece was complete and, in his eyes, his protégé had let him down.

'The group of boys of which Frank was a part, however, knew the truth, knew what it meant for any of Donnington's pupils who had to spend time alone in his company. And one of them, despite the unwillingness of the others to speak up, plucked up the courage to tell his parents, who approached the headmaster about what had been going on.

'You might imagine that at this point something would have been done. But, like I've said, this was fifty years ago. Attitudes were different and the safeguarding policies that have been put in place today just didn't exist. The unveiling of the painting had already been announced with a great fanfare about Donnington's generosity in giving it to St Peter's. The main concern of the headmaster and the governors – one of whom was the Reverend Simon Peabody, the Vicar of St Peter's – was to protect the reputation of the school and the church and to avoid a scandal. The boy's mother was persuaded to keep the matter quiet, believing that this would also be best for her son.

'The unveiling of *A Portrait of Pain* went ahead as planned. And even the initial wave of criticism from members of St Peter's who found the painting disturbing, and who might even have picked up rumours about the relationship of the artist to his young model, was quickly swept away when Donnington, possibly persuaded by the headmaster and the Vicar, made a substantial donation which covered the cost of the repairs to the roof, which had needed to be done for some considerable time. There might have been dark rumblings about his conduct, but the people in authority seem to have made sure that it never came to light.'

Eddie let out a sigh, a weary mingling of resignation and disgust. He looked drained, and for a moment Joe and Pippa thought he was going to leave the story there. But after a brief pause and a shake of his head, he pressed on to the end of his sorry narrative.

'And that gets me to what you really want to hear. Donnington left Penford Grammar the following year. I'm guessing he was encouraged to move on by those who were in on the secret and knew the truth about his conduct. He took up a similar post at a boarding school somewhere in Norfolk. As far as I can gather, he left there suddenly after another couple of years – similar problems, you can be sure – and I can't find any trace of him from there.'

He paused again and looked directly at Pippa, who was still waiting impatiently to discover the identity of The Intruder.

'And the young fellow who was the artist's model? Frank Cassidy remembers him well. Still feels guilty that he didn't have the courage to speak up and help him. His recollection is that he moved away just a week or so before the painting was unveiled. The last Frank heard of him – which was many years ago – he was living rough. From the description you gave that I shared with him, Frank's sure, even after all these years, that he's the man who broke into St Peter's on Saturday morning. His name is Josh Naismith.'

Pippa, who'd been so anxious for this final piece of the jigsaw, found herself lost for words when it actually came. She tried to think of an adequate response, but all she was able to do was to shake her head and repeat the words 'Josh Naismith' two or three times in a voice just above a whisper.

It was left to Joe to formulate a response to Eddie's story. 'I don't know whether we should thank you for that or not,' he said wryly. 'I mean, it doesn't show my school or our church in a very favourable light. But thanks for all you've done and what you've found out in just a couple of days. I guess the question for us now is, what do we do and where do we go with this information?'

'Well, clearly our first duty,' Pippa responded, 'is to help an elderly man who's been through so much and who's made his way back to Penford and back to St Peter's despite what this place has done to him. We certainly owe him something.'

Eddie was just about to suggest that they should leave the conversation there, take some time to reflect and meet again for half an hour in the evening to work out their next steps. Before he could get the words out, his phone rang. It was a number he didn't recognise and he excused himself, going into the hallway to take the call. Pippa and Joe, who were still trying to digest all they'd learned in the last hour, could overhear just enough to make out that it was very much a one-sided conversation in which the caller was obviously doing most of the talking. Joe even remarked under his breath to Pippa that it wasn't like Eddie to be out-talked by anyone.

When he did come back into the room, still with his phone in his hand, Eddie's normally ruddy complexion had lost its colour and his breathing was laboured more than usual. He half-staggered towards a chair. Pippa's first thought was that the stress of the last few days had brought on a heart attack and she quickly fetched a glass of water. Her suggestion that she should call a doctor was quickly dismissed.

'No, don't do that,' he insisted with a wave of his hand. 'Just give me a minute and I'll be alright.'

She felt an overwhelming wave of compassion for this man who'd previously made her slightly nervous, but who now seemed so vulnerable and fragile despite his considerable size and formidable presence. She would have reached out and taken hold of his hand had she not been afraid that such an expression of sympathy would only have embarrassed him. There was nothing to be done until he was ready to speak again.

'That was the police in Coniston,' he said, his voice hoarse and tired. 'This morning a couple of walkers found the body of Frank Cassidy in the woods near his house. He was hanging from a tree. Taken his own life...'

His voice wavered and he took some sips from the glass of water that Pippa had set in front of him.

'Oh, Eddie,' Joe gasped. 'I'm so sorry. I can only guess what a shock that must be to you.'

'You're right about that. Just hearing that news was bad enough, but what really hit me was the reason why the police phoned *me*. Frank asked me to leave him my mobile number before I left yesterday, which, of course, I did. He said he'd get in touch if he thought of anything else I needed to know. I thought it was a good sign. Thought he'd found some kind of release in talking about it, some hope for the future. Well, I was wrong on that one.'

His hand was trembling as he sipped again from the glass of water. He put it back on the table very carefully.

'His phone was in his pocket when they found him and, of course, the police checked all the phone activity over the last few days. He hadn't made that many calls in the last six months, and most of them were to suppliers of art materials. He didn't appear to have any close friends with whom he was in regular contact. And he sent even fewer texts.

'But the first thing the police found, the last text he sent, was the one he sent to me about one o'clock this morning. I was so tired that I switched my phone off in the motel last night and put it in my bag to make sure I brought it home – I've left it in motel rooms so often. I didn't bother to check it after I switched it on again this morning. So I didn't even know it was there until I got that call from the police.'

He scrolled down through the texts and pushed the phone across the table for Pippa and Joe to read the message.

Thanks for visit. Should've spoken out long ago. But shame & guilt have destroyed me. Media attention too much. Not yr fault. Pls don't blame yourself. JUST GET THE TRUTH OUT.

Pippa felt she should say something in response to what was turning out to have more far-reaching consequences than she had imagined when Billy Ross had come banging on the vicarage door and alerted them to the presence of The Intruder on Saturday morning. If only it had just been another break-in.

'They didn't cover this in my ordination training,' she said, in a vain attempt at dry humour. 'There wasn't anything in the pastoral care manual or the sessions on resolving conflict that prepared me for this.'

Neither of her companions responded with even a hint of a smile, and she wished she'd just said nothing. The truth was that none of them had words that were adequate and none of them was remotely prepared for this news – the terrible death of a gifted but guilt-ridden man who'd hanged himself at a place and time where even the darkness and bitter chill of the woodland could not match the black loneliness of his troubled soul.

It was left to Eddie to express the reality that each of them was being forced to acknowledge.

'If you do the kind of journalism that *The Dawn* specialises in, truth is nothing more than a cheap and expendable commodity. And if you believe politicians with their fine speeches and preachers with their passionate sermons, you can persuade yourself that the truth sets us free. Maybe it does in the long run. Let's hope so.

'But what I've learned as a journalist over the years is that exposing the truth can be a dangerous business. And what I've seen more clearly than ever today is that the truth sometimes comes at a terrible price. And, more often than we like to think, that price is paid not by the guilty but by the innocent. That's what happened in the woods outside Coniston last night.'

There was nothing to be added to Eddie's words. Their conversation could go no further, and each of them had something to do that required their immediate attention. Eddie had to talk to the police in Penford about what he'd discovered and what had happened, Joe had to pick up Harry and Zoe from the home of one of their school friends, and Pippa had a double appointment – a meeting with Katie Morgan at Penford Infirmary and a pastoral visit to the elderly man whose arrival in the town was threatening to turn everything upside down.

All three were grateful for the opportunity to do something practical, even though none of them had any idea how this strange train of events would turn out. The mood as they parted was sombre. When Eddie had left the vicarage on his previous visit, he'd done so with a hint of humour and a word of encouragement to hope for a happy ending to the story. On this occasion, however, neither he nor the couple who stood on the doorstep as he drove off had any idea what was going to happen next, how long events would take to unfold or what kind of ending there would be.

Six

A Visit to the Infirmary

Penford Hospital's long and colourful history had fascinated and amused Pippa ever since she'd picked up a leaflet on her first visit. It had been founded by a group of local philanthropists in 1830 and given the all-encompassing title of The Penford Infirmary Dispensary, Lunatic Hospital and Asylum. Records show that in its first year, despite the paucity of reliable medicines and the total absence of effective anaesthetics, its doctors and house surgeons treated more than 1,000 patients with different kinds of fever and performed more than fifty limb amputations. In that same period they also spent a total of £980 on salaries, £295 on wine and £287 on leeches. And though there were times in subsequent years when the mortality rate among patients soared as high as 15 per cent, there could be no doubt that the townspeople appreciated the ministrations of the hospital and its staff. When the famed operatic soprano Linda Jenson visited the town at the behest of the trustees in 1847, the concert she gave was so well supported that it raised a total of £1,511, enabling the construction of an additional wing complete with state-of-the-art hot water pipes and gas lighting.

By the time Pippa was driving into the hospital grounds just after two o'clock on the Tuesday afternoon of the week after Christmas, the only evidence of that rich history still remaining was the neo-classical tetrastyle portico with its four ionic columns that had once formed the impressive entrance to the main building. The architect of those bygone days had clearly heeded the wishes of the trustees who were determined that charity and civic pride should go hand in hand, and they had instructed him that The Penford Infirmary Dispensary, Lunatic Hospital and Asylum should be no less imposing than anything that could be seen in the big cities of Manchester or Liverpool. That once-imposing portico now formed only a humble and incongruous entrance to the present glass and steel structure, which had been opened at the beginning of the new millennium and now loomed over it.

Many of Penford's present-day residents protested that this attempt to blend old and new was a crass example of architectural dissonance unworthy of the town's much-loved Infirmary. In truth, had the matter been voted on in a local referendum, they would have preferred to have retained and refurbished the old building rather than see it demolished and replaced with what was often sarcastically described as an 'overgrown greenhouse'. Popular sentiment did, however, prevail when the powers that be elected to change the name to Penford *Hospital*. In an age of soundbites and political correctness, the original name had long ago been abandoned and shortened to Penford Infirmary. But Penford *Hospital* was a step too far. That might be the official designation; it might even be what appeared in the heading of formal documents and what was proclaimed in bold letters on the side of the building. But, to a man and a woman, everyone in Penford insisted on continuing to call it the Infirmary.

Unlike so many of those who had been born and bred in the town, Pippa liked the juxtaposition of old and new – nineteenth-century stone portico interlinked with twenty-first-century stark minimalism. For her it expressed a healthy acceptance of the need for progress allied to a proper appreciation of the past, and she sometimes wished that financial restraints and entrenched attitudes could be overcome to allow a similar transformation to be worked on the Victorian Gothic pile at St Peter's. It was something that often went through her mind when she came to the hospital on one of her regular pastoral visits.

Today, however, as she passed through the gloom of the portico and into the well-lit reception area, her thoughts were turning in a different direction. She was coming to visit an elderly man who'd returned to Penford after an absence of fifty years, an elderly man who in his youth had suffered terribly at the hands of someone now long since dead, an elderly man who'd been let down by people in authority who should have protected him, an elderly man whose arrival just a few days ago had brought the reality of the past right into the present.

If those civic authorities who had been charged with finding a place for the history of a building in its contemporary manifestation had struggled to balance past and present, how much more difficult would it be to provide justice for someone whose pain had endured for half a century? Grateful as she was for the love and support of Joe and the involvement and experience of Eddie Shaw, it was a burden that she sensed was being firmly laid squarely on her shoulders, and one for which she felt ill equipped and unprepared.

The geriatric ward was at the end of a long central corridor which ran through the heart of the building, exposing Pippa to the sights and sounds of life in a busy hospital: rows of noticeboards with posters clumsily attached with sticky tape that offended her fondness for tidiness and order; worried couples with troubled expressions walking slowly arm in arm, whose whispered conversations caused a wave of compassion to well up in her; porters conveying patients on trolleys and chatting as naturally as workmen pushing wheelbarrows. It was a world with which she'd become familiar and in which she'd gradually come to feel at home since the responsibilities of ordained ministry demanded regular visitation of sick and elderly parishioners.

But it was the distinctive smell of a hospital – the characteristic pungent aroma that she assumed to be a mixture of medicines, disinfectants and cleaning fluids – that always reminded her that it was *a world apart*, a parallel, sterile universe accessible from the everyday world we inhabit but governed by its own laws and moving to a different rhythm. It was a world in which things that were logically opposites – community and loneliness, sleep and wakefulness, health and disease, life and death – coexisted in a close and never-ending embrace. And as she pressed the buzzer and waited to be admitted to the ward to meet the man who'd broken into St Peter's on Saturday morning, she mentally added two more complementary contradictions – anticipation and dread.

The cheerful, if weary-looking, nurse who opened the door to the ward recognised Pippa immediately from her previous visits to the hospital. She greeted her warmly and led her to a room where Katie Morgan was waiting for her.

'Well, Pippa,' Katie said, shaking her head as she offered her a chair, 'we've got a really interesting case here. I've never encountered anything quite like this or anyone quite like this man in my professional experience. He's highly intelligent and he's able to articulate his thoughts better than many patients we deal with.'

'But are you OK to talk to me about it, to talk about him?' Pippa asked with a quizzical expression. 'What about patient confidentiality and that kind of thing?'

'Well, there's no problem there. Josh Naismith – you already know his name, I gather – has been talking to us. He's asked us to share what he's told us with you and he's anxious to talk to you himself. Clearly, St Peter's is really important in all this. And he's convinced that you've been instrumental in his return to Penford. So you're part of our team on this one!'

Pippa's eyes widened. To be cast in a central role in this rapidly unfolding drama felt less like a compliment than the imposition of a heavy responsibility on her. She instinctively searched in her mind for a legitimate reason to decline the honour.

'But I'm guessing he's still too confused. Not really in a place to make decisions. Still suffering from the memory loss thing. Some kind of amnesia, you called it…'

'Yes, dissociative amnesia,' Katie reminded her. 'Our psychiatrist tells me that my instant attempt at a diagnosis was pretty accurate. Of course, he's not completely recovered and we need to keep him here for observation for a few days yet. But he's much better than we would have expected at this stage. He was obviously exhausted when we got him in, and for the first couple of days, Saturday and Sunday, he just slept most of the time. But he's physically pretty healthy for his age and by yesterday he was wide awake and eating. And *talking* – definitely talking!

'From what he's telling us we know that his memory is returning. He knows who he is, he knows where he is, and he remembers his past except for the most recent bit. What's still missing are the weeks before he got here. But the last thing he remembers is almost certainly what triggered things off. And that's what he wants to talk to you about now.'

Pippa was grateful when Katie, sensing that she needed some breathing space, suggested that they should have a cup of tea before going to meet the patient in a private room at the other end of the ward. While they waited for the kettle to boil, she told Katie briefly of Eddie Shaw's visit earlier in the day and of the news of Frank Cassidy's tragic death. Then she did her best to clear her mind and prepare herself to meet the man who was apparently so keen to unburden himself to her.

'So how did you get him to start talking so freely?' she asked. 'Is that normal in cases like this?'

'It can vary, and we don't always get this kind of response so soon.' Katie paused, dropped teabags into both mugs and filled them with boiling water. 'We've got a range of therapies we can use in cases like this – drug-assisted question-and-answer sessions, even sometimes hypnosis to clear the blockage and get the patient talking. Tom Hartley, our resident psychiatrist, is very experienced at that kind of intervention. But he tells me that a few simple enquiries from him was all that it took.'

'And is that it? Does that cure him? Is he OK now?'

'Well, I wouldn't put it like that. Provided he doesn't suddenly discharge himself and leave as quickly as he arrived in Penford, we want to work with him for a bit longer. We use cognitive behavioural therapy, that kind of thing, to help patients understand whatever it is that's triggered their amnesia and how they might deal with the issues and avoid further trauma and stress in the future. We'd want to give him the tools to help him avoid a relapse, if possible.'

Pippa wasn't greatly comforted by Katie's explanation. The mug of tea would normally have been, if not quite the panacea for all ills, at least a soothing potion to be drunk before any stressful task. Now, however, it sat in front of her untouched.

'That all sounds very ...' she searched for the word, '... well, very *specialist*. Way beyond anything I can offer. I'm doing my best to become a half-decent vicar and to care for my parishioners. But I know my limitations when it comes to counselling. I'm always relieved to pass people on to those who're much better equipped than I am in that area. Of course, I can offer spiritual support and pray with him. But don't you think there's a danger that I might get in the way of medical professionals like yourself if I get any more involved than that?'

'Hmm... yes, there is that danger,' Katie said thoughtfully. 'But we medics need to know *our* limitations too. Just as much as you clergy. Do you remember your Shakespeare from school? Did you do *Macbeth*?'

'Yes, I think we did,' Pippa replied, unsure of the relevance of the question. 'But I don't remember much of it. And I'm not sure what it's got to do with this.'

'I've forgotten most of it too. But there's one bit that's always stuck in my mind. And I've been thinking about it since Josh Naismith made it clear that he wants to speak to you. So allow a doctor to give a vicar a lesson in English literature.'

'I'm not so hot on Shakespeare, but I can remember that bit from *Alice in Wonderland* about things becoming "curiouser and curiouser",' Pippa laughed, 'which is exactly what this whole thing is becoming! But go on. I'm listening.'

'Well, it's that bit in the play where one of her ladies-in-waiting fetches a doctor to watch Lady Macbeth who's been walking in her sleep and trying to wash the blood from her hands. The doctor watches for a while, but he's forced to admit that Lady Macbeth's troubled soul is beyond the scope of his medical skills. And he says – and this is the bit I've never forgotten, "More needs she the divine than the physician."'

Katie picked up her mug and held it in both hands. She looked out of the window for a moment, choosing her words carefully before placing the mug gently on the table and looking directly at Pippa.

'I think that's true about this man. He needs what you can give him, maybe even more than what we can offer. I don't normally talk in these terms in this office. But the truth is that we have the skills to help clear the blockage in his mind, get his thought processes working better. But this man's been hurt… damaged. There's something deep in his soul that needs to be healed. Medical science alone can't do that. Add that to the fact that his sudden arrival is surely bound up with St Peter's and the painting, and you'll see that there's no escape for you from this one.'

Pippa gave a long, resigned sigh and nodded in reluctant acquiescence. She suddenly thought that she, too, could remember a line from *Macbeth*. 'Lead on, Macduff!' she said, as she stood up.

'I think you'll find that's a misquotation,' said Katie, shaking her head. 'But it's the right sentiment.'

The two women laughed as they headed through the ward to meet the man of whom they'd been speaking.

Despite Katie's best efforts, Pippa was unprepared for what awaited them when they opened the door of the little side room. The man dressed in hospital-issue pyjamas and dressing gown was one and the same as the hunched and troubled figure she'd found kneeling at the communion rail in St Peter's a few days earlier. Now he was sitting in an armchair beside the bed and his distinctive features were thrown into sharp relief by the hospital's bright fluorescent lighting against the dark blue of the wall behind him.

But to Pippa it seemed that there had been a transformation. Her first sight of him on that cold morning in the church had revealed only a vulnerable elderly man, confused and fragile and damaged. And the story that Eddie Shaw had subsequently begun to uncover left little room for doubt that he had indeed suffered terribly and unjustly. All of that suffering remained etched on his face as deeply and as clearly as when she'd first seen him. But there was something else, something less immediately obvious, something that the casual observer might have missed. But for anyone who looked into his eyes, as she was doing now, it was unmistakable and inescapable. She could feel it in his piercing gaze. She could detect it in the way he carried himself as he stood up and stretched out his hand in greeting.

Pippa struggled for a word that would capture the impact of his presence on her. The only word that would come to mind was one that she could remember using only rarely. A word that sounded quaint and old-fashioned, even other-worldly. The word was *nobility*. Whatever had been done to this man half a century ago in Penford, and whatever had happened to him in his journeying since those days, had been painful and costly. It had hurt him, cost him dearly, probably almost cost him his life. *But it had not destroyed him.* Nor had he merely survived it. More than that, Pippa thought, it had shaped him and formed him like the blows of a sculptor's hammer, purified him like the searing flame of a refiner's fire. It was as if the evil done to him had somehow become part of him, had been gathered up into who he was. But in doing so its sting had been drawn, its malevolence stripped of its power to harm. And he had emerged transformed, the same elderly man she'd expected to see, but with a nobility – a fusion of dignity and grace and patience – that was entirely unexpected.

The effect on her was immediate. When they'd pushed open the door a moment before, Pippa's overriding emotion had been one of nervous anxiety. Now, as she stood before his penetrating gaze and felt the gentle firmness of his handshake, that initial unease was overwhelmed by a feeling that was deeper and richer, a sensation that was at one and the same time infinitely desirable and profoundly disturbing. And now she knew exactly the word to describe what she was experiencing. The word was *awe*.

She was unsure what to say, and it was a relief when he opened the conversation. 'Reverend Sheppard, thank you for coming to see me. You've already been so kind to me. And please accept my apologies for breaking into your church.'

Josh Naismith smiled at Pippa as he spoke. The same smile she'd seen at the communion rail on Saturday when he'd lifted his head and looked up at her. It was an expression of uninhibited and unfeigned gratitude. And, just as it had then, it threatened to melt her heart. She wanted to say something in reply to his greeting, but again she was afraid to speak for fear of crying.

'Please don't let me upset you,' he said, sensing that she was on the verge of tears. 'Can we sit down and chat, please? I owe you an explanation for my sudden arrival.'

He eased himself back into the armchair while Katie brought two plastic stacking chairs from the other side of the bed. Pippa regained her composure sufficiently to respond.

'I'm not sure about *you* owing *me* an explanation. But I'd certainly like to listen to what you have to say and get to know you better.'

Josh Naismith sat back in his chair and closed his eyes. Pippa was vaguely aware of the sounds of hospital life going on as normal beyond the door behind her and the steady hum of traffic entering and leaving the car park just outside the window. But the only sound in the room at that moment was the breathing of the man on whom her attention was fixed. For almost a minute he said nothing and she gave a questioning sideways glance at Katie. Had he fallen asleep? Had he lost consciousness? Or was he engaging in prayer or meditation?

Just when she thought he wasn't going to speak, he opened his eyes and sat forward. His face, which had been expressionless while he'd kept silence, came to life again with that smile that enthralled her and captivated her attention.

'I just needed to gather my thoughts,' he said. 'I still can't clearly remember exactly how I got here or how long it took me. It's still all rather fuzzy and indistinct. I hope it'll come into sharper focus in the next little while. But I *can* tell you how what you did prompted me to return to Penford at this time.'

Pippa was taken aback by his words. What had she done that would prompt a man she didn't even know existed and who was living in some other part of the country to return to the town where he'd been born half a century after he'd left? Surely this was just the product of his still fuddled mind. Her doubts must have shown on her face.

'Don't worry. I'm not getting confused here.' He shook his head and smiled at her again. 'You really did give me the prod I needed to come back to the town. It really was you who gave me hope and a sense of urgency.'

'I still don't understand.' This time it was Pippa who was shaking her head and smiling.

'Well, let me explain. For quite a while now I've wanted to come back to Penford, to tell my story and find some sort of closure, but it never seemed the right time. Apart from anything else, I'd no idea how I'd be received or whether people would believe my story. Or whether anybody would even care. But over the last ten years or so I've kept in touch with life in Penford. Even an old man like me uses the internet, and the online edition of *The Gazette* has proved to be very useful. A few weeks ago I read the article about Herbert Donnington's painting being moved from the entrance of the church into a side chapel.'

Now he sat upright, speaking quietly but articulating every word with the precision and intensity of a man making a final plea for his liberty before the jury leaves to consider its verdict.

'There was some stuff in the article about the vicar not liking the painting, being disturbed by it, insisting that it should be moved, even if some of the congregation thought it should stay right where it was. *That's when I started to hope*. Maybe she has a sense of what lies behind that picture, I thought. A sense of what it cost me, and of the hurt I've carried through life because of it. Maybe I can go back and tell her my story. Maybe she might even believe me. And maybe I can finally reach a place where I can completely forgive what was done to me fifty years ago.'

Pippa would always remember that moment in a side room in the geriatric ward of The Penford Infirmary. Whenever she tried to put it into words, on those few occasions when she even attempted to explain it to anyone, she would always end up feeling embarrassed, imagining that whoever was listening to her would think to themselves that they were in the presence of someone suffering from delusional thoughts, someone in the grip of religious mania of some sort. But she couldn't escape it that day and she'd never really doubted it ever since then – the sense that a discernment had been given to her about that painting, and a responsibility laid on her towards the man whose face stared out from the canvas.

Once again she found herself searching for a word, a word that shocked her when it emerged into her conscious mind. She had been *chosen*. The very idea sounded ludicrous to her then and no less absurd as she looked back on it. But try as she might, and however much cold logic might argue against it, she couldn't escape the conviction that Pippa Sheppard, the wife of Joe, the mother of Harry and Zoe, an ordinary vicar in an ordinary Anglican church in an ordinary town in the north of England, had been *charged with a particular responsibility* – she usually substituted that phrase when trying to explain it to anyone because it seemed less sanctimonious than *chosen* – a responsibility that could not be refused without rendering her guilty of treason to all that she believed and disobedient to the vocation she had accepted.

Josh spoke again. 'That's it, really. I went to bed that night determined to do something about it in the morning. My mind was in turmoil and I know that I didn't sleep well. Strange troubled dreams about places and people I hadn't seen since I'd left this town. But after that I remember nothing until I woke up in this room. I hope you can make sense of that. And I hope you don't think I'm just a crazy old man.'

Pippa wished she could have responded by expressing her profound sympathy but explaining that she was a busy wife and mother with a family to care for as well as a church leader with a congregation who already made demands that required her to have superhuman powers, an endless array of talent, and the patience and wisdom of Job. Consequently she would need to pass on responsibility in this matter to someone a little less busy and a great deal more qualified than she was. What she actually said was, 'I'm so glad you've come back to Penford. You're quite right. That painting has troubled me from the day I first set eyes on it. No, I don't think you're a crazy old man. And yes, I want to hear your story. In fact, I think I might already know some of what you want to tell us. But will you first let me ask you a question, please?'

There was an immediate look of relief on Josh Naismith's face at her response, and he nodded his agreement to her request. She asked her question in a tone that was as matter-of-fact as she could manage. 'Does the name Frank Cassidy mean anything to you?'

There was a fleeting moment when the elderly man's blank expression caused her to question whether she'd been wise to ask, or whether too many years had passed to allow him to recall the names of old schoolmates. Then, slowly but surely, a look of recognition passed across his face. He began to rock slightly backwards and forwards in his chair as recognition grew into a fuller recollection.

'Frank Cassidy... Frank Cassidy.' He mouthed the words quietly several times before he addressed Pippa. 'Frank Cassidy – yes. I haven't thought about that name for years. He was one of the boys in the art class. I think he might have been a month or two younger than me. But he experienced it too. He'd back up my story.'

As gently and sensitively as she could, Pippa told him of Eddie Shaw's visit to Coniston and of his conversation with Frank Cassidy. She tried to sidestep the precise details of what Frank had said to avoid colouring anything that Josh might subsequently reveal. His relief that there was someone who would be able to vouch for the truth of the story he had to tell was obvious. He nodded and slapped his hand on the arm of the chair in response to what she was telling him. When she finished he clenched his fist in a gesture of delight and triumph.

'Yes, yes, yes! Thank God! Thank God that there's someone else still alive who knows what we went through and is willing to tell the truth.'

Katie had kept silent all through this conversation, but now, seeing Pippa's discomfort at Josh's words, she leaned forward and took hold of Josh's hand as it came to rest on the arm of the chair. 'I'm so sorry, but this bit of the story doesn't have a happy ending. Sadly, we have to tell you that Frank Cassidy took his own life last night after talking to Eddie Shaw.'

As Pippa had related her account of Eddie Shaw's meeting with Frank Cassidy, his expression had become ever more animated. Now he was suddenly crestfallen. His eyes glazed over, the colour drained from his lips and his mouth sagged open. It was as if someone had pressed a mask of utter despair on to his face. Katie sprang to her feet, fearful of the effect her revelation might have had on him. At first he said nothing, seemingly ignoring her

124

expressions of concern. When he did speak, his voice sounded flat and lifeless.

'I'll be OK. It's just that for a minute I thought that this whole thing might be a little easier than I had feared. I should've known better than to get my hopes up after all these years.'

Pippa drew her chair closer and took his hands in hers. She looked directly into his eyes as she spoke.

'This must be a blow to you. I understand that. But what it means is that what *you've* got to say becomes more important than ever. And there's a little group of people in this town who'll do everything they can to help you.'

Josh Naismith nodded gratefully. He was tired after their conversation and there was no more to be said at that time. The nurse whom Katie had summoned helped him back into bed, and Pippa realised with a start that the figure of nobility who had aroused in her such a sense of awe had become once again just a fragile, elderly man whose vulnerability now provoked only feelings of sympathy and concern. But she also knew that she had experienced something when she had entered that room that made it impossible for her either to dismiss Josh Naismith as an inconvenient visitor or to ignore the summons that had been laid on her to play her part in ensuring that his voice would be heard and that the suffering of the years would be healed.

As Pippa walked away from the Infirmary into the gathering gloom of the late December afternoon and headed across the car park, she glanced back at the dark stone of the old portico entrance set against the brilliant light flooding from the wall of glass behind it. It was an apt metaphor for the daunting task to which she was now committed. The dark truth of Josh Naismith's past would forever stand. Whether it could be illuminated and given a life-affirming and healing purpose was another matter entirely.

Seven

Send for Sam

Wednesday began quietly enough for Pippa. Harry and Zoe were Joe's responsibility for the morning and, having first made sure the joiner who'd come to repair the door of the church that had been damaged in the break-in knew exactly what needed to be done, she set off to pick up some groceries. She was glad of the chance to be on her own and to be doing something that didn't require any particular thought or to expend any emotional energy.

To her relief, the supermarket wasn't busy, though she did have to curb her annoyance when she realised she still couldn't escape the same irritating medley of banal Christmas hits that had been playing on a seemingly endless loop since mid-November. The forced jollity of the music and the sight of the by now tired-looking decorations had a mildly depressing effect on her, but she consoled herself with the thought that it was, of course, New Year's Eve. Not too many hours from now the church bells would ring out the old year, bringing the festive season to an end, and at last life could begin to return to something like normal.

No sooner had that thought occurred to her, however, than the events of the last few days flooded back into her mind. Just thinking about all that had happened was enough to almost overwhelm her. An older clergy-colleague had once suggested to her that the challenge of pastoring a congregation made up of people of different ages and diverse personalities was akin to herding cats. She'd often thought to herself that it was a particularly apt metaphor. Now, however, it felt as if the cats had been infiltrated by some strange and wild creatures that threatened to scatter them in every direction, leaving the shepherd at a loss to know what to do next.

The emotional high of yesterday's encounter with Josh Naismith at the Infirmary had quickly evaporated in the cold light of a new dawn. The challenging prospect that she would have a major part to play as events unfolded had become instead a nagging fear which had only increased as the morning went on. And the emotional and physical dip of life's roller coaster had been made all the more steep. She tried to ignore the sense of mild panic that was rising in her and turned her attention back to the shopping list in her hand.

'Hello, Vicar. Penny for your thoughts.'

Pippa gave a start and almost fell over the shopping trolley of the woman whose voice had just broken into her troubled thoughts.

'Oh, Mrs Hesmondhalgh,' she said, her heart sinking as she recognised a regular member of her congregation with a not totally unjustified reputation for being something of a gossip. 'I'm sorry. I didn't see you there. I was miles away. How are you today?'

She was hoping that the white-haired old lady standing in front of her would say that she was well and then hurry on with her shopping. But Mrs Hesmondhalgh, who spent too much of her time alone in her flat, was always grateful to chat with someone, and an opportunity to talk to the vicar wasn't one she was about to miss. She began her answer to Pippa's enquiry by listing just a few of her many ailments and the various treatments, successful and otherwise, required by each of them. Then she moved on to the topic of greatest interest to her at the moment – the recent break-in at the church.

'It must have been awful for you, Vicar, to find that dreadful man in the place. We can do without that sort, can't we? And you've got enough to do trying to cope with running the church and looking after your husband and children. I don't know how you do it all, to be honest. I just don't understand those folk in the congregation who persist in criticising you. Some of them seem to think it needs a man to do your job properly. "She's doing the best she can." That's what I always tell them. And they couldn't do any better themselves …'

She would have gone on indefinitely in that vein had not Pippa interrupted her with as much politeness as she could muster.

'Well, it's good to know I've got your support, Mrs Hesmondhalgh. But I must let you get on with your shopping and not take up any more of your time. You take care, now. And I'll see you on Sunday.'

Mrs Hesmondhalgh was about to protest that it was really no trouble and that she was in no particular hurry, but Pippa had already made her escape. She reached the safety of the fruit and vegetable aisle without looking back, where she paused while she took some long, slow breaths. Of course, she knew well enough that conversations like the one she'd just had, conversations that were barbed with criticism masquerading as encouragement, went with the job and should be ignored. The trouble was, she never found that easy in practice. Try as she might to push such encounters to the back of her mind, they always left her with a knot in her stomach that would last for the rest of the day and sometimes well into the night.

Ever since childhood, her self-confidence had been fragile and easily damaged. She'd always felt herself to be a failure in comparison to her older sister, Ann, who was both clever and pretty and who succeeded at most things, to the delight of her parents. Pippa was always their 'other daughter'. Not unloved or ill-treated in any way, just their 'nice ordinary child'. That's how she'd once overheard her mother describe her when she was fifteen years old to a friend to whom she'd been proudly showing some awards that Ann had won for gymnastics. When the friend had asked if their other daughter was as talented as her older sister, Pippa's mother had responded sweetly, 'Oh no. She's just a nice ordinary child. Average at most things, not outstanding at anything in particular. Give her a good story to read and she's happy. But she's not strong in any of the subjects that really matter – science or maths, that kind of thing.' Then she'd added as an afterthought, 'But she's good-hearted and she'll probably manage to get decent enough grades in her exams to do something useful. You know, nursing or social work, that kind of thing. Nothing too academic or intellectually demanding.'

If her mother had intended her words to be a compliment, it had been at best a back-handed one, and it had an immediate wounding effect on the awkward teenage girl listening outside the room. She'd been intending to meet a classmate that evening. Instead, she hurried out of the door, trying unsuccessfully to fight back the tears, and went for a long walk on her own, painfully aware that even though nobody was close enough to notice, her cheeks were flushed with embarrassment. The sting of those words had never really left her. To have mentioned it to her parents would have seemed petty and would only have increased the humiliation she felt. So she kept it bottled up deep inside her, where she managed to suppress it most of the time. But it would take only the slightest cutting comment for the lid to come off and the bitter toxin of shame and failure to spill out and erode her self-confidence for days.

In fact, she'd been a hard-working and diligent student and had managed to get a place at university, where she had graduated with a BA in English and History. It made little difference to her. In her own eyes her achievements paled into insignificance when compared to her sister's first-class Law degree from Cambridge.

Her mother had been right about one thing, however. She loved good stories. And there were fleeting moments when she allowed herself to dream. What would it be like, she wondered, not just to read the tales told by others, but to become a writer herself? It always aroused in her a puzzling mixture of emotions, a tangle of sadness and excitement, when she thought of creating her own stories. But she always quickly dismissed it as a childish fancy, something for people far more gifted than she was. Even into her late teens and early twenties she still felt like the 'nice ordinary child' who was unlikely ever to do anything remarkable.

However, something happened in those three years at university that boosted her confidence far more than academic success ever could. It was there that she met Joe. To her amazement he'd been attracted to her immediately, and their relationship had progressed steadily from their first meeting at a freshers' week party to the day they got married a couple of weeks after graduation. There were two things about the happy, uncomplicated young man with the unruly ginger hair and ready smile that had both captivated her and puzzled her in equal measure. The first was simply that he was drawn to her despite the fact that there were other girls in their circle of university friends that Pippa always considered to be far more glamorous than she was. Whenever she mentioned that to Joe, he would shake his head and laugh and tell her that he was a better judge of what made a woman attractive to a man than she was.

The other thing that had emerged very early in their relationship was that he had told her, to her great surprise, that he was a member of the Christian Union. Pippa's family always considered themselves to be Christian in much the same way as they regarded themselves as English – an unquestioned part of their cultural identity that didn't require any particular thought or action. And they would have described themselves as Anglican on any form that had a question on religious affiliation. Their religion, however, was very much of the nominal variety, requiring no greater active commitment than a visit to church at Easter or Christmas, and no deeper theological reflection than that living a respectable life was the Christian thing to do.

Joe's faith was of an altogether different ilk, unlike anything that Pippa had previously encountered. It wasn't just that he genuinely seemed to *believe* the stuff. He actually tried to live by it too. What surprised her even more was the fact that he found his beliefs to be a source of strength in his efforts to live well. What he believed provided both the inspiration and the dynamism for how he lived his life. And, whether in casual conversation or deeper discussion, he was firm in his convictions without being in any way piously dismissive of the opinions of those who differed from him.

It was as far from the aggressive evangelism of the street preacher who regularly accosted students and demanded to know if they would 'go to heaven if you died tonight' as it was from the anaemic version of Christianity with which she'd grown up and that had seemed to her to be of some consolation to the sick and elderly, but completely irrelevant to the everyday life of a normal young woman. And, little by little as they got to know each other better and talked about life together, it began to stir something in her, a longing that she could neither easily define nor totally ignore. Long before graduation she'd come to share the faith of the man who was to become her husband in just a few weeks' time. There had been no 'Damascus Road' experience, nothing that she would have identified as a definite moment of conversion. Just a gradual process, at the end of which she was happy to describe herself as a believer and a passionate, if imperfect, follower of Jesus.

Her new-found faith gave her a sense of purpose and a moral compass by which to live. It was a comfortable and comforting place to be in life, and had it stopped there she would have been content. To Pippa's surprise, however, over time it became an increasingly unsettling place. Something was beginning to trouble her that she was afraid even to acknowledge. At first she tried to dismiss it as just the familiar sense of inadequacy reasserting itself as she faced the challenges of being a wife, a teacher and, just over a year later, a mother. It was an inevitable dip, she tried to persuade herself, after the excitement and euphoria of graduation and marriage. But as weeks passed into months, it persisted and grew into a constant irritant that simply couldn't be ignored. And as it began to form itself into something identifiable, she was embarrassed even to put it into words.

Eventually she plucked up her courage and blurted out to Joe as he was falling asleep one night that she felt she should apply for ordination. He might have been almost asleep a few moments before. Now he was sitting bolt upright with his eyes wide open. Pippa's recollection of the moment was that in his shock he'd even uttered a mild oath, though Joe always insisted she'd imagined that. There was, however, no disagreement between them about the fact that they didn't get much sleep that night, as Joe tried to recover from the shock of this unexpected revelation and they began to take on board what it might mean for them as a couple.

The next eighteen months were something of a blur in both their memories – a seemingly endless series of meetings and conversations, two days of being questioned and assessed by the Bishops' Advisory Panel, and then the arrival of the brown envelope in the mail telling her that she'd been recommended for ordination training. They both resigned from their teaching jobs and moved with their two young children to Oxford, where Joe took up another teaching post and Pippa began her training for ordained ministry. The years that followed were no less eventful, with ordination and three years' curacy before their move to Penford and Pippa's first experience of the demands of being what Joe, with a mixture of pride and amusement, described as 'a fully fledged vicar' for the first time.

The life of 'a fully fledged vicar' set alongside the demands of being a wife and a mother, she very quickly discovered, could have stretched her beyond her limits had she not learned to recognise when a build-up of stressful situations could leave her vulnerable to those deeply ingrained and debilitating feelings of low self-esteem. With Joe's support, she'd begun to develop a routine in which periods of intense activity were followed by times of retreat and recuperation. It was a rhythm that served her well. But it was moments like her unexpected encounter with Mrs Hesmondhalgh and the sting of such throwaway comments that could catch her off guard and leave her feeling exposed and inadequate for the task. She left the supermarket and drove home, her self-confidence at a low ebb, wondering if the events of the last week would prove to be more than she could handle.

Joe was standing at the door waiting for her when Pippa arrived at the vicarage, and after they'd unloaded the shopping together he told her he had a surprise for her.

'I wondered why you were waiting by the door for me,' she said. 'I usually struggle in with all this stuff before you eventually emerge from upstairs. Don't tell me you've decided to buy me a New Year's gift. Or have you broken something?'

'Nothing like that,' he laughed. His expression became more serious. 'Don't be annoyed, but I've invited someone I think you might be glad to see. He's in the kitchen having a cup of tea.'

Pippa felt a surge of irritation at what she considered the unnecessarily cryptic nature of Joe's words. A surprise visit from a mystery guest was the last thing she felt like at this moment. She managed to stifle her annoyance and fix a smile on her face as she dutifully followed her husband into the kitchen.

She wasn't at all sure who or what she'd been expecting to see, but it certainly wasn't the tall, elderly man with stooped shoulders and wispy grey hair who rose unsteadily to his feet to greet her. He was dressed in a well-worn tweed jacket with leather elbow patches, an Argyle sweater and grey flannels. His appearance immediately reminded Pippa of her grandfather, who'd died while she was still in her teens, a memory that was reinforced when she noticed his hand trembling as he put his cup down on the table. When he began to speak she recognised the same slow, quiet monotone in his voice that she'd observed all those years ago in the man she'd called 'Gramps'.

She'd really had enough of unexpected visits from old men for one week, and she couldn't imagine why Joe had invited another one on New Year's Eve, especially one who was obviously suffering from Parkinson's disease and who looked like a time-traveller from the 1950s.

'You must be the Reverend Pippa Sheppard,' he said, with a faint trace of a smile on his face. 'I'm Sam Andrews. Bishop Gerald alerted me to what's been going on and I've seen some of the stuff that's got into the newspapers. Your husband called me this morning. He thought I might be of some help. So I got my grandson to drive me over. I don't drive myself these days – Parkinson's, you know. But I think you've already noticed that.'

Pippa's irritation gave way to embarrassment and a rush of shame at her impatience. She was sure that, despite his frailties, the man standing in front of her knew exactly what she'd been thinking, and she remembered what Bishop Gerald had said about him being 'a bit scary until you get to know him'. She felt herself blushing and she tried to think of a suitable excuse for her initial annoyance. But Sam Andrews had noticed her discomfiture, and before she could say anything he spoke again.

'Now, I've no doubt that the last thing you need is an old codger like me hanging around the house. My lift will be here to pick me up again within the hour, so why don't we sit down and talk about things? I'm sure this isn't an easy time for you both. So you talk and I'll listen, and let's see where we go from there.'

For the next half hour, sitting around the kitchen table, Pippa and Joe talked about all that had happened in the past week, and Sam listened intently. Pippa understood enough about Parkinson's to know that the slow movement of his eyelids and his infrequent blink were typical symptoms of the disease. She sensed nonetheless that his steady, unbroken gaze had been a lifelong characteristic of the man. Like others before her, she noticed that he had a way of looking and listening, a quiet and steady stillness in his person, despite the tremor in his hands, that made you say more than you had intended to, that drew things out of you that you'd never properly articulated before.

They told him about the break-in at the church, about the sensational and inaccurate reporting in the press, about Eddie Shaw's interest and involvement, about what he'd learned from Frank Cassidy and the tragic outcome of their meeting, and about Pippa's visit to Josh Naismith at the Infirmary yesterday. And all the time they were speaking, Sam was listening intently, seeming to absorb every detail.

They reached the end of their account and Joe went upstairs to check on the children, leaving Pippa alone with Sam. His tea must have been cold by now, but he lifted his cup shakily to his lips and slowly took a drink before he spoke. His words were brief and to the point. 'So what are you going to do?'

'I wish I knew,' she replied. 'To be honest, I haven't a clue. I haven't got any answers. Just questions. How do we best help this man who's come back to the town where he was so badly hurt? What do we do about the mixed reactions of people? I mean, some folk think he's a kind of Messiah and some think he's just a con man. How do we stop this thing getting completely out of hand in the newspapers? And how do we stop this damaging the church? I don't know the answer to any of those questions.'

She looked at Sam, hoping that this man her husband had invited without consulting her would provide some answers to her questions or, at least, offer some wise counsel. She waited, but he said nothing. His reaction, when it came, took her completely by surprise. First he smiled at her, then his smile became a chuckle, and then grew to a laugh. She certainly hadn't expected this from a man who'd been recommended by the Bishop, or from someone with his particular medical condition. As he continued to laugh, her surprise changed to annoyance. Her guest didn't appear to be taking seriously anything of what she'd just said.

He took a deep breath and, not without some difficulty, curbed his mirth. 'I'm sorry,' he said, panting slightly. 'I don't mean to treat what you've said lightly. Far from it. Give me a moment to get my breath back and I'll explain.'

When Joe came back into the room, he immediately noticed the silence and the air of tension and wondered why the conversation had stalled. Sam beckoned to him to join them again at the table and took another sip of cold tea.

'I've just apologised to your wife for laughing when she said she's no idea how to answer all the questions this business has raised,' he said, still smiling. 'I laughed because I was delighted to hear what she was saying. Not knowing how to answer those questions is halfway to dealing with this thing.'

Joe and Pippa looked at each other and then at him, his explanation having left them none the wiser. Sam chuckled again.

'Here's the thing,' he said, as the smile faded from his face. 'It's a mistake made by people in all walks of life, but particularly by those of us in the Church. We spend too much time and energy trying to find an answer to every question that people throw at us and trying to come up with an argument to refute every criticism they make of us. Oh, I know we have to do some of that. Dialogue is important and apologetics has its place. I've had to do a fair bit of that stuff myself over the years. And goodness knows, we've made some mistakes over the centuries for which we simply need to put up our hands and apologise.

'But if I'm learning one thing as I get older it's this – *that's not who we are and it's not what we're meant to be doing*. It never achieves what we think it does and it puts us constantly on the defensive. Sometimes I think the Church resembles nothing so much as those paintings you sometimes see of the Battle of Little Bighorn. You know the one: there's Colonel George Armstrong Custer and the 7th US Cavalry, encircled by the enemy, fighting valiantly, but they're dropping one by one, and they'll keep dropping until the last man falls and the flag falls with him. It looks heroic, but the truth is that everybody knows that defeat is inevitable. When I was a lad we even used to sing a hymn about trying to hold the fort in the desperate hope that reinforcements would eventually arrive.'

He paused in mid-flow as his voice began to croak. Pippa and Joe sat spellbound at what they were seeing and hearing, hardly able to believe that a man of his age and with his medical condition could speak so passionately and expend so much energy. But Sam was just warming to his subject and he'd no intention of stopping yet. He drained the last of the cold tea from his cup by way of refreshing himself and turned directly to address Pippa as he resumed speaking with renewed vigour.

'It's time for you to do in this situation what we who call ourselves the Church should be doing all the time. Don't try to answer all the objections, don't try to solve every problem and don't hold back for fear of how people might react. *Just tell the story*. Tell it as truthfully and as persuasively as you can, but make sure you tell it. Let Josh Naismith tell you his story and then you tell it to everyone else. That's your responsibility in this. How people react to it is their responsibility. Of course, it'll cause a bit of division. Telling the truth always does that. Some folk will believe it, some will refuse to believe it and some won't know what to do with it. But a good story – a true story – has the power to challenge people and change the world.'

His voice was beginning to weaken and he paused again. Joe, sensing that he hadn't finished, filled a glass of water from the tap and put it down in front of him. Sam gratefully gulped down several mouthfuls before taking up from where he'd left off.

'I know what's worrying you about all this. Josh Naismith's sudden appearance, his likeness to the face of Christ in the painting, the seeming stigmata, the dark stuff that's hidden in Penford's past – that's a pretty potent mixture, I can see that. The last thing you want is some kind of sect sprouting up proclaiming that the Messiah has appeared in Penford. You can just imagine what the tabloids would do with that! And you certainly don't need the backlash that would come with it. So you'll need to be careful how you tell Josh's story.

'But tell it you must. You've got to tell it because a man who's suffered like he has deserves to have his story told. And you've got to tell it because, from all you've told me today, it resonates with the big story that the Church exists to tell and that everybody needs to hear. You won't find the answer to what we do with suffering and pain and injustice in philosophies or programmes, but in stories. The stories we tell will inevitably guide the actions we take. And, if I know anything at all, it's that the best of them will echo the story we've been trying to tell for the last 2,000 years. You might just have one of those stories right here.'

When they talked about it later that evening, Joe confessed that he'd wanted to stand and applaud at that point in Sam's speech. Pippa said she knew exactly what he meant and that she might have done the same thing if she hadn't been trying to work out just what kind of man Sam was. When Bishop Gerald had recommended him, she'd imagined someone in the shape of a counsellor. Someone who'd spend most of the time listening, interrupting only to clarify what he'd heard, and making brief comments to help them reach their own conclusions. Clearly Sam Andrews had been cast from a very different mould.

In the event, neither of them had time to respond to Sam's words before Pippa had to answer the doorbell. The tall young man in his early twenties who stood on the doorstep smiled at her. His smile was exactly like that of the elderly man sitting in their kitchen and the resemblance between the two men was uncanny.

'Hi, I'm Ryan Andrews. I've come to collect my grandfather.'

Pippa stared at him without saying a word and his smile immediately broke into a laugh.

'Don't tell me. He's been making one of his orations. That's enough to make anybody speechless. And then I turn up at your door looking like a younger version of him. I get this kind of reaction all the time.'

The expression on Pippa's face left him in no doubt that he'd assessed the situation perfectly, and he began to laugh. His laughter was infectious, and when they reached the kitchen Pippa was laughing with him. By the time they were saying goodbye to Sam, all four of them were laughing.

Having waved their visitors off, Joe and Pippa sat down again at the kitchen table and looked at each other, wide-eyed with wonder at what had just happened. In contacting Sam, Joe had broken the rule they'd always tried to follow in their marriage that neither of them would ever make a significant decision or issue an invitation to anyone to visit their home without consulting their spouse. And Sam had broken all the rules of good counselling they'd learned and tried to follow with his authoritarian monologue.

So how come, they asked each other, did they feel such a lift in their spirits? It wasn't as if the situation had suddenly changed and become less complicated. Yet, somehow, things just felt a little better.

Joe tried to sum it up.

'Here's the nearest I can get to it,' he said, reaching over to hold Pippa's hand. 'When I've had any kind of counselling before it's felt like someone has helped me start walking on the right path. And that's good. It's been just what I needed at times. But when Sam talks, it's different. It's like suddenly coming on a signpost when you're lost. You've still got to do all the walking. But you know the right direction to head in. And you know that there is a destination and that you'll get there eventually if you keep going.'

'That sums it up pretty well,' Pippa agreed. 'The only problem is, it doesn't tell you what the destination will be like when you get there. Or even how difficult the road ahead will be.'

The overcast skies of the last few days had given way to a chilly but bright afternoon and they grasped the opportunity afforded by the break in the weather on the last day of the year to take the children to the nearby park for a couple of hours. Pippa and Joe sat on a bench, watching as Harry and Zoe ran around and called out happily to each other, oblivious to the impact of the last few days on their parents. When they decided to move from the roundabout to the climbing frame, Joe got up and hurried across to keep a closer eye on them, leaving Pippa alone with her thoughts.

Ever since childhood, New Year's Eve had made her pensive, even a little melancholy. The prospect of the old year yielding to the new was a poignant reminder of the ongoing stream of time, an irresistible current with the past for ever flowing into the present and on into the future. Attempting to separate past, present and future, she often

144

reflected, was like putting a cup into a river and trying to separate the waters from the tributaries that had flowed into it upstream. It was an impossible task, for now they flowed together, all part of the same onward surge.

The impact of Josh Naismith's unexpected arrival and its possible consequences for the coming year made her train of thought more pertinent than ever. Less than one week after the discovery of The Intruder at the communion rail, she knew that she was being changed by what had happened. And just a few hours from the beginning of another year, she knew in her heart that, as the story of the man who broke into St Peter's was told, it was impossible that her church and her town would ever be quite the same again.

Eight

The Art of Storytelling

The town of Penford always struggles to rouse itself and get back to everyday life after the festive season. When people pass in the street or meet in the supermarket, their exchanges normally amount to little more than asking each other how their Christmas has been and commiserating with each other that it's time to return to work. And, after a few brief pleasantries, they hurry on their way to face the dark January days and the mundane tasks of another year.

This year, however, there was an unusual buzz about the town and an additional topic of conversation for Penfordians as they greeted each other. 'What about the goings-on at St Peter's?' was the question on the lips of more than a few. And rarely was the enquiry met with a shrug of the shoulders that indicated a lack of interest in the subject. Even those townspeople who couldn't remember the last time they attended a church service, and for whom anything to do with religion was an irrelevance, had an opinion about the mysterious visitor whose coming had brought the glare of publicity on Penford.

Everyone, it seemed, was putting two and two together and coming up with an array of answers anywhere between four and forty-four. Many were adamant that the stranger was nothing more than a con man with an eye on the main chance. More cynical observers were firmly of the opinion that the whole affair was a publicity stunt dreamed up by a dying church willing to resort to any trick in an attempt to boost declining attendance. Others expressed sympathy for an unfortunate individual who'd obviously fallen on hard times and deserved to be shown a little kindness. And some even dared to wonder if their town had become the site of a visitation that had a supernatural dimension that defied rational explanation. But all were in broad agreement that it was time to get back to the business of normal life. However interesting, the story would have to remain incomplete until some other time.

Not everyone in Penford, however, was able to put the matter to one side. Late in the afternoon of Friday 2nd January, while their fellow citizens pushed the events of the previous week to the back of their minds, Pippa Sheppard and Eddie Shaw were once again sitting facing each other at the well-worn oak table in the vicarage kitchen. For them, getting back to business meant turning their minds again to their unexpected visitor and the issues raised by his sudden arrival in the town.

Together they'd spent the first hour of that morning with officers from the local police force who'd interviewed them regarding the man who'd broken into St Peter's. Since Pippa was clear that she had no desire to press charges, they were happy to close their investigation into what they had at first assumed was another burglary of a vulnerable church building. And, while they were certainly interested in the story that was emerging about the relationship of Herbert Donnington to his pupils fifty years before, the fact that it had all happened so long ago meant that it was highly unlikely that there would be anyone still alive against whom charges could be brought.

The officers also shared the news that their colleagues in the Cumbria force who were looking into the sudden death of Frank Cassidy had concluded that there was little room for doubt that the cause of death was suicide. There would, of course, need to be an inquest. But in the light of their findings, there was no reason to extend their investigations unduly.

As Pippa and Eddie were leaving Penford Police Station, the senior officer present, Chief Inspector Mike Barraclough, rose to say goodbye. He knew Eddie well from previous meetings and thanked him for the sensitive manner in which *The Gazette* was trying to handle its reporting of the affair. Then he turned to Pippa and gave her his card.

'Vicar, please call me directly if you need any help from us. But I've got a feeling that this is one of those instances where your involvement will be more important than that of either the police or the press.' He paused and nodded towards Eddie. 'He can do a lot to make sure that people are informed in the right way. And we can make sure that people are protected and the law isn't broken.'

Pippa noticed his expression change. Up to that point she'd been looking at a competent police officer who was practised in conveying the impression that he had everything well under control. Now she was trying not to stare at someone whose air of professional confidence had momentarily deserted him.

'This is different. It's really made an impact on the town. And for some reason I can't get it out of my head. I like to get things tidied up – you know, get all the facts sorted out – but there's something about this one that I can't get to the bottom of. I spent half an hour talking to Josh Naismith at the Infirmary yesterday. I don't know quite what to make of him. But I'd stake my life on the fact that he's not a rogue. There's more to him than meets the eye, and I think you might be the only person in this room with the perspective to understand what it all means.'

Now, sitting at the kitchen table with Eddie Shaw, she couldn't get those words out of her mind. They served only to reinforce what Katie Morgan had said to her at the Infirmary about the limitations of medical science and the importance of her role in all of this. Pippa was finding it impossible to escape the conclusion that she was being pushed irresistibly to a place where she was being handed a commission that couldn't be refused. But there was still one possible way she could see that would let her off the hook. She told Eddie about the visit of Sam Andrews, making sure to emphasise what he'd said about it being vital for them to tell Josh Naismith's story. Surely that's where Eddie would have to take central stage, she suggested. After all, he was the journalist, the one with the writing skills.

Her hopes that she'd found an escape route were quickly dashed. As soon as Eddie took his hands off the table and put them on his knees, she recognised the familiar signs that he was about to say something she didn't want to hear.

'You're right, Pippa,' he said, before breathing loudly through his nose. 'I am a journalist. I know how to get to the facts. Sort out what's important from what's not. And you already know that I'm committed to seeing this thing through to the end. But you're the one to tell the story.'

She tried to protest that she had neither the skills nor the training for such a task, but Eddie was having none of it.

'No, I'm not letting you get away with that.' He wagged his finger to emphasise his point. 'I make it my business to find out about people. And I've found out a thing or two about you. I know you've got a joint degree in English and History. That's not a bad combination for what's needed here. And another thing: I've talked to one or two folk who sit in the pews every Sunday. You know what they tell me?'

Pippa hoped that this was just a rhetorical question, but Eddie was waiting for a response before he was willing to reveal what he'd discovered from her congregation. She confessed that she'd no idea what they'd said and steeled herself to receive the anticipated criticism.

Eddie noticed her anxiety and shook his head.

'Nothing to worry about. Far from it, in fact. They actually like your sermons. And what they like is that you don't just give them abstract theology or heavy moral instruction. They say that you flesh it all out with stories and real-life stuff that they can relate to. One of them who said that you're a natural storyteller even went so far as to say I'd enjoy it if I came to church!'

That was enough to set him off in a fit of wheezy laughter that left him gasping. Pippa brought him a glass of water. It took him more than a minute to recover his composure and get his breath back. When he did speak again the smile had gone from his face and his manner was unmistakably serious.

'Let me tell you something. Sometimes I have a hunch that one of my young reporters is just right to handle a particular assignment. And sometimes they'll come back at me saying that it's too big a story for them or that they don't have the experience. When that happens I've got a little phrase that I use.' He leaned across the table and wagged his finger at Pippa again. 'I say to them, "You've got to do it. This story's been looking for you."'

'I've been thinking about that since I first called on you. Seems like you started something when you decided that painting needed to be moved from the entrance of St Peter's. Whether or not the timing of Josh Naismith's arrival is a coincidence, it's clear that his story is tied up with the painting. I'll give you all the help I can, but I'm telling you, just like I tell those young reporters, "This story's been looking for you." You've got to tell it and bring it to some kind of conclusion.'

'Well, since you put it like that…' Pippa laughed, trying to sound more confident than she felt. 'But seriously, how do I do it? And where do we start?'

Eddie dug in his pocket for his notebook, opened it to a blank page, clicked and poised his pen, ready to write. 'Now's the time to think about that. There isn't any time to waste if we want to get the truth out before the tabloids can do their worst. Let's put some ideas together.'

By six o'clock that evening they'd decided what they should do, and by ten o'clock the following morning they'd begun to do it. A discussion with Katie Morgan had confirmed that the hospital would be happy to discharge their patient on condition that he would be well looked after and remain under their care. A call from Pippa to a local retirement complex had obtained suitable temporary accommodation for Josh Naismith which would be available for the next few weeks. A lunch at the best restaurant in town, paid for by *The Gazette* and hosted by Eddie at his most charming and persuasive, had been enough to convince the chair of trustees of a local charity that funding the short-term care of Penford's unexpected visitor fell well within the parameters of their terms of reference.

By Monday of the following week everything was in place and they were ready to put their plan into operation. That's why they were sitting in a bright and pleasant room in the appropriately named Oak Woods Retirement Community on the outskirts of Penford, listening to Josh Naismith talk. Eddie, who had his notebook in his hand, occasionally interrupted to ask a question or clarify something he hadn't fully understood. Pippa, who took responsibility for the voice recorder placed carefully on the arm of Josh's chair, was content just to listen. It would be the first of many visits in the course of the month as Josh drew them ever deeper into his world. Little by little, as they gained his trust and as he recovered his memory, a vivid picture emerged of a man who'd suffered greatly, travelled countless miles, faced many obstacles, taken a few wrong turnings and come eventually to a place – both literally and figuratively – where he was able to confront the past and embrace the present.

After every visit, Eddie would type out his notes, highlighting anything that he deemed of particular importance. Pippa would listen to the voice recorder several times, absorbing every word and following every nuance of what she was hearing. And one day each week the flock at St Peter's would try in vain to contact their pastor who would be hidden away in a tiny attic room in the vicarage where even Harry and Zoe couldn't find her. From nine o'clock in the morning until early evening she would listen again to the recordings and read through her draft outline before typing four or five thousand words, which she would then email to Eddie for his comments. The fruit of her labours would be a special insert that would appear in *The Gazette* over the next four Fridays, telling readers a very different kind of story to those they were used to seeing when they opened their newspapers.

Before those sessions in Josh's room at Oak Woods, Pippa had always thought of him as *The Intruder*. But over the weeks of listening to him, that name faded in her mind, to be superseded by one that carried an altogether different connotation – *The Pilgrim*. For she had come to know him as a man on a journey of the most profound significance. A journey that had changed him and, in ways she was still to discover, would change her and others too. And that became the title for her four-part series in *The Gazette* – *The Pilgrim's Tale: A journey of transformation*.

Throughout the entire period, Pippa was beset by misgivings. As the weeks passed she recognised that she had at least a modicum of ability as a writer, and there was no denying the thrill of doing something she'd longed to do for so many years. But writing for a local weekly newspaper, she knew only too well, was a particular skill, and not one that she possessed. She had no knack for constructing the short, snappy sentences and attention-grabbing headlines of popular journalese.

More than once she appealed to Eddie, whose idea it had been in the first place, that they should abandon the project. If she were to be honest, she told him, she was afraid it would make them both look ridiculous and do further damage to the man they should be seeking to protect. But he was adamant she should write it and that he would publish it in *The Gazette*.

She even shouted at him, during one of their heated discussions on the matter, that it had become a kind of crusade for him. 'It's like you've got some kind of religious conviction about this,' she yelled, only half-joking. 'You remind me of a 1970s-style evangelist!'

For a fleeting moment she thought she could see him blushing. But he quickly shook his head, gave one of his wheezy laughs, insisted that his main motivation was that it might sell a few hundred more copies of the paper, and hurried off saying that he'd got too much to do to stand around listening to such nonsense.

A few weeks later, under a front-page headline 'THE STORY PENFORD NEEDS TO HEAR', *The Gazette* drew the attention of its readers to an editorial announcement:

> The recent break-in at St Peter's Church has aroused an unusual level of interest in Penford and beyond. There have been rumours and counter-rumours as various stories, many without any foundation, have circulated. It is time for readers of this newspaper to know the truth. In keeping with

The Gazette's tradition of reporting on important local events in innovative and informative ways, the next four issues will come with a free insert featuring a series of articles written by the Reverend Pippa Sheppard, the Vicar of St Peter's. We have asked her to contribute this series because of her close involvement in the events, and the relationship of trust she has been able to form with Josh Naismith, the man at the centre of the story.

The series will be entitled *The Pilgrim's Tale* and will provide readers with a full and exclusive account of all the matters surrounding the break-in at the church. Readers will immediately recognise that it is very different from the usual style of reporting in *The Gazette*, coming as it does from a member of the clergy rather than a journalist. But we believe that the Reverend Sheppard's perspective is an important one, we believe that this is a story which is at one and the same time disturbing and encouraging, and we believe that our response to it will impact the kind of community Penford will become.

We will follow up the series with a further insert in which we will publish readers' responses.

As Penfordians turned to the centre pages, few could have guessed what they were about to read.

The Pilgrim

Nine

The Pilgrim's Tale:

A journey of transformation

Week one: A portrait of pain

Joe Naismith was in his late twenties when he came from Yorkshire to work in the Penford Mine shortly before the outbreak of war in 1939. The British government's decision to make coal mining a 'reserved occupation' meant that, like everyone else in that industry, he was exempted from conscription to the army. And the risks inherent in working underground, as well as the importance of a plentiful supply of coal to the nation's war effort, were such that no one in the town ever thought of Joe and his fellow miners as less patriotic than their countrymen who took the King's shilling. They faced danger every day as real as those who fought the Führer's army on the frontline.

They did, however, have one undeniable advantage over the young men who left their homes and filled the troop ships that carried them across the English Channel, one that the tall, good-looking but shy miner from Yorkshire took full advantage of. With so many of their contemporaries in the army, the miners, he would later joke to his friends, faced less competition for the attention of the attractive girls who worked in the mill. That's why, he would go on to explain, looking proudly at his wife, he managed to win the affections of Mary Howarth, who was ten years his junior and widely regarded as a local beauty and a prize catch for any young man fortunate enough to steal her heart.

The couple married in the summer of 1941 and their first and only child, Joshua, was born just over a year later. Some of the members of their wider family questioned why he hadn't been named after his father, as was the custom at that time. But his parents were adamant that the name was the right one for their son. As he grew up through childhood and into puberty, it became ever more obvious that Josh, as he was always known, was like his father physically and temperamentally. By his mid-teens the awkward, gangly youth began, as his mother put it, to 'fill out nicely'. His natural shyness and diffidence only added an extra charm to his increasing good looks, causing neighbours and teachers who knew the family to smile and remark, 'He's definitely Joe Naismith's boy. No doubt about that.'

But father and son were alike in another way. Both shared a passion that few of Joe's workmates or drinking companions at the George and Dragon were aware of. From childhood, while Mary sat reading or knitting by gaslight in the old leather armchair beside the coal fire, Josh would kneel on a chair drawn up to the table, watching his father paint in watercolours. The boy looked on amazed that a coal-miner's hands, marked with the blue scars caused by coal dust getting into cuts, could hold a brush so lightly and produce pictures of such delicacy and accuracy. And as year followed year, he progressed from being merely an admirer of Joe's work to become his eager and responsive pupil. Both parents recognised early that the boy's budding artistic talent was just one manifestation of a deep and broad intelligence allied to an insatiable hunger to learn, and they resolved to do everything in their power to ensure that their only child would have the best education possible and to give him the opportunities that had been denied to them.

When Josh passed his eleven-plus exam and moved up from primary school to Penford Grammar School, his parents' assessment of their son's ability was quickly confirmed by his teachers. Only once before in the school's history had a pupil gone on to study at Oxford. Now their unanimous opinion was that they had discovered their second Oxbridge candidate. He excelled at subjects across the board and, as his academic prowess flourished, he began to overcome his natural diffidence and to develop into a confident and likeable young man. The Naismith boy, everyone agreed, had a glittering academic future ahead of him. For Josh, however, though he applied himself diligently in every subject, academic achievement was never his goal. Those evenings spent at home watching and learning from Joe had stirred something he could not ignore, and his heart was set on going to art college and becoming a painter.

For all that, the pressure from well-meaning teaching staff and an ambitious headmaster who regarded him as a potential standard-bearer for the school might have pushed him in the direction of academia had not Herbert Donnington arrived as head of art at Penford Grammar in 1957 when Josh was in his mid-teens. Donnington was well known in educational circles as a charismatic teacher with a talent for inspiring budding young artists. He also had a growing reputation as a painter of considerable merit whose style was very much of the mid-twentieth century but whose subject matter was primarily of a religious character.

There were some senior members of staff who questioned why he'd left his previous teaching post with little warning of an impending move. But any reservations they had were quickly swept aside by the near-euphoria among the school governors at securing such a high- profile figure who could breathe new life into the art department which, despite a long tradition of excellence, had been in the doldrums for some years.

Donnington immediately recognised in Josh someone with an unusual degree of talent whose personality and passion for the subject would make him ideal material in the hands of a strong and forceful mentor such as himself. Again, several of the more experienced teachers expressed concern about the degree of influence their new colleague was beginning to exert on the handful of boys with whom he was surrounding himself. And yet again those anxieties were swiftly stifled when the outstanding quality of work that Josh and others were beginning to produce under Donnington's tutelage became apparent.

It was towards the end of Donnington's first year at the school that tragedy struck the Naismith family when Joe was killed in a mining accident. A heavy stone weighing more than a ton fell on him from the roof of the coal seam in which he was working, pinning him to the ground. He was rushed to Penford Infirmary, where he was found to have sustained spinal and internal injuries. He died three days later with his wife and son at his bedside, never having regained consciousness.

Josh, who had remained close to his father throughout his teenage years, was grief-stricken. His mother feared that he might never recover from the blow, and she was at a loss to know how to bring him through this difficult time. But help was at hand in the shape of Herbert Donnington, who emerged as something of a surrogate father in the weeks that followed. Josh became the 'favourite son' among the family of boys he'd been gathering around him since his arrival in Penford, and gradually he seemed to become once again the talented and valued member of the school community everyone admired so much. Mary Naismith could not have been more grateful. When Donnington suggested that Josh should be allowed occasionally to stay overnight with him and his wife in order to receive more personalised tuition, she was delighted to agree.

Her pleasure at her son's apparent emotional recovery, however, was short-lived. Over the succeeding months she slowly began to notice a disturbing change in his personality. His natural shyness had always been an attractive quality, a winsome diffidence that made it well-nigh impossible for people not to like him. Now he was becoming morose and withdrawn. At first she tried to tell herself that it was just the natural moodiness of a teenager, particularly one who'd experienced the loss that he'd recently come through. But in her heart she knew it was something deeper. There was only one person to whom she felt she could turn. Herbert Donnington would understand. When she plucked up the courage to go to see him he listened sympathetically to her, promised to take an even greater interest in the boy, and vowed that he'd do everything he could to bring him through this difficult time and continue to develop his undoubted talent as an artist. She left his classroom encouraged by his sympathetic words and hopeful that things would improve.

The sad truth was that she had unwittingly handed Donnington carte blanche to surrender to his dark impulses and indulge in his hideously perverted practices. The concerns of those members of staff who feared that his close involvement with some of his favoured pupils was decidedly unhealthy were not without foundation. The man was a devious paedophile with a predilection for teenage boys. The respect generated by his standing as a nationally regarded artist, an unwillingness to acknowledge the full extent of his abuse and a misguided concern on the part of the authorities to protect the reputation of their schools meant that when rumours of his behaviour began to surface, as they inevitably did, he was simply allowed to move on to another post in another part of the country. By the time he arrived in Penford, his abusive behaviour, left unchecked for years, was deeply ingrained in his personality and his actions. A recent interview by the editor of *The Gazette* with Frank Cassidy, a gifted professional artist and also a former student of Donnington's around this same time, revealed a catalogue of serious offences committed against young male pupils at Penford Grammar School. And the circumstances surrounding Frank's recent untimely death bear witness to the lasting effects of his offences.

Appalling as their treatment was at the hands of Herbert Donnington, none of the other boys suffered to the extent that Josh Naismith did. Citing his conversation with Mary Naismith as a parental request that he should keep a close eye on the boy, he had a ready explanation for the headmaster and other members of staff who questioned why he was spending so much of his time with one particular pupil. Were they convinced by his answers, uncertain as to how to deal with a tricky and embarrassing matter, or simply choosing to look the other way? It's impossible for us to be sure at this distance in time. What is beyond any doubt is that no action was taken and his hold on a vulnerable boy struggling to come to terms with the sudden death of his father became ever stronger.

There is one aspect of Donnington's character that has become clear in recent days, both in the editor's research through the archives of this paper and through the recent conversations he has been able to have with the handful of men who are still alive and who still carry the hurt of what was done to them in our town and at our school so many years ago. It's something that troubles me deeply as a committed Christian and a clergyperson in the Church of England, and something that I wish with all my heart was not the case. But it must not be ignored.

To those who knew him, both in his personal and professional life, Herbert Donnington was, to all intents and purposes, a devout and practising Christian. He was active in his local church in every town in which he lived throughout his teaching career, he was open and forthright in his defence of orthodox Christian beliefs and traditional morality, and he was generous in his support of a wide variety of charities and good causes. Perhaps even more significantly, as an artist he concentrated almost exclusively on painting scenes and images of a religious and spiritual nature. One art critic of the day said of him that his style merged 'the eccentric religious vision of Stanley Spencer with the disturbing biblical imagery of Francis Bacon in a unique manner that unapologetically declares, as none of his contemporaries have been able to achieve, the timeless relevance of faith in an age that has witnessed the violence of two world wars in less than half a century.'

The easy response to Herbert Donnington's abuse and control of countless young boys would be to dismiss him as a hypocrite – someone who merely pretended to be religious and who callously used his so-called faith as a clever cover for his terrible wrongdoing. And that may be partly true. But I suspect that explanation is too glib, too simplistic, too naïve. I'm grateful for the fact that in my life, I haven't personally encountered anyone in the Church, or outside it for that matter, whose misdeeds have been as pitiless and evil as Donnington's. But I have come across people who've behaved in ways that hurt other people.

What fascinates and concerns me is that hardly ever would I describe them as hypocrites. At least, not in the way we normally understand that word. What I've seen, particularly in some people with genuine religious beliefs and high principles, is something much worse and much more worrying than hypocrisy. I haven't got a word for it. But I'll try to explain it. *Hypocrisy is trying to fool others*, pretending to believe something you don't really believe, pretending to hold to standards you don't actually live up to. And all so that you can use them as a camouflage for your wrongdoing. There's something sad about that. Sometimes it's even so ridiculous that it can be funny. And in the end it's usually easy to spot.

It's a far more dangerous thing, and it always results in far worse evil, when people get to a place where their selfish or

166

hurtful or perverted behaviour becomes so ingrained, so much a part of who they are and how they live, that they manage to *fool themselves*. Then their religion, or their principles, or the great cause they believe they're serving, becomes not just a cover that hides the truth; rather, it actually compounds the problem, reinforces their behaviour, enables them to convince themselves that what they're doing is not really so bad, or even that it's necessary to further the work they've been called to do. It's a way of thinking that's so devious and all-consuming that people can actually reach the place in their heart and mind where evil becomes good, where lies become truth, and where other people become expendable. And it's why the worst sins are often committed by those sold out to what they believe is a noble cause and by those who are convinced that they're carrying out God's will.

It's only when we allow ourselves to enter into that kind of thinking, I believe, that it becomes possible to comprehend the depraved and cruel behaviour of Herbert Donnington towards Josh Naismith and the other boys within his orbit. From all I've been able to learn about him, it's clear that there were three things that motivated him. He was, in the first place, passionately religious. Perhaps being raised in a particularly narrow and exclusive Christian sect had imbued him with a cast of mind in which religious belief, rather than being the dynamic for a journey of faith with many unknowns along the way, became a rigid structure of immovable and interlocking certainties. To have questioned one thing would, he feared, have brought down the whole edifice in a pile of rubble. Then there was his artistic talent. He was, in the opinion of many experts, a brilliant artist who saw his talent as a gift from God to be devoted to his service. That's why his work focuses almost exclusively on scenes and topics of a religious character. And thirdly, he was by all accounts an exceptionally able teacher who was naturally drawn to young people whom he believed to possess artistic potential that he could develop.

Had that been the whole picture, Herbert Donnington's life would have been an entirely productive one, and he might well have left only a legacy of great paintings and grateful pupils. There was, however, a terrible flaw in his character: his overpowering physical attraction to adolescent boys. Had he been able to acknowledge the dark forces that never left him alone, to seek professional help and spiritual counsel, perhaps even to find employment outside of teaching that didn't involve spending so much time in the company of young people, it might have been possible for him to restrain the urges that controlled him. But the intertwining of his inflexible religiosity, his all-consuming passion for his art and his pride in his ability as a teacher formed an ever-strengthening mesh that suffocated his rational mind, smothered his conscience, enfeebled his will and trapped him in a web of deceit and destructive behaviour. It was a web into which Josh Naismith was drawn and trapped with horrifying consequences when Donnington decided it was time to embark on the project that he hoped would be his magnum opus.

Donnington began working on *A Portrait of Pain* about a year after the death of Joe Naismith. He had used those twelve months when Josh was at his most vulnerable to ensure that he was well and truly ensnared. His mother was grateful for the attention he was giving to her son following her conversation with him. The increasingly frequent invitations for him to stay overnight at the Donnington's home seemed innocent enough to her. After all, Mrs Donnington and her daughter were always present, as far as she knew, and the boy was being given individual tuition from one of the country's leading painters. She tried to tell herself that everything would be alright.

But in her heart of hearts she knew that Josh's mood wasn't really brightening. Indeed she could see that, if anything, he was withdrawing into himself more and more. She would attempt to engage him in conversation when he came home at the end of a school day only to be met with curt monosyllabic answers before he took himself off to his room. When she cooked what she knew was one of his favourite meals, he would have little appetite and would get up from the table with his food half-eaten. Nothing seemed to give him much pleasure. But she herself was still mourning the loss of her husband, and since his death she'd had to return to full-time work in a local draper's shop which, added to her grief, left her feeling constantly tired. Her own emotional reserves were too low for her to be as proactive as she would have wished, and she resignedly put her son's black moods down to the inevitable reaction to the loss of his father.

The truth, had she known it, would have horrified her. Donnington's abusive treatment of Josh had not only continued but increased and worsened after his father's death. It wasn't a term that was used back then, but he was well-practised and skilled in *grooming* his young victims, biding his time as he gained their trust and won the confidence of their parents, making them feel they were part of an elite group with its own code of conduct and what he called 'our special secrets'. And all the time he was slowly but surely increasing the level of his sexual abuse until their wills were broken and his control over them became almost absolute. There is little point in providing a catalogue of his offences here. Suffice to say that had his crimes been uncovered in these times, the sentence he would have received would have meant that he would have been unlikely to be released from prison in his lifetime.

But now we come to the most sickening part of this sorry tale. The point in the story where his distorted view of religion, his obsession with his art and the sickening depravity of his deeds merge to terrible effect. Donnington often referred to his long-held ambition to paint a portrait of Christ in his passion, to produce a work that would not only echo the great religious paintings of past centuries, but that would also reinterpret and depict the agony of the crucifixion for a generation whose sensitivities had been blunted by the horrors of the Holocaust and the scenes of a thousand conflicts played over and over again on their TV screens.

Not content to portray the face of Christ in a way that would simply replicate the traditional image of Jesus wearing the crown of thorns, he was determined to find someone to be his model whose face would show a depth of agony and despair that would lodge itself for ever in the minds of those who viewed his painting. And, whether it came to him gradually over time or in a moment of intuition, he realised that he could the see the pain and suffering he had been looking for in the face of Josh Naismith.

It is impossible to enter fully into the mind of a man who has been dead for many years, a man whose warped thinking and emotional dissonance put his mental processes far beyond the understanding of ordinary folk. But the evidence we have strongly suggests that from the moment he chose Josh to model for him, the pain to which he was prepared to subject his victim steadily increased. The sexual abuse alone must have been terrible enough, but there is one detail that I would willingly omit from this account were it not essential to understanding the depth of suffering that was inflicted on Josh and the lifelong damage that it would cause him. Donnington had him come to his home two or three evenings a week to model for the painting he'd decided to call *A Portrait of Pain*, insisting that he should stand throughout every session and never allowing him to change his posture. It was, he explained, essential that he should experience a level of discomfort if he was to fulfil his role properly. But his obsessive demands went much further.

On the fifth evening – Josh still remembers it vividly – he unlocked a drawer in his desk from which he brought out two hand-forged rosehead nails, each about three inches long. He handed them to Josh, saying that these were to help him enter into the sufferings of Christ more fully and to reflect them more realistically in his facial expression. Then he watched without any sign of emotion as he instructed the boy to twist the nails into the palms of his hands until the skin was broken and they began to bleed. The physical pain must have been acute, but the mental anguish being perpetrated on a young person already tortured by confusion and self-loathing resulting from the sexual abuse is beyond comprehension. It was to be repeated many times in the weeks that followed, and it triggered a pattern of self-harm that would continue in the years ahead.

The painting was finished in just under four months. A few weeks after its completion a number of prominent citizens of Penford received an invitation printed in embossed lettering on a gilt-edged card to *An Intimate Soiree at the Donnington Residence*. The purpose of the evening, it went on to explain, was to enjoy an exclusive advance viewing of *A Portrait of Pain*, a major new work by Penford's nationally respected artist. The guest list included the headmaster of Penford Grammar School, Dr Edward Vernon, and the vicar of St Peter's, the Reverend Simon Peabody, and their respective spouses. The daughter of one of the other dozen or so people who were present contacted *The Gazette* after she read about the recent break-in at St Peter's. She recollects hearing her father speak about the event years later, shortly before he died. It's something she had never shared with anyone until prompted by the report in this newspaper. The account she passed on sheds additional light on the story.

The atmosphere that evening, aided by the guests' glasses being topped up regularly and generously with an expensive vintage from the Donningtons' well-stocked cellar, was convivial and the conversation flowed as easily as the wine. The mood changed dramatically, however, when Dr Vernon, at Donnington's request, unveiled the painting they'd come to see. After what seemed like an eternity, the shocked silence eventually gave way to a few embarrassed comments. 'It's... different. Not quite what I was expecting,' was one. 'It certainly makes an impact,' was yet another. But it was left to Dr Vernon, still with the velvet cloth in his hands that he'd just removed from the picture, to articulate what several people in the room were thinking. 'It's uncannily like young Naismith,' he gasped.

The attention of the entire company shifted instantly from the canvas standing on its easel to the artist standing proudly beside it. If the stunned reaction of the group and the headmaster's recognition of the boy who'd modelled for the portrait perturbed him in any way, he didn't allow that to show in his response.

'You're right, headmaster,' he said with a self-assured smile. 'Josh Naismith learned of my intention to paint this subject and was keen to model for me. At first I was a little reluctant. But the more I thought about it, the more the idea grew on me. It would be good for him to watch me at work. And he's been through some difficult times since the death of his father, and that experience has given him a wisdom beyond his years. I promised his mother I would keep an eye on him. Allowing him to sit for me gave me another opportunity to support him.'

Donnington's confident reply to the headmaster's observation eased the tension in the room sufficiently for the conversation to resume and for more considered and approving comments to be made regarding the artistic merit of the portrait.

It wasn't, however, enough to bring closure to the matter. From this distance in time, it's impossible to know precisely what happened in the succeeding weeks, but it is possible to reconstruct a likely sequence of events leading up to the formal unveiling of *A Portrait of Pain* at St Peter's on Good Friday 1959. Inevitably, word of the evening at Donnington's house and the reaction of those present to the painting began to circulate among members of staff at Penford Grammar, and this resulted in the rumours and concerns regarding his conduct resurfacing.

There was a series of meetings of the school governors, chaired by the Reverend Peabody, of which no minutes were kept. At one of these, Donnington was questioned as to the nature of his relationship with Josh. Of course, he strenuously insisted that there was no cause for concern. Whether everyone was convinced by his repudiation of any suggestion of wrongdoing isn't clear. It's safe to assume that the governors had no stomach for the kind of enquiry that would have been needed to investigate the matter fully. What's even more certain is that their overriding concern was not to search for the truth or to safeguard vulnerable pupils, but rather to protect the reputation of their school. Everything that followed resulted from that misguided sense of priorities.

Donnington's obsession with the painting he'd just completed meant that there was no way he would allow it to be hidden away from view. So he moved swiftly to stem the tide of suspicion that would have exposed his deeds. He immediately made it known that his latest work had been a labour of love and that he'd decided that it should be a gift to the town and should be on permanent display in St Peter's. At the same time he abruptly ceased all contact with Josh Naismith, a decision that left the boy even more confused than he already was.

Unable to think of any other course of action, and fearful of doing or saying anything that would arouse local interest or attract the attention of the media, Dr Vernon and the Reverend Peabody went along with Donnington's seemingly generous gesture. It's difficult not to come to the conclusion that the help of other influential citizens of Penford was enlisted in maintaining what was essentially a cover-up of the truth. And even when the initial negative reaction of the congregation at St Peter's at the unveiling of the painting threatened to kick-start the controversy once more, a substantial donation by Donnington to the repair fund of the church was enough to ensure that leading members of the congregation were happy to use their influence to ensure that any unrest was dampened down as quickly as possible.

How differently the rest of this story would have turned out if anyone had taken the time and trouble to speak to Josh and find out what had really taken place is anyone's guess. But nobody seems even to have thought of that. What did happen was that someone was delegated to speak to Mary Naismith about the school's concerns for her son who, they gently put to her, 'seems to be having some kind of a mental breakdown'. It was then suggested that it might be best for her and beneficial to her son's health if they were to make a new start in another part of the country.

Fortuitously, she was informed, Dr Vernon had a colleague who was headmaster of a small boarding school in the West Country and was looking to employ a live-in housekeeper at a decent salary. Not only would the job come with excellent accommodation, but there would also be a place for Josh in the school free of charge. How much, if anything, she knew of the truth, we don't know. And whether pressure was exerted on her or she simply felt that such a move would indeed be in their best interests, Mary agreed to the suggestion that was put to her. The week before *A Portrait of Pain* was unveiled on Good Friday, she locked the door of the miner's cottage where she'd lived since her marriage to Joe for the last time, leaving a neighbour to dispose of the furniture and forward any money that was raised by the sale.

Herbert Donnington moved from Penford Grammar School just over a year later. The reason stated publicly was that he was taking up a post at a school in Norfolk so that he and his wife and daughter could be nearer his elderly mother-in-law who was growing increasingly frail. The records show that he stayed there for less than two years before moving on again. We can find no record of him being employed by another school anywhere in the country. Not before time, we must hope, his career in education had come to an end. For Josh Naismith, on whom he had dealt so much hurt, a long and winding journey was just beginning.

Ten

The Pilgrim's Tale:

A journey of transformation

Week two: The lost years

Mary Naismith fell in love with Langborne the moment she and Josh stepped off the train on a perfect spring day. The station, which she thought must have changed little since it was built a century before, was tidy, with everything maintained in immaculate order. The paintwork on doors and window frames was in pristine condition, the platform had been swept clean of any litter, and there were tubs of freshly planted flowers and shrubs carefully placed at regular intervals that were obviously looked after by someone who took pride in their work. A stout and rosy-cheeked man in a stationmaster's uniform greeted her with a cheery 'Alright, my lover?' as they passed the ticket office. He chatted with them in a broad West Country accent for a minute or two and happily pointed them in the right direction for Langborne School in response to Mary's enquiry.

They walked slowly through the town, pausing frequently and putting their suitcases down to rest for a moment under the late afternoon sunshine. And each time they stopped and looked around, Langborne continued to work its magic on Mary. The pleasingly random assortment of medieval and Georgian buildings, most of them constructed in the honey-gold Hamstone so characteristic of Dorset, produced in her a sense of delight she had not felt for a very long time. It was impossible for her to imagine anything in greater contrast to the sombre buildings of Penford.

Here, surely, was an opportunity to put the sadness of Joe's death behind her and make a fresh start. Even Josh felt his spirits begin to lift within him as he walked alongside his mother. They'd left early in the morning and the complexities of the railway timetables had meant that they'd had to change trains twice. And each time they boarded the train, lifted their suitcases up on the rack and settled into their seats, Penford and Herbert Donnington had felt just a little further away. They'd said very little to one another on the journey, each of them either dozing off to sleep or lost in their own thoughts as the English countryside sped past them.

Since his mother had told him of the proposal that they should leave Penford, Josh's feelings had been a confusing contradiction of utter relief at the possibility of escape from all that was happening and an all-consuming anger – anger at Donnington and his cruelty, anger at his own failure to stand up to him, anger about the attention being given to the painting, anger at his mother for not knowing what had been going on, and anger at himself for not being able to tell her. Now, standing beside her in this quiet street more than 200 miles from Penford, where no one knew him, he thought he could detect a faint whisper of hope underneath the clamour of his warring emotions. Perhaps it would just all go away. Perhaps he'd begin to feel better in a new place. Perhaps he'd go to sleep that night and wake up in the morning and it would be as if none of it had ever happened.

When he did wake up the next morning it was in a spacious bedroom overlooking the school playing fields. The whole of the top floor of what had once been a minor stately home and was now the headmaster's residence had been adapted to provide separate living space for the housekeeper, and it offered more than adequate accommodation for two people. Compared to the miner's cottage they had just left, where space was at a premium and home comforts were basic, to say the least, it felt to Josh and his mother like living in a mansion. And that morning they sat down to eat breakfast with the sun streaming in through the windows of a kitchen which was almost as large as the entire ground floor of the two-up two-down cottage they had left the day before.

Mary had just gone downstairs to report for her first day at work and Josh was at a loss as to how to occupy himself when he heard the sound of someone running up the stairs, followed by a loud knocking on the door. He opened it to be greeted by a confident, fair-haired youth who introduced himself as James Willoughby-Smith and explained that, unlike the other seventy or so boarders who'd all gone home for Easter, he was staying in school since his parents were working in Africa. He'd come, at the request of the headmaster, to offer to show the new boy around the school.

Grateful for the company and for something to do, Josh gladly followed him downstairs, through the playing fields and into the main school block. James chatted easily as they threaded their way along the corridors and in and out of the various classrooms. Everything about his guide – his languid, world-weary air and the lazy swagger that perfectly matched his public school accent – made Josh acutely aware that he'd suddenly arrived in an alien environment where a lad like himself from a working-class Lancashire family could easily feel out of his depth.

He was beginning to regret that he'd allowed himself to be persuaded to leave Penford when James closed the door of the classroom in which they were standing, lowered his voice to a whisper and asked him if he was interested in seeing his 'stash'. Without waiting for a reply, he led him to a wooden shed in which the sports equipment was stored, assuring him that what he was about to show him would make the Easter holiday much more interesting. He pushed the door open before producing a set of keys from his pocket that unlocked a cupboard half-hidden behind a pile of cricket nets. The door of the cupboard swung open to reveal the nature of his 'stash' – a supply of bottles and cans that wouldn't have looked out of place in an off-licence. Normally, he explained with a wink, he sold these to other pupils for a small profit. Today, however, as an expression of welcome to his new-found friend and to ward off the boredom of what would be an otherwise uneventful day, drinks would be 'on the house'.

I need to pause at this point in the story. Readers of *The Gazette* may well be thinking that this is just an example of schoolboy bravado and wondering why I've devoted so much space to it. Some might even be questioning whether this is just the oversensitivity of a vicar who's out of touch with the conduct of normal teenage boys. The truth is that there's a much more important reason for the prominence I'm giving to this episode. Not only is it a scene that stands out vividly in Josh Naismith's memory, but it's also a moment that was to dictate the direction of his life for the next twenty years.

Mary Naismith, like many of the miners' wives, was constantly concerned by the culture of heavy drinking that existed in a mining community and was anxious to protect her son from the temptations around him. Her husband had not been a particularly heavy drinker and had been happy to acquiesce to her wish that they shouldn't keep alcohol in the house. And, largely as a result of her vigilance and his respect for her anxiety on his behalf, Josh had never so much as tasted a drop of alcohol in his life.

But that moment when James opened one of the bottles and passed it to his surprised companion was to change everything for Josh. His heart began to beat faster and his breathing started to quicken as his hands caressed the smooth contours of the pleasingly cool bottle. He was nervous but excited. It was as if he was being invited to join a secret brotherhood from which he'd previously been excluded. Not knowing what to expect, he lifted the bottle to his lips and tasted beer for the first time. The malty yet bitter flavour took him by surprise and his first instinct was to spit it out. But James was watching him with an unwavering gaze and he knew immediately that he was being subjected to a test, undergoing an initiation rite. After all that he'd been through, after the pain and isolation he'd experienced, here was the chance to be admitted to a fellowship in which secrets, rather than being repressed and leaving you isolated, bonded you with other initiates. It was an opportunity he would not allow to pass. He forced himself to look James in the eye before he put his head back and drained the contents of the bottle.

For the next hour the two boys lazed around and chatted until Josh made the excuse that his mother had some things she needed him to do. The truth was that he was feeling nauseous and, as soon as he reached his new home, he rushed to the bathroom and threw up with his head in the toilet bowl. His first thought as he got up from his knees and washed his face was that he would never do that again.

But there was another voice, deeper and more persistent than logic, whispering seductively that there was something about this unfamiliar taste that mattered more to him than whether or not he liked it. Something that might help him bury the secret that haunted him every day. Something that could release him from his prison of isolation and usher him into a fraternity of fellow conspirators, safely hidden from the scrutiny of abusive and controlling adults. The upshot was that every day throughout the Easter holidays he and James would make their way to the shed at the far end of the sports field where they would drink together while James would regale him with tales of life at Langborne School.

By the end of the holiday, James had quickly become the friend Josh had always longed for. And for his part, James seemed to be just as pleased with Josh's company, though he was at pains to make sure it was understood that his generosity could not continue through term-time and that Josh would need to begin paying for his drinks, just as all the other boys did.

As the term went on and the long summer break began to draw nearer, Josh occasionally wondered if James was quite as keen on his company as he had been at the beginning, but it was a thought that passed swiftly when they met, sometimes on their own and sometimes with up to a dozen other boys, for their regular drinking sessions in the sports equipment shed.

With the arrival of the long summer holidays, James went off to stay with his parents in Africa and, for the first time, Josh was the only boy still at the school. It took only a couple of days for him to realise that he was missing what had become almost a daily intake of alcohol. Now, in the face of boredom, loneliness and the endless effort to shut out the memories of his abuse by Herbert Donnington, the craving to drink became ever stronger.

For most of the term he'd been paying for the cost of his drinking by secretly withdrawing money from the Post Office account that his mother had set up for him a couple of years before. Now, however, that relatively meagre sum was all but exhausted. He was able to earn a little by doing odd jobs for the school caretaker, and all of that went to fund his regular trips to the off-licence in the village. Even the paraphernalia surrounding alcohol fascinated him to the point where it became a fixation. He would find himself standing in the shop looking at bottles, admiring their shape and colour, and reading the labels with an obsessive interest as he waited to be served.

At first, his height and the fact that he looked older than his years allowed him to make his purchases without too many difficult questions from the person behind the counter. But, as his visits to the shop became ever more frequent, he could see that the proprietor was beginning to regard him with some suspicion. The only solution was to walk to the shop in the next village, a round trip of almost six miles. And that in turn obliged him to come up with a list of credible excuses to explain his frequent lengthy absences to his mother. He'd been able to keep the secret of Donnington's abuse from her simply by keeping silent, and he could justify that kind of deception to himself as something he had to do to protect her from the shock and the shame of the truth. Now he was choosing not just to keep silent, but to cover up a different kind of secret by actively lying to her. And this time his deceit was to protect himself. The burden of guilt on an already deeply troubled young man would prove to be too much for him to bear.

He'd hoped that the return of James and the other boarders at the beginning of the new school year would distract him from his inner struggle and help him to feel better. To his bitter disappointment, however, it quickly became apparent that all pretence of friendship had disappeared and that to James he was now no more than just another customer. As the months passed and his drinking increased, he grew more and more lethargic, losing all interest in his work and finding little in common with boys from very different backgrounds to his own, most of whom regarded him as nothing better than an interloper. As one of them sneeringly told him when it was rumoured that word of the drinking den had reached the headmaster, 'Our parents pay good money for us to be here, so nothing will happen to any of us. But you're only here because your mother's the old man's cleaner. You're both for the high jump if anything gets out.'

That was when he decided that he couldn't handle the situation any longer. One Friday evening in spring, when Mary was out enjoying a meal with some of the women she'd got to know in the town, he broke into the bursar's office and stole £50, put some clothes in a bag, left his mother a note saying he'd get in touch when he got himself settled, and went to the station where he boarded a train to London. He was eighteen years old. And he never did get in touch with his mother.

Josh Naismith describes the two decades that followed his sudden departure from Langborne as his 'lost years'. At first he managed to find cheap lodgings in a run-down block of flats and to hold down a succession of casual labouring jobs. But, as his alcoholism careered out of control, his life spiralled ever downwards. He was eventually evicted from his flat for failing to pay the rent and lived in a Salvation Army hostel for some years. But his drinking and his occasional violent rages led to him being blacklisted for the protection of the other residents, and he ended up sleeping rough on the streets of London.

He was hardly ever sober. He drank to forget the abuse that had been done to him, he drank to escape who he'd become, he drank because he despised himself, and he drank because it was the only thing that afforded him any kind of temporary pleasure. Once or twice he heard from other vagrants that a woman called Mary with a Lancashire accent had been asking questions and looking for him. Sometimes it stirred a longing in him to make contact with his mother. And sometimes he was so drunk that he couldn't think who Mary was or what her search had to do with him.

A few more years of this existence would surely have resulted in his early death. He himself feels that it's remarkable that he survived as long as he did, given the inevitable effects of alcohol abuse on his body and mind. But almost twenty years after he'd walked out of Langborne School, Josh Naismith's life was to change dramatically once again. He has charged me with telling his story, but this is a moment when

I must stand aside and let him describe a life-changing encounter on a London street in his own words.

It's just another typical day for an alcoholic living rough on the streets. And it's a typical English summer's day – cold and wet! I'm pretty well soaked to the skin and feeling miserable because I need a drink. By this stage I've resorted to begging, and by early afternoon I've got just enough money to buy a couple of bottles of cheap wine. The soles of my shoes are hanging off and my feet are sore and wet. So I'm hobbling along the street clutching my money and heading for a shop where I know they're not fussy about who they serve as long as they can pay.

Suddenly I'm vaguely aware of a man coming towards me, looking straight at me. I'm thinking this is unusual, because most people step aside to avoid you when you're in the state I'm in. But he keeps coming until he stops right in front of me. I cuss at him and tell him to get out of my way. But he just stands there, staring at me. Then he holds out his arms and takes me by the shoulders, still staring straight at me. I try to take a swing at him to knock him out of the way. But I'm so sozzled that I almost fall over, and he just keeps his hands on my shoulders and holds me up. I'm still trying to wriggle free when I hear him say my name.

'Josh Naismith… Josh Naismith. It is you. I've spent the last week of my life looking for you.'

But my mind's fuddled and I'm desperate for a drink. I've no idea who this is. The only thing I can think of is that this is someone I've stolen from and he's come after me. But I look at him again and it's obvious, even in my muddled state, that this guy's not living rough. He's clean and tidy and he certainly doesn't look like he's been drinking.

'Who the... Who are you?' I ask him. 'What d'you want?'

'Josh,' he says, shaking his head. 'I'm James Willoughby-Smith. Do you remember me? I need to talk to you.'

It takes me a second or two before some hazy memories begin to form themselves in my confused mind... the Easter holidays, the old cricket shed, the drinking sessions...

I'm stuck for words; my head's all over the place. I've no idea why he's come looking for me after all these years. And I certainly don't realise right there and then how important this is going to turn out to be...

It's hardly surprising that the befuddled, rain-soaked alcoholic who was accosted on the street on his way to his next drink failed to appreciate the significance of what had just happened. It was an unexpected and unlikely reunion with an acquaintance from his past. And it makes sense only when we know something of James Willoughby-Smith's own story and why it became an obsession for him to track down the boy whom he'd introduced to alcohol so many years earlier. We can sketch out that story in just a few paragraphs.

James had gone on to university from Langborne School. He'd no real interest in scholarly pursuits and consequently his academic achievements had been mediocre. He had, however, used the time to hone his undoubted entrepreneurial skills and utilise his natural talent for making contacts. After graduation and a succession of different jobs, he eventually moved into property development. It was a line of work that suited his personality and abilities perfectly, and within a few years he'd become sufficiently wealthy to afford the kind of lifestyle that made him the envy of his contemporaries. From the outside he appeared to be the very embodiment of success – rich, talented, charming, with a glamorous wife and two children.

But all was not well with James. His drinking, which had begun as an expression of youthful bravado and a quick way of making money when he'd been a boarder at Langborne School, had become a dependency on alcohol. It was both the lubricant that oiled the wheels of his business deals and a convenient escape from the pressures of a life lived at a frantic pace. Only when his drinking began to threaten his marriage did he accept that something had to be done. He put his business on hold and checked himself into a drug and alcohol rehabilitation facility.

It was an experience from which he emerged, not just as a recovering alcoholic with the tools to confront and control his addiction, but also as a man who'd reassessed his lifestyle and realigned his values. Integral to his change of direction in life was an awareness of his previous selfishness. That stimulated a desire to help his peers in the business world whose stressful lives might be making them as vulnerable to addiction as he had been. His one-day seminars for business leaders had attracted the interest of the media, and the resulting publicity had led to him accepting an invitation to return to Langborne School as the guest speaker at the Annual Prize-giving Ceremony.

At the end of the afternoon's event, he'd been invited to a meal with the senior teaching staff in the headmaster's residence. He knew barely anyone around the table, most of the teachers of his day, including the headmaster, having moved on or retired. He did, however, vaguely recognise one of the women who was waiting on table. It took him most of the meal to figure out who she was before it came to him that she must be Josh Naismith's mother. The memory of Josh's sudden disappearance from school came flooding back, and with it an overwhelming surge of guilt at his own behaviour towards him.

When the meal was over he made a point of asking her about her son. She thanked him for his concern and quietly told him of her repeated but unsuccessful efforts to discover his whereabouts and make contact with him. All she had been able to gather was that he was somewhere in London, that he was drinking heavily and that he didn't want to be found. Her weary, dignified resignation at the prospect of never seeing Josh again only added to his remorse for the part he'd played in setting his fellow student on this road.

James made no rash promises to Mary Naismith that afternoon, but as he was driving home he resolved that he would try to make amends for the past and do what he could to bring about a reconciliation with the son she hadn't seen for twenty years. Something told him there was no time to lose. So the next day was spent in the office with two of his senior colleagues, ensuring they knew what needed to be done in his absence. Early the following morning he headed to London. He was a man who was used to asking questions and finding the right answers, but he quickly learned that talking to people in the shadowy netherworld of rough sleeping and hard drinking was very different from conversations in the boardroom.

He was almost on the point of giving up when an elderly man sitting on a wall outside a pub told him that six months earlier he'd met a tall, skinny guy called Josh and remembered him saying something about a public school in Dorset. They were dossing in a derelict house in east London at the time and he thought the tall, skinny guy might still be squatting there. It took James another full day and another dozen encounters with groups of men sheltering in doorways and under archways before he finally tracked Josh down on that rain-soaked London street.

It might have taken him twenty years to decide that it was time to make restitution for past wrongdoings and a week of trudging round the most dismal streets in the capital city before he found the man for whom he was looking, but his timing couldn't have been better. He'd succeeded in finding Josh at a moment when he was as close as he ever came to being sober and, just as importantly, when he'd reached his lowest point of despair at the misery of his existence. Before the day was over, James had bought him a change of clothing and cleaned him up sufficiently to put him in his car and drive him the 150 miles to the private drug rehabilitation clinic where he himself had been treated. He couldn't persuade his passenger to remove the worn and damp fingerless gloves he was wearing or to let go of what looked like a small, leather moneybag he was clutching. But in the larger scheme of things, he deemed that to be a battle not worth fighting.

It was dark by the time they arrived at the clinic and Josh, who never did get the drink he'd set out to buy that afternoon, was sweating and shivering and feeling nauseous as the effects of withdrawal kicked in. Since James had already contacted the clinic earlier in the day to ensure a place was available and to arrange payment for Josh's stay, two members of staff were waiting for them, ready to receive their new patient and to begin the detox treatment immediately. James said a quick goodbye and headed for home, knowing that there would be a long journey ahead of Josh but hopeful that he'd been able to set him on a road where recovery was at least possible.

Twenty years of drinking takes a toll on the strongest of men, and the early days spent in detox, even with the help of medication expertly administered by skilled health professionals, were difficult and unpleasant as the alcohol poisoning was flushed from his body. But, as he emerged from that initial phase of the treatment, Josh began gradually to feel stronger mentally and physically. Under a regime of counselling and therapy that focused on identifying the reasons behind his addiction and developing strategies for achieving and maintaining sobriety, he was able for the first time to open up about the abuse he'd suffered.

He was, however, unable to speak about his experience in detail. He didn't tell the psychiatrist about Donnington's painting or reveal the true reason for the odd-looking wounds in the palms of his hands. He would not and could not try to explain to anyone else what he could not explain to himself – how the very existence of *A Portrait of Pain* which carried his image on the canvas and the scars he carried in his hands somehow turned the sexual abuse into something even worse: a deeper invasion of his privacy and a more brutal corruption of his personality. It would be many more years and much further along his journey before he could begin to address those things.

Throughout the four months he was in rehab, James visited him almost every week. The more Josh learned of his benefactor's wealth and his successful business, the more surprised he was that he'd taken time away from his work to trudge around London looking for someone he could so easily have forgotten. In one of their conversations he tried to express his appreciation. James stopped him, explaining that he was the one who should be the more grateful – grateful for the chance to make amends, albeit belatedly, to someone he'd wronged.

'Here's the thing, Josh,' he said as he got up to leave. 'We're both in need of something that the other one can give. You need to recover sobriety and I can use some of the money I've made to help with that. But I've learned that my good fortune means little to me without the forgiveness I need from the people I've hurt. And when I talked to your mother that day at Langborne School, I knew I had to find you, give you what I could and ask you for the forgiveness I needed.'

Josh thought about those words long after his visitor had gone. They made him feel more alive, more human, than he'd done for many a long year. And he was grateful that, against all the odds, he'd reached a place where he could offer forgiveness to someone, and he determined, as soon as he was able, to go to someone whose forgiveness he needed to seek.

Eleven

The Pilgrim's Tale:

A journey of transformation

Week three: Mother and child reunion

The last time Josh Naismith had stepped off a train at Langborne station he'd been seventeen years old and he'd arrived with his mother from Penford. They'd set their suitcases down on the platform on a warm day before setting off on the short walk to their new home. The stationmaster had greeted them warmly and made sure they were heading in the right direction for Langborne School. Now, two decades later, he was alone, his belongings in a backpack and his memories weighing far more heavily on him than his sparse luggage. No one spoke to him or even seemed to notice him as he turned his collar up for warmth and hurried through the driving rain on the cold November morning. His mother had offered to meet him at the station. But he was nervous as to how he'd control his emotions when he saw her and he'd asked her to wait for him in her rooms. It would be easier for both of them, he'd told her, if they were completely alone when they saw each other for the first time in more than twenty years.

The town, like the station, had changed little since he'd left, but now the charm of the ochre-coloured Hamstone buildings was lost on him. He was no tourist come to view the sights and wallow in nostalgia for a time when the world had been a rosier place. The England of his past wasn't a green and pleasant land. For him it was much more like a cold and barren landscape bereft of beauty and without any redeeming feature. He'd spent his youth in Penford and lived in London for the past two decades with barely a year in Langborne sandwiched between those times. All three places held unhappy memories that he'd been trying to shut out of his conscious mind. Only in the last few months spent in the rehab clinic had he dared to hope that he might one day walk free from the long, dark shadow of the past, maybe even come to a place of healing from the hurts inflicted upon him.

The rain began to ease a little when he reached the wrought-iron gates of the school and walked up the path by the side of the sports field that led to the headmaster's residence. As he approached the house, he glanced up and caught sight of a slight movement at one of the windows on the top floor of the impressive three-storey building in front of him. It was the merest twitch of a curtain, but it was enough to disarm him, to weaken his resolve to stay in control of his emotions. Tears welled up in his eyes. He knew his mother was watching, looking for him, just as she must have done on many a day. He climbed the stone steps leading up to the heavy oak front door and hesitated just for a moment before he leaned his shoulder against it to push it open. It groaned slowly on its hinges, just as it had done on that Friday evening long ago when he'd tried to stifle the noise in the hope that he could slip out of the building without anyone noticing his leaving. This time he was glad there was no need for such secrecy.

He reached the bottom of the stairs to find that his path was blocked. His mother had run down three flights of stairs to greet him and was standing in front of him. She looked smaller than when he'd last seen her – diminished was the word that came to his mind – and her hair had turned white. But apart from that she'd changed little. Her face was flushed, she was panting for breath and her arms were wide open. Josh took a moment to throw off his backpack and fell into her arms. For two or three minutes they were locked together in an embrace. Several times he tried to say sorry and each time she silenced him by patting his back and making a quiet but insistent shushing sound. No words were spoken and none were needed.

Eventually, reluctantly, she released him from her arms. He picked up his backpack and they climbed the stairs together, arm in arm. Mary Naismith had been anticipating this meeting ever since James Willoughby-Smith had got in touch to tell her that he'd found Josh and that he was safely ensconced in rehab. She would have visited him immediately she received the news, but Josh had been adamant that he didn't want her to see him while he was undergoing treatment. He'd promised her that he'd come to Langborne as soon as he was discharged from the clinic. Never before had she waited so impatiently for a promise to be fulfilled.

They talked for a long time that day. Mary told him that Langborne School had treated her sensitively and kindly after his sudden departure. She'd immediately paid back the £50 he'd stolen from the bursar's office and handed in her notice, only to be summoned to the headmaster's office and told that her work was appreciated, that her job and her accommodation were safe, and that they wanted her to stay. The police had been informed that Josh was missing, and in the course of their investigations the existence of the late-night drinking sessions had been discovered. A number of parents, including the Willoughby-Smiths, had been contacted and warned about their sons' future behaviour. But, just as one of the boys had boasted to him, no further action had been taken against any of the pupils.

The local constabulary had passed on word to the Metropolitan Police of Josh's disappearance, but nothing had ever come of whatever searches they might have made. Mary herself had travelled to London several times in the first few years to look for her son. Each time she'd picked up hints and rumours, but her hopes were always shattered and ultimately her efforts had proved fruitless. In the end she'd returned to Langborne with only her prayers to keep those hopes alive. Now, as he clutched her hand, Josh could see in her eyes and hear in her voice the relief she was feeling at their reunion. And he knew that everything she'd ever longed for was fulfilled in this moment.

Josh had come to Langborne with no clear idea of whether or for how long he might stay, but it soon became clear to him that his mother needed him to be around for a while. As things turned out, the school was looking for someone to replace the caretaker who was just on the point of retirement and, when they offered him the job, it seemed only sensible to accept. The regular daily routine and the practical nature of the work was exactly what he needed after the chaotic lifestyle he'd led over the previous twenty years. It also meant that he had time to spend with his mother after neglecting her for so long. For her part, she was just grateful to have him around and to be able to cook for him and look after him. By the summer of the following year he'd put on some much-needed weight and was looking and feeling healthier than he'd done since his youth. He was even beginning to wonder if this might prove to be the end of his travels and if he'd spend the rest of his days in this quiet and pleasant Dorset town. Then life changed again for Josh.

The school had paid for him to have driving lessons and had put him through his test so that he could be available for additional duties, picking up deliveries from the town and taking pupils on study trips. Driving opened up a whole new world for him and gave him a sense of independence and freedom he'd never had before. It also gave him the opportunity to do something for his mother. He'd noticed recently that she was looking more tired than usual, something he put down to her commitment to her work and her determination never to be idle. A drive to the coast, he thought, would do her no end of good. She'd always talked fondly of childhood outings to the seaside, so the day after the summer term ended he borrowed a car from one of the teachers and drove her to Weymouth for the day. They followed a leisurely meandering route through some of Dorset's country lanes and side roads, chatting and laughing together as she regaled him with tales of his childhood. It occurred to him that he'd never seen her so relaxed or carefree.

The weather was warm, and after lunch she asked if they could take a stroll along the prom. She took Josh's arm and drew in long deep breaths of sea air as they walked along slowly together. But after just a few hundred yards he could see that she was already getting tired. He half-expected her to resist his suggestion that they should get a couple of deckchairs and rest, but she seemed relieved and gladly accepted his offer. And this again is one of the points in the story where I need to allow Josh to tell it in his own words, just as he told it to me.

> Even after all these years I can still see it, still hear her speaking, still remember exactly what she said. She took her time to get settled into the deckchair and to make sure that the brightly coloured cotton skirt she was wearing was arranged just right. She made sure it was covering her knees – she was always very careful about what she called 'a woman's proper modesty' – tucked it neatly under her, drew her knees together and clasped her hands on her lap. Then she asked me to turn my chair towards her so that she could look at me while she was speaking.
>
> 'Now, Josh,' she said, 'I need to talk to you and I need you not to interrupt. So sit still and listen.'
>
> I suddenly started to feel nervous at what she was about to say, but she gave me a beaming smile and I thought it couldn't be anything to worry about.

'Today's been a lovely day,' she said. 'Just what I needed, thank you. And the last few months have been the happiest time of my life. When I lost your dad, that was bad enough. But when I lost you, too, that was almost more than I could bear. But my work at the school kept me occupied and I never gave up hope. Every day I prayed that you'd come back and every day I looked out of the window hoping that I'd see you coming along the path. And when I heard from James that he'd found you... and then when you did come home – well, I can't put into words how I felt.'

I thought that was it, that she just wanted to tell me how glad she was that I'd turned up. But she beckoned to me to lean closer, like she was about to share a secret. And when she began to speak again her voice was unusually quiet, really calm. Just matter of fact, as if she was telling me where to find something she'd put in a safe place. She told me that five years earlier she'd been diagnosed with cervical cancer. The treatment, however, had been successful and she'd had five good years since then. But she'd recently been feeling more tired than usual and had gone for some further check-ups which showed that the cancer had not only returned but had also spread to other parts of her body. The doctors had told her that she had only a few months to live.

I did what most people do when they hear something like that – you know, all the usual stuff you say – maybe they'd got it wrong, maybe we could get a second opinion, maybe we could find enough money for her to be treated privately. But she just took hold of my hand and shook her head.

'No, Josh. They haven't got it wrong and there's no point in going to any other doctors. The people at the hospital have looked after me very well. And I've made them promise that they'll always tell me the truth. I can feel that I'm getting weaker. So let me just enjoy this next little while without us having to pretend to each other.'

She stopped speaking and opened her handbag – she never went anywhere without her handbag – and pulled out an envelope that she handed to me.

'I've written it all down for you, so you'll know what to do when I'm gone. I've sorted everything out. I've spoken to the headmaster and given in my notice. He's a good man and he's happy for me to stay in the house for as long as I've got. And he's also said that when I'm gone, there'll be some accommodation for you if you choose to stay on in your job.'

By this time, I'd started to tear up. But she wasn't having any of that.

'Josh Naismith,' she said trying to sound stern like she did when I was a kid, 'stop that right now. Or you'll get me started. There's something else you need to know. But there's a breeze getting up and I'm getting tired. Let's walk back to the car. Not too quickly, so I can talk as we go.'

I helped her out of her deckchair and she took my arm as we strolled back along the prom. I can still remember every word.

'Now, there's something else you need to know.' She squeezed my arm as she said it as if to emphasise the point. 'I've got a bit of money put by. I never needed to spend much, living in as I did. And I never went very far on my days off. The headmaster was always trying to persuade me to take a holiday. Said I deserved a break from the place. But I never did go away. I love Langborne and I couldn't think of anywhere that would be nicer. And I knew you'd come back one day. I couldn't bear the thought of you walking up to the house and me not being there to meet you. So I never once spent a whole day away from the school. Anyhow, like I said, there's a decent amount of money that'll help you get on your feet. All I need you to do is to pay for my funeral. And I'd really like it if you could do something nice for the school, something that'll show how grateful I am for all the years I've spent here. But it needs to be something practical. Talk to the headmaster about it. Between you, you'll think of something. The rest of the money is for you to do as you see fit.'

You know what really made the biggest impact on me that day. I still can't get over it now. It wasn't just that she'd waited and watched for me every day for twenty years – though that was more than I deserved. And it wasn't that she was leaving me her money. It was that little sentence: 'The rest is for you to do as you see fit.' You'd think she might have said, 'But don't spend it on booze', or even put it in some kind of trust fund where it would only get released to me if I was staying sober. But she trusted me. They did a lot for me in the rehab clinic, taught me things about staying off alcohol for which I'll always be grateful. But it was only when she said those words to me that I really believed for the first time that I could stay sober. It gives you the strength to believe in yourself when someone else believes in you.

The last conversation she had with her son was shortly before her death. She was agitated and it was clear that something was troubling her. Josh knelt by the bed and put his ear close to catch what she was saying. Her breathing was shallow and the words wouldn't come easily. At first he couldn't believe what he was hearing. She was saying sorry to him! He wanted to tell her that he was the last person to whom she needed to apologise. But there was something she needed to say and she wouldn't be put off.

She told him that she'd suspected 'things had gone on' at Penford Grammar all those years before. But she couldn't bring herself to speak about it then. She was just too embarrassed and didn't even know the words to use. And when the opportunity had come up to leave Penford and come to Langborne, that had seemed the perfect solution. She'd hoped that whatever it was that had happened, Josh would be able to forget in time, 'just get over it and get on with life'. But now she knew that he'd been hurt too deeply for that to happen, knew that it had led to his drinking, knew he would have to carry it for the rest of his life. And she knew that she'd failed him as a mother. 'Can you forgive me?' she asked. 'I don't want to die with it on my conscience.'

He wanted to tell her that there was nothing to forgive. But he knew that would have denied her the one thing she needed more than anything else at that moment. She needed him to *forgive* her. She needed to be absolved and freed from the guilt that she carried.

'Yes, Mum,' he said, squeezing her hand. 'I forgive you. And I need to ask you to forgive me for all the pain I've put you through. Neither of us knew how to deal with it. Will you forgive me?'

She breathed out the words, 'Yes, yes. Thank you.' For a second or two she smiled at him. It was an expression that reminded him of when he was a child and how she would sometimes look at him when he was painting with Joe. It was a look in which pride and gratitude were mingled with utter contentment at what life had given her. Then she closed her eyes and fell into a deep sleep. She didn't speak again and died peacefully a week later on an early autumn evening when the leaves were falling from the trees just outside her bedroom window that she'd loved and watched across the years of waiting through the changing seasons.

It wasn't until her funeral that Josh began to appreciate the impact of his mother's life on Langborne School. The service was held, as she'd requested, in the school chapel, and it was standing room only. Every member of staff and every boarder was there, former pupils had travelled considerable distances to be present, and townspeople with whom she'd become friends added to the more-than-capacity congregation. She might have been employed as a housekeeper, but her influence had been felt far outside the walls of the headmaster's residence. Teachers would often ask her to have 'a motherly word' with troubled pupils, particularly new boys who were missing home and finding it hard to settle, and she'd become a kind of surrogate mum to several generations of grateful boarders. The comfort was often nothing more elaborate than a gentle but firm word of encouragement and a slice of homemade fruit cake wrapped in greaseproof paper, but it was enough to get many a boy through a difficult time in his education.

One 'old boy' of the school, now the CEO of a large company, had been asked to pay tribute to the woman everyone knew as 'Mum Naismith'. He produced from his pocket a handwritten note that she'd sent to his parents in response to a letter from them expressing their thanks for the help she'd given their son. It said simply, 'You're welcome. I'm glad to help. I've got a little boy of my own somewhere and I hope someone's being nice to him.' Josh, who was sitting in the front row between the headmaster and James Willoughby-Smith, was not the only person who shed a tear at that point.

Mary Naismith was buried in the graveyard of the sixteenth-century parish church on the other side of a stone wall, no more than a couple of hundred yards from the house in which she'd lived during her years at Langborne School. Josh had agreed with the headmaster that a headstone should be erected which would read, *Wife of Joe, Mother of Josh, and Mum to countless boys*. And on a glorious evening some weeks later, as the fiery glow of the autumn sunset deepened the gold lettering in which those words were etched on the marble of the gravestone, Josh stood alone, confronted by the mystery of life and death and trying to resolve the contradictions of joy and sadness that the last few months had highlighted. The pain of what had been done to him at Penford Grammar School had all but destroyed him. It was still present with him, would always be with him, and the injustice of it all threatened at times to dominate his every waking moment. The perpetrator, he guessed, might even be dead now and would never be held to account for his wrongdoing. Nothing could ever make things right.

And yet, and yet… Some good had come of it. His mother, bereaved of her husband and deserted by her son, had nonetheless found a place that gave her a purpose for her life, a place where she was respected and loved and where she would be long remembered. And he was alive. Yes, he was a recovering alcoholic whose future was unknown and whose only certainty was that he hadn't had a drink today. *But he was alive*, and that last conversation with his mother had changed things. Not only had she forgiven him for his disappearance and his long absence, she had also conferred on him the dignity of asking for his forgiveness. All through his drinking years there had been fleeting moments when he would wonder if he ever could be or would be forgiven. It had never once occurred to him that he would be asked for forgiveness by anyone, especially the person who loved him the most.

And then there was James – the last person he would ever have thought would even have remembered him. Yes, James Willoughby-Smith had come looking for him, searched until he had found him, taken him to a place of recovery and paid for his care. It reminded him of the story of the Good Samaritan and, for reasons that he couldn't quite fully figure out, that struck him as being funny. It had been a time of mourning and tears, but now he was smiling to himself as he stood in the fading light. All that was missing from his story was the donkey, he reflected ruefully. Though, as he turned and walked slowly away, he consoled himself with the thought that the plush leather upholstery of James' Mercedes was probably a good deal more comfortable and secure for a man under the influence of alcohol than the back of the Samaritan's donkey.

After his mother's funeral he quickly settled back into life as the school caretaker. Being part of a close-knit community with his regular daily responsibilities provided him with a welcome distraction from his grief. His twice-weekly attendance at a local Alcoholics Anonymous group gave him the support he needed to maintain his sobriety, and the school doctor made sure he was taking proper care of his health. He ate lunch with the rest of the ancillary staff, which ensured he had at least one good meal each day and, to his surprise, he even learned to cook some basic dishes for himself. The school was as kind to him as it had been to his mother and the bursar tried to persuade him to regard his job as a long-term position. It was an appealing prospect for a man who had slept rough for twenty years, had it not been for the growing sense of restlessness he felt.

Things came to a head one night as he was carrying out his regular duty of tidying up the school library after all the boarders had headed to their dormitories. It was a task he enjoyed and over which he always took his time. As the bright and intelligent pupil he'd once been, he'd read avidly any book he could put his hands on. But all the time he'd been living rough, his only reading material had been the newspapers, usually several days out of date, that he found lying on the street. Now, as his body grew stronger and his mind recovered something of its old sharpness, he longed to read again. The times he spent alone in the library gave him opportunity to do just that.

On this particular evening, he came across an old copy of John Bunyan's *The Pilgrim's Progress* that one of the boys had left lying around. It had been a prescribed text for an English examination when he was a schoolboy. To most of his class, unable to fathom the allegorical depiction of Christian's journey to a place of redemption, the story had been difficult and inaccessible. But Josh had loved the simplicity of the language and the steady, measured cadences of Bunyan's seventeenth-century English prose. He turned to the first page and read the opening sentence aloud:

> As I walked through the wilderness of this world, I
> lighted on a certain place where was a den, and laid
> me down in the place to sleep; and as I slept, I
> dreamed a dream.

As he heard himself speak out the words in the stillness of the empty library, he remembered how that phrase had enthralled him when he'd first read it in the English class at Penford Grammar: 'As I walked through the wilderness of this world ...' Back then it had charmed him just by the simplicity and beauty of the language. Now it had a deeper resonance for him. For he, too, had walked through the wilderness of this world and laid down in many a den, though his dreams had been more fitful and fretful than those of the Bedford tinker-turned-preacher who'd written those words. He sat down at one of the tables and thumbed through the pages, smiling to himself as characters and scenes long forgotten came back to mind.

He reached the part where Christian, after many ups and downs on his journey, arrives at the House Beautiful. He paused and read more slowly, running his finger along the lines of print, searching for another phrase that had lodged itself in the dim recesses of his memory. It was a phrase that had awakened in him a longing for a place of safety all those years ago when the hurt inflicted by his abuser was at its worst. At last he found it – the words of Christian as he sought entry from the porter at the gate of the house:

> By what I perceive, this place was built by the Lord
> of the hill for the relief and security of pilgrims.

That was what had been denied to him back then. And that was exactly what Langborne School had become for him now – *a place of relief and security*. He read the words over and over again, sad for the past, thankful for the present and wondering what the future might hold.

He sat in the library late into that night with *The Pilgrim's Progress* open in front of him long after everyone else was asleep. Eventually he roused himself into action, signed his name in the borrowers' register, slipped the book into his pocket, turned off the lights and headed for bed. It was neither regret for the past nor even gratitude for the present that was dominating his thinking by the time he reached his room that night. What he had just been reading had brought the reason for the restlessness he'd been feeling into sharp focus. Langborne School had been *his* House Beautiful – the place in which he'd been cared for and treated with grace, the place in which he'd been allowed to brighten his mother's last days and to lay her to rest. But it was not to be the end of his travels. It was a place in which to be refreshed and renewed for the journey ahead. He fell asleep knowing that it was time to leave the place in which so much kindness had been shown to him.

The next morning he met briefly with the headmaster and the bursar and told them of his intention to resign his position and move on. They were somewhat surprised at what seemed to them like a sudden decision, but they could see that his mind was made up and that there was no point in trying to dissuade him. He agreed to their request to work on for another month so that a replacement caretaker could be found, and they, in turn, complied with his wish that no announcement of his departure should be made, to allow him to leave quietly without any fuss.

And so it was that on a breezy November morning, as the first effects of winter were beginning to be felt, he put his belongings once again in his backpack and locked the door of his room at Langborne School for the last time.

First he went to the library with the copy of *The Pilgrim's Progress* that he'd been reading for the past month. He sat for a few minutes and flicked through the pages that followed the description of the House Beautiful, nodding to himself at the succession of fierce battles and life-threatening struggles that confronted Christian on his journey before he reached the next place of welcome and rest. He paused and read Bunyan's description of his hero's arrival at the delightfully named Delectable Mountains.

> So they went up to the mountains, to behold the gardens and orchards, the vineyards and fountains of water; where also they drank and washed themselves, and did freely eat of the vineyards.

He smiled at the thought of such a prospect as he got up and returned the book to the librarian, who asked him why he was looking so happy on a wintry morning.

'Well,' he replied, beginning to walk to the door, 'if I survive what's waiting for me out there, I'm hoping to reach the Delectable Mountains.'

The librarian, who'd never actually read *The Pilgrim's Progress*, was about to ask him to say the name of his intended destination again. But Josh had already gone.

He walked slowly across the playing field and sat for five minutes under a chestnut tree on a brightly painted wooden bench that carried the inscription:

Langborne School
A House Beautiful and a place of relief and
security
In loving memory of Mum Naismith

Then he stood up, turned up his collar against the wind and strode purposefully out through the wrought-iron gates of the school.

Twelve

The Pilgrim's Tale:

A journey of transformation

Week four: Return to Penford

When Josh Naismith walked through the wrought-iron gates of Langborne School a few weeks after the death of his mother, he just kept on walking. Literally! He walked the thirty miles to the village of Abbotsbridge on the Jurassic Coast where he spent the night in a local Bed and Breakfast. In the morning he ate a hearty breakfast, walked out of the front door, turned left and, with the sea on his right, kept going through sun and rain for the next five years of his life.

He walked along the south coast past Portland Bill and Beachy Head, all the way up the eastern seaboard leaving Harwich and Cromer and Whitby in his wake, crossing the border into Scotland at Berwick-upon-Tweed, on to Aberdeen and Wick, all the way to John o' Groats on the north-eastern tip of Britain, along the bleak northern shores of Scotland to Cape Wrath, turning south down the west coast by long lonely paths until he reached picturesque towns like

Mallaig and Oban and Largs, then through the dusty outskirts of Glasgow, into the clear skies of Ayrshire and placid beauty of the Scottish borders. On and on he walked – down the breezy shoreline of Cumbria, quickly past the gaudy glitz of Blackpool and the bustling waterfront of Liverpool, across the sandy beaches of Wales, over the Severn Bridge and back into England, and finally south-west through Somerset and Devon to the Atlantic Coast of Cornwall before turning sharp left and heading back to the Jurassic Coast where he'd set off five years before.

He turned inland only when the absence of a coastal path made it absolutely necessary, driven on by a desire not only to keep moving, but also to stay on the edge of things, to be an observer rather than a participant in the everyday business of life. He quickly traded his small backpack for something much larger in which he could carry his tent, his sleeping bag and his cooking utensils. Mary Naismith's frugal lifestyle meant that what she'd described to him as 'a decent amount of money' actually amounted to just short of £90,000 – much more than Josh had ever anticipated. But this was something he needed to do on his own and from his own resources. The small fortune he'd just received was left untouched.

So whenever his money ran out he would stop off in a town or village where he could find some casual labour until he'd made enough to allow him to get back on the road again. Sometimes he lodged with a farmer who offered him work or with someone who just happened to have spare living space that they were willing to rent out cheaply to a traveller who looked as if he meant no ill and kept himself to himself. At other times he would camp in some secluded spot where he could be alone with his thoughts. He was always polite and courteous in his dealings with the people he met, though he spoke as little as he could and said nothing about himself other than that he'd decided 'to go travelling round the country for a time'.

Whenever he tried to explain to himself what he was doing, the best he could come up with was that he was on 'some kind of pilgrimage'. But, despite his quip to the librarian as he was leaving Langborne that he was hoping to find the Delectable Mountains, he wasn't really trying to reach any particular place. He was just walking. And it was, he had to admit to himself when he realised that his journey was turning into a round-Britain hike, an odd kind of pilgrimage that went round in a circle – even if it was a very big circle – and would inevitably end up where it began.

It was no easier to find an answer when he attempted to work out *why* he was doing it. Of course, it was beneficial to his health. It felt good to be sober and clear-headed and there was no doubt that he was stronger and fitter than he'd been for a long time. There was a sense of freedom after so many years of being driven by the need to find his next drink. Each day he could decide whether to stop where he was or start walking again. Just making those simple choices was deeply satisfying to a recovering alcoholic.

He'd been on the road for almost a year before he began to grasp with his mind what he'd known deep in his soul from the moment he'd taken the first few steps on his journey. It worked its way slowly into his consciousness every time he shouldered his rucksack and straightened his back and set off again. *That was the real reason he was walking.* He needed to carry that load, needed to get used to its weight on his shoulders, needed to accept it, not just as a piece of essential gear for a walker, but as a part of him without which he couldn't be fully himself. Walking on the edge of the country with a heavy and unforgiving load on his back was, he slowly began to realise, a metaphor for his life. This pilgrimage, if that's what it was, wasn't about trying to get to some holy place where he might experience a mystical moment or a life-transforming miracle. It was all about accepting the load he had to carry, acknowledging that it couldn't be wished away, recognising that it had to be shouldered every day.

He would occasionally pass people on the road who were out for a leisurely half-hour stroll, who carried nothing on their backs, and who would greet him with a cheery wave and a jocular comment on the size of his load. And he would feel a momentary pang of envy at the lightness of their step and their carefree manner. But the further he travelled the more he would come to believe that nobody could walk any distance without shouldering their own burden. You could put it down whenever you stopped. You could rearrange the contents to make it a little more comfortable. But if you wanted to move on, you had it pick it up, put it on your back and start putting one foot in front of the other all over again.

One moonlit night, towards the end of his long journey, he pitched his tent on a cliff overlooking a sandy bay. He was tired after a full day's walking, and the sound of the waves lapping on the shore far below lulled him into a deep sleep in which he had a troubling dream. In the dream he was sitting in his tent, when he became aware of someone opening the tent flap from the outside. All he could see were the person's arms as they reached in, emptied the contents of his rucksack and scattered them across the tent.

He wanted to lunge forward and stop whoever it was. But, try as he might, he was unable to move. He watched paralysed and transfixed as they replaced his belongings with large, heavy stones before sealing up the bag again and closing the tent flap. It was only when they withdrew their arms that he was able to move. He leapt forward and ripped through the walls of the tent just in time to catch a glimpse of the prowler's face as he turned and hurried into the darkness. It was a face he recognised immediately. A face that filled him with fear and loathing. It was the face of Herbert Donnington.

There was no more sleep for him that night. Through the hours of darkness the scene he'd just witnessed in his dream played over and over again in his mind. At the first light of dawn he packed up his tent, put his rucksack on his back and began walking. And with every step his subconscious mind was forcing him to face the thing he'd been trying to shut out of his thoughts throughout his drinking years.

We all walk through life carrying the weight of our strengths and our weaknesses, of our wise choices and our foolish mistakes, of our good deeds and our evil actions. And, since none of us lives in isolation, we all have to accept the additional weight that's added to our burden by the things that others do to us. But many of us, because of some terrible sins inflicted upon us by someone else, have to bear a crippling load beyond what should be demanded of any man or woman.

We hope and we pray that we live in a moral universe in which those who perpetrate such hurts will sooner or later be brought to justice. But one insistent question remains, and it was the question that Josh couldn't avoid any longer. What can we do with such a load? Is the best we can expect only that we manage to limp through life without collapsing and being completely crushed under the weight? Or can we hope for something better? Can any man or woman bear the burden in such a way that it strengthens the one who carries it, helps those who walk alongside, and even touches and changes those who placed the load on us? To such perplexing dilemmas Josh had no immediate answers. But he knew that he would never again be able to ignore the question.

He arrived back in Abbotsbridge at the end of his walk on a summer evening with no thought in his head other than that he'd travelled far enough and that it was time to sleep in a proper bed again. By seven o'clock, he'd booked into the same Bed and Breakfast where he'd spent the night five years before at the start of his walk. He went straight to bed and slept for the next twelve hours.

The next morning he strolled just a couple of hundred yards along the main street that ran through the village – without his backpack – and liked what he saw. The seventeenth-century thatched cottages on one side of the road, many of them constructed with stones from the ruined abbey that had been destroyed by fire in Tudor times, faced a long row of Victorian terraces on the other side that had been built in the 1850s. He noticed that one of the cottages, with a bright blue door and leaded windows, had a *For Sale* sign outside. It awoke within him a longing for a permanent home that startled him with its intensity and forced him into immediate action. Without a moment's hesitation, he walked across the street to the estate agent's office and two hours later emerged as the owner of the cottage, and Abbotsbridge's newest resident.

In the twenty-five years that have elapsed since then, the cottage has been both his home and his art studio. After he ran away from Langborne School, he never once picked up a paintbrush in the ensuing years. But within weeks of taking up occupancy of his new home, he began to paint again. Though at first it was simply for his own pleasure and satisfaction, his impressionistic landscapes of the countryside immediately surrounding the village soon aroused the interest of local residents and visitors to Abbotsbridge, and within a year he was earning a comfortable living from his paintings.

His burgeoning reputation brought him to the attention of a wider audience, and for the past two decades he has continued painting under the alias of Joshua Howarth Walker. The works of J H Walker can be found in some of London's most prestigious galleries and regularly fetch prices upwards of £5,000. Some critics have suggested that his lack of tutoring beyond his schooldays has freed him to discover what has been described as his own unique 'primitive-impressionism' that might otherwise have been stifled by a more formal art education. The artist himself dismisses such labels as pretentious and is simply content that people like his paintings enough to buy them.

J H Walker, as he insists on being known when his work is being discussed, is a familiar figure in Abbotsbridge, walking through the village carrying his easel, and with his brushes and paints in a well-worn and far-travelled backpack, as he heads out to paint *en plein air*. Those villagers who have known him longest sense that he is sometimes distracted, as if his mind is elsewhere, like a man with a task that he has neither finished nor knows how to complete. For all that, he is unfailingly courteous and will spare a moment to share a pleasantry with anyone who shows an interest in what he is doing. Everyone who knows him likes him, and many have watched him at work in the nearby fields and country lanes. But no one knows him well and few have been in the little room that serves as his studio and where he adds the finishing touches to what was begun outdoors.

Those few who have been admitted to that inner sanctum have noticed with some interest what seems to be a kind of shrine. On each side of a triangular table in the corner of the room opposite the window is an old, framed photograph. One is a sepia-toned snapshot of a couple on their wedding day. The husband looks a few years older than his wife. The other is monochrome black and white, a picture of the same couple a few years later, with a tall, alert-looking teenage boy standing between them. From what can be seen in the background of these photographs, it appears as though both were taken in a northern industrial town. Between them on the table is an old, pocket-sized, black leather moneybag. And on the floor, just in front of the table, is a pile of stones that looks like a miniature version of a cairn you might find on some mountainous path. No one who has visited him has ever had the courage to ask the significance of this odd display.

But if anyone was to visit the cottage today hoping to meet the well-known painter, they'd be disappointed. They would find that the door is locked and J H Walker is not at home. And if they were to peer through the window trying to catch a glimpse of the strange tableau described above, they would see only the two photographs on the triangular table in the far corner of the room. For on the first day of December, J H Walker put the leather moneybag in his pocket and loaded the pile of stones into the old backpack he'd carried around Britain so many years ago, before closing it up and lifting it slowly and carefully on to his back. Then he set off walking, this time away from the sea and in a northerly direction. It would not be until two days after Christmas, having been almost a month on the road in one of the coldest months of the winter, that, exhausted and confused, he would reach his destination: St Peter's Church, Penford.

Anyone who isn't a resident of Penford and who has just picked up this final instalment in what I have called *The Pilgrim's Tale* will inevitably be asking the obvious question: 'Why would a man in his late sixties, respected and regarded with affection by his neighbours, and with a deserved reputation as an artist, leave his comfortable home on the south coast of England and set off on a 250-mile trek to the northern town of his birth?' The key to unlocking this mystery is to be found in the objects that were on display for so many years on the triangular table in J H Walker's studio. But it's best to let the man himself, Josh Naismith, to give him his proper name, tell you the story as he told it to me.

> I knew that the dream I had about someone leaning into my tent and filling my backpack with stones had to be significant. Whether it was just my subconscious mind or some kind of divine revelation, you can decide for yourself. But I felt it was telling me something about the pain I was carrying. I didn't know what to do with it, but I knew it was too important to forget.
>
> It might seem silly to anyone else, but after I got back to Abbotsbridge I gathered a pile of stones and set them up in the corner of the room so that I'd see it every day, keep it in my mind. The photographs on the table were just to remind me of who I was and where I'd come from. Calling myself

J H Walker was just a way of protecting myself, something to help me preserve my privacy. The middle initial for Howarth was, of course, my mother's maiden name because I owed her so much. And Walker – well, that was just my attempt at humour, I suppose, having spent so long walking round the country.

I looked at those stones every day for twenty-five years. Again, that might sound crazy, but it didn't feel crazy to me because I was still carrying that weight with me every day. The abuse wasn't just something that had happened a long time ago when I was in my teens. It had become part of me. It shamed me, made me feel soiled. If I'm honest, I guess to a great extent it's defined me.

I was never able to have a relationship with anyone of the opposite sex. There was one woman in the village I was really attracted to, and I think the feeling might have been mutual. I'd have loved to get to know her better. But I couldn't. I felt there was something dirty about me that could contaminate her. I didn't even know how to make an approach, didn't know any chat-up lines – that's what they call it, isn't it?

At this point in his story, I interrupted Josh and asked him why he hadn't mentioned the leather moneybag that sat on the table between the photographs. Had he forgotten about that, I wondered? He shook his head slowly before responding.

No, I didn't forget it. In some ways, that's the hardest thing of all to speak about. I think you can probably guess what was in there – the two rosehead nails that Herbert Donnington forced me to push into my hands when I was the model for his painting of Christ. I've kept them all through the years. From time to time I've suffered bouts of depression, and when that happens I find myself taking those nails out again…

His voice trailed off and his expression changed. He was no longer the peaceful elderly man I'd been listening to for more than an hour, telling his story with a detachment that came from having reached a place of quiet resolution. The man I could see before me now had suffering etched deep into every feature. Over the years in my work as a vicar, I've had to watch people in pain. I always find it difficult. But never have I witnessed anything like the grief and anguish I saw on the face of Josh Naismith at that moment. Thankfully, it lasted only for a second or two and he quickly recovered sufficiently to continue what he was saying.

The truth is that I've been self-harming ever since I sat for that painting. I don't do it all the time. But when I get hit by depression everything is just black despair and shame. It's a way of punishing myself for being who I am. I know it doesn't make sense to anyone who hasn't been there. My logical mind tells me that I'm punishing myself for what someone else has done. But he did it to me, used my body to do it. And he did it in the name of religion, which makes it worse. I'm carrying somebody else's sin and abuse. And there's a price to be paid for that. I can't explain it logically. I can only tell you how it's felt all these years. Those nails have been a symbol of how I was abused and broken physically and emotionally.

Again he sat quietly for a time. It was clear that telling all this was taking a toll on him physically, mentally and emotionally. I asked him if he wanted to stop. But he was determined we should hear his story and understand his actions. He took some long, slow breaths and began to explain what had prompted him to set out on his long walk home.

For a few years now I've had a longing to be in touch with my roots again. You know – wondering what life in Penford was like these days. Wondering if anyone knew anything about what had taken place all those years ago or remembered me. Wondering if Donnington's *A Portrait of Pain* still existed and where it might be. I started to read the online edition of *The Gazette* each week just to find out what might be happening in the town. Then I read the article about the controversy that still surrounds the picture and about the decision to move it to a different part of the church on the first Sunday of the New Year.

Well, you can probably guess that triggered off a whole range of conflicting emotions in me. My mind was in turmoil. I didn't sleep for a couple of nights. Maybe it was the lack of sleep, maybe it was just an old man overreacting in a crazy way, maybe it was something deeper than that. But in the end, I knew what I had to do. I had to get back on the road again. Not just going round in a big circle like I did quarter of a century ago. This time I was going to walk to Penford. I was going to deal with the guilt – not just my own, but also Donnington's guilt and the guilt of all the people who either covered it up or just didn't want to know. I'd reached a point where, whatever it cost me – even if it cost me my life – I was going carry it to a place where I could leave it for ever.

So one morning at the beginning of December I got up early, put the stones in the bottom of my old backpack, threw some clothes in on the top and set off north. For the first ten days or so I was OK. I did about ten or twelve miles a day. I had my old tent with me and sometimes I slept in that. Two or three times I managed to find a Bed and Breakfast where I got a proper night's rest and a good meal.

But the emotion of it all and the sheer physical exertion must have got to me. I can remember beginning to feel stressed and disorientated. I wasn't sure where I was or even who I was. After that I don't remember anything about the journey. The only thing I knew was that I had to get to St Peter's Church in Penford and get rid of what was in my backpack. The rest you know.

But there was something I didn't know. What had happened to the backpack filled with stones? I could clearly recall his words as we led him out of the church on that Saturday morning just after Christmas: 'The stones, they've gone! Thank God, they've gone!' But I'd had no idea what those words meant then, or if they were just the meaningless ramblings of a confused and tired old man. I hadn't given them any thought until I heard him tell his story. And now this detail seemed so personal, even *sacred*, that I was uncertain as to whether I should raise it. But it seemed too important – too central to the story – to ignore. So I asked my question a little hesitantly: 'What happened to the backpack and the stones?'

> You know, I've been hoping you wouldn't ask me that. I just don't know. I'm certain I carried them for most of the way. And it was only when you helped me out of St Peter's that I realised they weren't still on my back.

Josh's expression was a mixture of embarrassment and bafflement and his tone was apologetic as he struggled to offer some kind of explanation for the disappearance of the bag and the stones.

> Now this might be just my imagination. It's not even strong enough or clear enough for me to call it a memory. But way at the back of my mind I have some kind of recollection of them sinking into deep water and vanishing from sight. It wasn't something I did. It just seemed to happen despite me. I'm not sure if that really tells you anything, but it's the best I can do. I'm pretty certain that I wouldn't have made it all the way to St Peter's if I'd still had to carry them.

It was clear that Josh had told us everything he could. I switched off the voice recorder and Eddie Shaw, *The Gazette*'s editor, closed his notebook. We both knew that what we'd heard was something much more than a narrative of a remarkable feat of physical endurance, of a 250-mile trek by a man in his late sixties from Abbotsbridge to Penford. It was, in truth, the moving account of one man's odyssey from youth to age, a man who had suffered greatly but learned much.

For a full five minutes we sat without speaking. Eventually it was Josh who broke the silence, and there was an intensity about his words that took us by surprise.

'I want you to tell my story,' he said, looking at us directly. 'I want you to tell it for my sake. For too many years I've carried the pain of what happened in this town such a long time ago, carried a lot of anger at what was done to me, carried the guilt of someone else. Now I want to let it go. I want to be free of it.'

He paused momentarily, leaning heavily on the arms of his chair and pulling himself forward. He seemed to be summoning reserves of energy that would allow him to draw up something that was deep within him.

'And I want you to tell it for the sake of Penford. I wasn't by any means the only boy in my school who was abused. I'm pretty sure that there are others who've been hurt in all kinds of ways in this town since then. Other folk will call for justice and punishment for those who've done wrong. And they're right to do so. But if justice is all there is, we're all done for, because we're all guilty. We all share the responsibility for the stuff that happens to people around us.'

He hesitated again and we wondered if the exertion had been too much for him. But he hadn't finished. Now he spoke like a general addressing his troops, calling them to the final push that would stretch them to their limits, but without which the battle would never be won.

'I've come to the place now where I believe we need something bigger, something much more costly, something that does what justice alone can never do. We need to forgive. And I've discovered that means accepting the pain of what's been done to me, not bottling it up, but accepting it in order to release it. I know that'll sound too passive, like weakness to some people. But I suspect that it's only forgiveness that can begin to break into whatever it is that makes us do such terrible things to one another.'

He reached the end of his sentence and sat back in his chair. In less than a minute, he'd fallen asleep, exhausted by the effort of speaking.

As we gathered up our things and tiptoed out of the room, Eddie Shaw looked at me, clearly moved by what we'd just heard.

'Well, Vicar,' he said, trying unsuccessfully to stop the tear in his eye and keep his tongue in his cheek, 'I guess that's the message that you and your colleagues are supposed to preach every Sunday. If only I'd heard someone preach it with as much conviction and credibility as that man just did, I might have been a faithful member of your flock rather than becoming the cynical old newspaper man that I am.'

'Mr Editor,' I replied, trying equally unsuccessfully to sound flippant, 'if I thought it would give me the chance to meet more people like Josh Naismith who understand and embody what I try to expound from a pulpit, I'd be a full-time newspaper reporter rather than the cynical clergy person I sometimes fear I might become.'

The question I leave with you, the reader, is this: What does Josh Naismith's story mean to you? And what does it mean for Penford?

EDITOR'S POSTSCRIPT

We've come to the end of what has certainly been the most unusual series of articles ever printed in *The Gazette*, and possibly in any local newspaper in this country. We know from the responses we've already received that many readers have appreciated it. Some, however, have questioned why I commissioned a local clergyperson to write the series rather than assigning it to one of our reporters or doing it myself, and why we've given such prominence to this unusual story. Since the Reverend Pippa Sheppard has left *you* with a question, it seems only right that I should answer the question that readers have asked of me.

As the editor of this newspaper, I decided to ask the Vicar of St Peter's to write these articles because she has been more directly involved in the story and has got to know the man at the centre of it better than anyone else. In addition, although personally I have no religious commitment, I felt that as a faith leader in Penford, she was in a unique position to interpret the events that have unfolded.

As to why we've chosen to feature the story so prominently, I can answer that very easily. Many of us have spent our entire lives here and know that there is much to be proud of in this town. But Josh Naismith's story has shone a spotlight on the darker side of life in Penford. We can choose to dismiss it as something that happened long ago and has no relevance to us today. Or we can, individually and corporately, consider what our response should be to the story of this remarkable man who has returned after so many years not to demand the justice he deserves, but to offer the forgiveness he believes we all need.

As someone who is committed to the belief that one of the chief purposes of a free press is to ensure that we have an opportunity to hear and respond to truth, I am convinced that the space we have given to this series of articles is fully justified.

The Guest

The Quest

Thirteen

Catch the Wave

Even before *The Gazette*'s four-part weekly series *The Pilgrim's Tale* was halfway through, the debate had not only started, but was already threatening to turn into fierce argument. Initially the discussion centred on whether or not the series should have been published at all. A small though significant minority felt that the editor had made a serious misjudgement in giving so much space over the course of a month to the story. It was a sentiment that was articulated with typical northern candour in a letter to the paper by someone signing themselves as 'Disgruntled Reader'.

> Who does Eddie Shaw think he is, publishing this stuff? I buy *The Gazette* every week to keep me up to date with local news and sport. If I want to read the sob story of some old man who can't get over what happened to him fifty years ago, I'll go to a bookshop and buy a proper biography. If we get any more of this kind of thing, I for one will be cancelling my subscription.

That negative reaction was immediately countered by a score of letters the following week expressing the writers' appreciation for a moving human-interest story. It wasn't clear whether or not Mrs Eagleton of Primrose Gardens had engaged with the deeper issues raised by the articles, but she felt that she spoke for many when she thanked the editor for printing the kind of story that 'gave me the chance to have a really good cry'.

Other letters, however, addressed a wide range of topics arising from Pippa's recounting of Josh's story. Why, in our multifaith culture, was an Anglican vicar allowed to 'take over' a local paper for a month? How could we be sure that the recollections of an elderly man, who wasn't just a recovering alcoholic but who'd also had some kind of breakdown and memory loss, could be trusted? Was *The Gazette* just jumping on the bandwagon by digging up yet another instance of historical sex abuse? Since it was too late to change what happened or to be sure of all the facts after so many years, was there any point in publishing something that could damage the reputation of Penford? And what about the impact on the remaining family members of those whose conduct had been criticised in these articles?

The controversy continued not only in the letters page of *The Gazette* but also wherever Penfordians assembled together. For some weeks it was well-nigh impossible to sit in a pub or stand in a supermarket queue where the story wasn't the main subject of sometimes heated conversation. It was after the final instalment of *The Pilgrim's Tale*, however, that the discussion became more focused and more thoughtful. Josh's comments, quoted verbatim in the article, that forgiveness was ultimately more important than justice, provoked a reaction that neither Pippa nor Eddie had expected.

The letters that now began to arrive at *The Gazette* were of an altogether different character to the earlier correspondence. There was a perhaps not surprising number that took the line that there would always be bad people – the kind who would abuse children or inflict what almost all these writers described as 'mindless violence' on others – and neither justice nor forgiveness would make any difference to people like that. The only answer was to 'lock 'em up and throw away the key', although, in the minds of most of these correspondents, that was definitely a second-choice solution. Hanging would get the job done more quickly and more efficiently, make sure they never got the chance to do whatever they'd done again, and save the country money.

Other contributors offered more considered reflections on the issue. Many put forward the point of view that without justice, forgiveness simply didn't make any sense. It stood to reason, they argued, that you couldn't expect a person to forgive if they were still being treated unjustly. The task facing the allied governments in the Second World War was not to ask those who were interned in Nazi concentration camps to forgive their oppressors, but to bring those oppressors to justice and set their surviving captives free.

Still others equally cogently reasoned that forgiveness meant nothing until the perpetrators recognised the evil of their ways and repented of their wrongdoing. Some questioned whether justice and forgiveness could meaningfully sit side by side in the same sentence, either as alternatives or as related concepts. Surely, they insisted, justice is a public responsibility, something to be achieved by society as a whole through good laws and proper restraints. Forgiveness, on the other hand, is an entirely personal thing, something an individual extends to or withholds from someone who has wronged them.

It was comments like those that were uppermost in the minds of the three people who sat round the scuffed and scratched oak table in the kitchen of St Peter's vicarage, poring over the letters pages in the latest issue of *The Gazette*. The Reverend Pippa Sheppard sat on one side, facing two men of contrasting appearance. One was short, obese and dressed as always in a crumpled navy-blue pinstriped suit and grubby shirt and tie. Pippa sometimes wondered if he wore the same clothes every day or whether he had several suits all of the same material and in the same shabby state. The other man was tall and thin and his tweed jacket, Argyle sweater and grey flannels gave him the look of a retired academic – which indeed he was – who cared little about keeping abreast of fashion – which of course he didn't.

Pippa had asked Eddie Shaw and Sam Andrews to meet her at the vicarage because of her concern as to how they should respond to the reaction to Josh's story and the ongoing discussion about justice and forgiveness. It was clear that the ripples had spread beyond St Peter's and the pages of *The Gazette*. Something had been set in motion that they couldn't just ignore and hope would go away. The question was, what was to be done? And while she readily acknowledged that Eddie's editorial expertise and Sam's unconventional wisdom would be invaluable, she had also come to accept, albeit somewhat reluctantly, that the mantle of leadership in the matter had fallen on her. She needed their counsel, but she knew that she wouldn't be able to escape the responsibility of making the final decision.

They'd looked at various options – from publishing another series of articles to setting up a conference and inviting some nationally respected authority, perhaps a theologian or a philosopher, to be the keynote speaker. Nothing they came up with, however, seemed to be quite right. Their deliberations had ground to a halt when Sam began to chuckle. Pippa knew from his previous visit that this was likely to be a signal that he was about to suggest there was something they'd missed.

'We're missing the obvious.' His chuckle expanded into laughter and he had to pause for breath before continuing. 'We're missing the obvious,' he said again. 'We don't need to come up with a cunning plan. We don't need to make something happen. We just need to be like surfers. All *we* need to do is to catch the wave. Let it carry us where we need to go.'

It was a figure of speech that set all three of them laughing. There was an absurd incongruity in the image he'd conjured up of an untidy and overweight newspaper man, a retired academic with Parkinson's and an Anglican vicar in her mid-thirties surfing together that brought an abrupt halt to any sensible conversation. When they stopped laughing, Sam was keen to explain what he meant by his metaphor.

'What I'm trying to say is that our job isn't to try to *make* something happen. It's happening already.' He turned and addressed his words to Pippa. 'I'm sure you've often wished you could get your congregation focusing on the really important things instead of all the trivial stuff that so often takes up people's attention in our churches?'

Pippa nodded in agreement and Eddie grinned, beginning to see where Sam was going with this.

'Well, it isn't just your flock here at St Peter's that's talking about forgiveness and justice, Pippa. Half the population of the town is taking part in this debate. All because something happened a few weeks ago that's turned out to be more significant than any of us could have realised at the time. All because *you* took the responsibility for telling the story, Pippa. And all because *you* had the courage to publish it, Eddie.'

Sam was determined to make his point. He pushed himself up out of his chair, breathing heavily from the effort the action demanded of him, and leaned forward on the kitchen table. He looked first at Pippa, then at Eddie. 'We might never get a chance like this again. Probably not in my lifetime. So let's not miss it. This town is already talking about justice and forgiveness. People are up for a debate. So let's make it a proper debate. Let's catch the wave.'

On a Friday evening three weeks later, the challenge of Sam's words had been met. Originally it had been planned to hold the event in the town hall, but the demand for tickets was so high that it had to be moved to the largest indoor venue in the town. Nearly 4,000 people were crammed into the sports hall at the Penford Leisure Centre.

The entire floor area had been covered with protective matting and the usual sports equipment had been replaced by rows of chairs.

A stage had been erected under a banner stretched along the back wall which was emblazoned with the words 'Catch the Wave' in large gold letters. The strapline under the main heading read 'A debate sponsored by *The Gazette*' and, though it was in a smaller font, the editor of Penford's local newspaper had made sure it was still clearly visible from the back of the hall. Such was the level of interest that local radio was recording the proceedings and the regional television station was filming highlights for the following day's news bulletins.

At precisely 7.30, Pippa Sheppard, Eddie Shaw, Sam Andrews and Councillor Betty Ormerod, the recently elected Mayor of Penford, entered through a side door, mounted the temporary steps and took their place on the platform. After Councillor Ormerod had welcomed everyone and given her stamp of civic approval to the occasion, Eddie stepped forward to explain that since *The Gazette* was underwriting the event, he would take the role of chair for the evening. There was some good-natured heckling from the members of the audience sitting on the front rows who could see that their host was wearing a freshly ironed shirt and tie and was looking smarter than they'd ever seen him. But Eddie drew a round of applause by assuring the audience that he'd already forgiven the hecklers for their unkind comments, and things settled down quickly.

The first person to be invited to the stage was the local imam, as a representative of the town's largest faith group after Christianity, much to the delight of the considerable number of Muslims in the crowd. For others in the audience whose only previous understanding of Islam had come from news reports of Islamist terrorism, the thought of being addressed by someone robed in an ankle-length white *thobe* and wearing a *kufi* on his head was at first disconcerting. But it took only a few sentences for them to appreciate that the softly spoken man standing at the microphone was very different from the hate-preachers who sometimes appeared on their television screens.

He began by suggesting that Islam and Christianity had a similar though not identical view of human sinfulness as essentially an offence, not just against other people but also against a God who would judge wrongdoers for their deeds. He spoke briefly about the importance of God's justice, then very quickly he moved on to explain that the most frequently used titles for God in the Qur'an were ar-Rahman and ar-Rahim, names which emphasised his great compassion and mercy. He made reference to the prayer, taught by the Prophet Muhammad, that he often made his own: 'O God, You are most Forgiving One, You love to forgive, so forgive me.' And he left the stage to applause as he suggested that it was a prayer that everyone needed to make, and that everyone needed to offer such forgiveness to each other.

Pippa, who'd been anxious that the event should not be allowed to become an academic lecture or an abstract discussion, or even an escape into religious piety, interviewed three people who were known to her and who had real-life stories to tell of their first-hand experience of forgiveness. Christine, a mother of two young children, who was known to many in the audience and whose husband had been killed while walking home in a hit-and-run accident, spoke honestly about the bitterness and anger she'd felt towards the teenage driver of the stolen car and how she'd had to deal with it.

'It was destroying me and affecting my kids,' she acknowledged in response to Pippa's questioning. 'I had to reach a point of forgiveness for my own sake. I realised that unless I forgave and released the resentment I was feeling, the driver of that car would not only have killed my husband, he would have been controlling me for the rest of my life. I went to visit him in prison and told him I forgave him. He didn't say anything. Just looked at me blankly. But that's his responsibility. Mine is to forgive and get on with my life. I did it for me and my children.'

The next person who joined Pippa on the stage was Ron, a prosperous-looking businessman in his sixties. He began by admitting that it wasn't easy for him to tell his story, but that he did so with the permission and, indeed, the encouragement of his wife who was in the hall. About ten years into their marriage, he confessed, he'd got involved in an affair with his secretary. Eventually a work colleague had seen them together at a hotel and informed his wife. Despite the hurt and sense of betrayal she felt, she forgave him, telling him that she loved him and would not lose her marriage because of his infidelity.

'My trouble was that I couldn't forgive myself,' he told the audience. 'I was utterly ashamed at what I'd done. The fact that she was ready to forgive me almost made things worse. I felt I didn't deserve her forgiveness or her love. It got to a point where I started to think she'd be better off without me. For a time I had very strong suicidal feelings. Fortunately, someone put me in touch with a counsellor who helped me to begin to forgive myself.'

Pippa could sense from the stillness in the hall that Ron's words had struck a chord with his hearers, and she asked him if he could give three simple guidelines for people who, as he had been, were struggling to forgive themselves. He thought for a moment and nodded as he began to answer her question.

'Yes, I can. Firstly, just talking to somebody who knew how to listen meant that I wasn't bottling it up inside like I had been doing. Secondly, recognising that there's a time for guilt and regret. That's right and as it should be. But you can't stay there. I had to leave that behind for my wife's sake as much as for my own. And thirdly, this might sound trite, but it really works for me. Every time the old guilt feelings rear their head – and they still do from time to time – I replace them with thoughts of gratitude. I offer a quick prayer to say I'm sorry for the mistakes of the past and then make a list of all I have to be grateful for right now. It really works for me!'

Both of these storytellers were given the courtesy of polite applause as they returned to their seats in the hall, but nothing that compared to the stomping and clapping that erupted after Pippa's third interviewee had made her contribution. When Stella Brown had mounted the steps to the platform, there were some who wondered what the frail little woman in her late eighties who walked with the aid of a stick could add to the discussion. They didn't have to wait long for an answer. Pippa introduced her with the words, 'Mrs Brown, just tell us about how you've managed to reconcile justice and forgiveness over the years,' and handed her the microphone.

She told her tale with an energy and humour that surprised everyone in the hall. When she was in her mid-sixties, having recently lost her husband, her house was broken into by a teenage addict, out of his mind on drugs, who vandalised the place and smashed up many of her most prized possessions. He was still in the house when she returned but, despite his threats, she somehow managed to keep hold of him for fifteen minutes until the police arrived. And when he appeared in court she testified against him, demanding that since he had a string of previous convictions for burglary, he be given a custodial sentence. The court duly delivered that sentence and the young burglar was sent to a youth custody centre.

By this point, to the interviewer's delight, the audience was split down the middle. One half were ready to get to their feet and applaud the elderly woman who'd demanded justice, while the other half were puzzled and disappointed at her apparent failure to give any place to forgiveness. At this point Pippa stepped in again, this time to ask if that was the end of the story. Mrs Brown shook her head, smiled sweetly and continued.

'No, it isn't the end. It was right that he went to prison. You can't break into people's houses and think you can get away with it or that it doesn't matter. I believe in justice. If we don't have justice the world will just fall apart. But justice and punishment isn't enough. There has to be forgiveness and the chance of a new start.

'I visited him in prison to tell him that I forgave him, and I found out he'd spent most of his life in and out of children's homes. I knew that my forgiveness had to be more than just words.'

'So what did you do?' Pippa asked with a knowing smile.

'Well, on the day he was due to be released, I met him at the prison gates and took him home with me. People said he was a bad lot and I was crazy. But how could I tell him I forgave him and then just walk away? I helped him to get an apprenticeship with a plumber I know and he did really well. He stayed with me for the next six years until the day he got married.'

Pippa laid her hand on Stella Brown's shoulder and beckoned to a man sitting in the front row to stand up. 'Ladies and gentlemen,' she announced, 'let me introduce Mike Brown. The teenage burglar is now Mrs Brown's adopted son, happily married with three kids, and the owner of the plumbing business in which he served his apprenticeship. I don't think anyone needs me to spell out the moral of this story.'

The applause that broke out did not stop until Stella Brown had made her way to the empty seat in the front row beside her son, who stood to embrace here.

Eddie Shaw now invited Sam Andrews to lead into the next part of the evening, and Sam responded, much to the amusement of the audience, by telling Eddie it was time he got off the stage and got some exercise. Eddie duly did what he was told and, to a round of ironic applause, went into the audience, mic in hand, to take questions and comments from the floor. The crowd quickly warmed to the tall, scholarly looking man on the stage who, despite showing signs of advancing years and physical frailty, carried an authority seasoned with a touch of humour, and possessed an ability to interject exactly the right word whenever it looked as if someone might try to hog the mic or forget the etiquette of courteous debate. The evening was going better than the three presenters had dared to hope.

It was almost nine o'clock when the moment everyone was waiting for arrived and Pippa introduced the main guest for the evening.

'Ladies and gentlemen, everyone in this hall is aware, I'm sure, that the recent focus in Penford on the issues of justice and forgiveness has come about because of what happened a couple of days after Christmas when an unexpected visitor turned up at St Peter's Church. I know many of you have read his story in the pages of *The Gazette*.

'Eddie Shaw and I have very different perspectives – some might even say diametrically opposed points of view – on many things. But we have both come to believe that the return of this man to his place of birth and the story he has told us have something very significant to say to us as individuals and as a community. A few short weeks ago we encountered him as The Intruder. Now we welcome him as our very special Guest in our town. Please welcome Josh Naismith to the stage.'

For a moment or two the hall was silent. But then, as people began to catch sight of Josh entering through a side door and making his way to the stage, there was a sustained and growing burst of applause. Pippa couldn't help but think how different he looked to the dishevelled and confused man she'd first seen kneeling at the communion rail of the church just three months earlier. His weathered skin and well-lined features still evidenced the rigours and hardships of his past. But tonight he seemed, if anything, a little younger than his years, and his charcoal, shawl-neck cardigan, hanging loosely over his checked shirt and corduroy trousers, gave him the appearance of the artist he was.

The applause began gradually to subside and Pippa beckoned to him to take one of the leather barrel chairs at the front of the stage. She settled herself in the other and waited while he took the mic from the table in front of him and clipped it carefully to his shirt. In front of such a large audience and with the local media present, Pippa was more than a little nervous as she embarked on what she hoped would be the climax to the entire evening. Josh, on the other hand, seemed relaxed and at ease with the situation. So, after a few initial pleasantries to break the ice, she came straight to the point and posed the first of the two questions that she'd written in block capitals in her notes.

'When we talked together a few weeks ago, Josh, you said something that I quoted verbatim in the fourth instalment of your story in *The Gazette*. It's aroused a lot of interest and even a little controversy. Let me read it to you.' She looked down at the clipboard on her lap. 'You said, "Other folk will call for justice and punishment for those who've done wrong. And they're right to do so. But if justice is all there is, we're all done for, because we're all guilty." Can you explain what you mean by that?'

Josh leaned forward, nodding in agreement that those were his words. It was a gesture that allowed him a moment to gather his thoughts before he spoke. The only noise in the hall came from the constant low hum of the heating system. For almost everyone in the hall it would be the first time they'd ever heard the voice of the man who'd made such an impact on their town, and there was an air of anticipation as they waited for him to speak.

'Yes, those are my words,' he said eventually. 'It's something I've thought about more and more. After what happened to me at school here in Penford, for so long all I wanted was justice. Wrong had been done to me and others and I wanted the person who'd done it, and the people who'd covered it up, to pay the price. And they should have been held to account. They should have paid for it.'

The sound of applause, shouts of 'Hear, hear!' and the noise of feet-stamping could be heard from different parts of the hall. But Josh had more to say on the subject. He waited for the noise to abate and continued.

'The problem was, nobody was listening to me and I was powerless. And it began to eat at me. I couldn't have explained it to you then, but looking back I can see that what was happening to me was what can happen to anybody in a situation like that. The demand for justice can just morph into a desire for revenge. And when that happens, somebody gets hurt. Either you get to the person who did you wrong and you hurt them, or if, like me, you can't get to them, you start to hurt yourself. That's what happened – the running away, the drinking, the self-harming – they were just the ways I hurt myself.'

He stopped to take a drink from the glass of water on the table and Pippa took the opportunity to follow up on her first question. 'But surely you're not suggesting that the demand for justice is wrong? Surely we should never back away from that?'

'Of course not. People *should* be held to account. But justice has to be a bigger thing than just punishing individuals or groups of people who've done something wrong. And what happens when it's not possible to get that kind of justice? The man who abused me is long dead. And all those people who turned a blind eye or covered it up, they're dead too. They'll never be brought to justice. At least not in this life…'

Pippa could sense a restlessness in the audience, who weren't sure where this was heading. She jumped in with another question before he could go any further. 'So what's the *bigger justice* that you're talking about? What does that mean?'

Josh smiled at her eagerness to push him hard for an answer.

'Well, now, I'm glad you've asked me that,' he replied, smiling as he delivered the sentence in the mock-patronising tones of an evasive politician trying to avoid giving a straight answer. But he quickly resumed his previously thoughtful manner. 'Seriously, I really *am* glad you've asked me that. The point I'm trying to make is that meting out punishment and locking up evildoers is a necessary part of justice. I guess you could call it the negative side of justice. But justice itself is a *positive* thing. It's much more about *creating a just society* where everyone is treated fairly and people can flourish.

'I've come back to Penford and I've asked you and Eddie to tell my story, not so that we can find the offenders and punish them. It's too late for that. But maybe my story and my being here will help Penford to be a better place to live in, a more just town. The kind of town where what happened to me and those other lads fifty years ago is less likely to happen again. That would be the best outcome of all this; that would be the "bigger justice" I was talking about.'

Again his words drew a rumble of general approval from the audience. Pippa knew from her previous conversations with Josh, however, that they hadn't yet come to the heart of his thinking on the matter. It was time for the second question she'd written in her notes.

'You've highlighted an important distinction for us, Josh,' she said as she leaned over the arm of her chair and put her clipboard on the floor. 'But I know from speaking to you that you see forgiveness as going beyond that, being in some ways even more important than justice. Have I got that right, and can you talk to us about that?'

Sam and Eddie, who were sitting together on the side of the stage, glanced at each other. This was the crest of the wave they wanted to catch. Neither of them had more than a passing knowledge of the sport of surfing, but they'd seen enough on their television screens to know that it always climaxed either in the ultimate adrenaline rush or in an awkward and sometimes painful fall. They could only wait nervously to see what would happen on this occasion.

Josh pulled a sheet of paper from his trouser pocket and unfolded it very carefully before he began to speak.

'I guessed we'd get to this question in the end. I wanted to keep my answer as clear and brief as possible, so I've actually written it down. Do you mind if I read it out?'

Pippa assured him that she'd be happy for him to do so. He cleared his throat and began to read.

I'm not a politician or a philosopher or a theologian. But, having heard my story, I'm sure you will understand why I have thought long and hard about how justice and forgiveness relate to each other. I can sum up my thoughts in a sentence:

Justice sets the world to rights, but forgiveness sets people free.

Let me try to explain what I mean by that. Justice is all about making sure that society is governed well, that there are good laws, that evildoers are held to account and that people are treated fairly. And those are all really important things without which any community cannot hold together. But I don't believe that any community – whether it's a family, a city or a nation – can survive and flourish without forgiveness.

We all hurt each other at some time and in some way, even when we don't mean to, just because we're human. And, if we don't learn to forgive, justice will never be strong enough to restrain our baser instincts or contain the bitterness and revenge that will be set loose. We've all seen enough evidence of that in the conflicts that have torn nations and peoples apart in recent years.

We need forgiveness. Forgiveness liberates the person who forgives, if they're willing to pay the price. And forgiveness liberates the person to whom it is offered, if they're willing to receive it.

Josh was about to fold up the sheet of paper until Pippa reached over and took hold of his hand. 'Please don't put it away,' she requested. 'I'd like you to read it again, even more slowly, so we don't miss anything. And then I've got one last thing I need to put to you.'

He obligingly did as he'd been asked before slipping the paper back into his pocket and waiting for the final question.

'Thank you,' Pippa said, checking the notes she'd made while he was speaking. 'I wanted to make sure I'd heard what you said right at the end. Forgiveness, you said, liberates both the person who forgives and the one who is forgiven. But you were careful to make it *conditional* in both cases. You very deliberately said the forgiveness works only *if* ... Now I want to know what that *if* is all about.'

'You really *are* listening carefully,' Josh acknowledged with a smile. 'Well, the second *if* is the one just about everybody agrees on. You can only truly receive forgiveness if you're willing to stop doing whatever it is that's causing hurt to the other person. That's pretty obvious to most people. I guess you'd call that repentance, Pippa.

'But it's the first one that doesn't get enough attention. I said that forgiveness liberates the person who offers it, but only if they're willing *to pay the price*. It's one of the biggest lessons I've ever learned. When you've been hurt – *really hurt* – by someone, there's a price to be paid if you're going to forgive them. You have to be willing to carry that hurt in yourself rather than lashing out at someone. You've got to contain the hurt, stop it going any further. And then you've got to find a way of releasing it. It's a hard thing to do, and just as hard to put into words that make some kind of sense. It's something you grasp with your heart rather than understand with your head.

'But that's why I carried that backpack with the stones all the way from Abbotsbridge. It was a way of expressing physically what I knew I had to do emotionally and spiritually.

'After what was done to me here in Penford by someone who claimed to be acting out of religious devotion, it turned me against any kind of religion, but especially Christianity, for a long time. I was really glad to hear the imam speak of the importance of forgiveness in his faith and to hear him say that the God he believes in is merciful and loves to forgive. I guess all the great world faiths agree on that. But there's more to forgiveness, I suspect, than just that it's what God loves to do. I don't think forgiveness is easy, even for God!'

There was an audible gasp from someone in the audience at that last sentence, and Josh suddenly ground to a halt. He looked at his interviewer, wondering if he'd gone too far. But Pippa wasn't about to let him off the hook.

'No, don't stop,' she insisted. 'I sense you've got something more to add. Let's hear it before Eddie winds up the evening and sends us all on our way.'

'Well, I'm slowly coming to understand that the faith that became so difficult for me to accept because of what I'd suffered at the hands of someone who claimed to be religious, actually emphasises the cost of forgiveness. If I've got it right, the gist of the story that the Church will be telling at Easter a few weeks from now is that forgiveness is so costly that even God can't manage it without paying a terrible price. I can't fully understand that intellectually and I certainly can't explain it theologically, but I recognise it from my own experience. And it gives me hope. I've managed to find my way back to Penford. Maybe I can even find my way back to a God like that.'

Pippa had half-expected some applause at the end of the interview, but there was only silence.

Eddie Shaw got to his feet to wind up the evening with some appropriate words. But all he could think of were two simple sentences. 'There's nothing I can really add to that. Thanks for coming, everyone.'

He turned and walked off the stage and the audience began to file quietly out of the hall.

Sam Andrews just smiled.

'In my experience,' he whispered to his companions as they watched the hall slowly empty, 'when people leave like that after an evening like this, they're either preparing themselves to catch the wave or they're trying to slip out quietly to catch the bus home. I've no doubt we'll find out which it is sooner rather than later.'

Fourteen

Saturday Morning Visits

It was just after eight o'clock on Saturday morning and Joe and Pippa Sheppard had an unmistakable sense of déjà vu. They'd gone to bed late after the previous evening's event at Penford Leisure Centre, and they were looking forward to sleeping soundly, rising late and spending a leisurely morning with Harry and Zoe. But someone, having rung the doorbell several times, was beating heavily on the door and shouting loudly. The hoarse voice and strong Glaswegian accent left no room for any doubt as to the identity of the person demanding admission. It could be no one other than Billy Ross, the church caretaker, recently restored to his post following his much regretted relapse following the unexpected discovery of the man who broke into St Peter's.

By the time she reached the bottom of the stairs and opened the door, Pippa's reserves of Christian charity had already drained completely away. 'Billy Ross,' she snapped, 'you'd better have a very good reason for banging on our door at this time on a Saturday morning. And please, whatever you do, don't tell me that you've found another intruder in the church. Or so help me, I'll strangle you with my own two hands.'

Billy looked more than a little put out by this reception. The fact that he was in his standard all-weather working attire of shorts and T-shirt with a bunch of keys dangling from his belt was a clear indication that he'd already been hard at work for some time. And it hadn't occurred to him that the vicar would be less fastidious in carrying out her duties.

For a second or two Pippa wondered if she'd offended him and if he was going to turn on his heel and walk away. She had a sudden panic and in her imagination she could already hear the rumour sweeping round the town about how rude the vicar could be to staff and volunteers at the church. She was just about to summon up a less than totally sincere apology for her off-handed manner when Billy's face broke into a smile.

'Ach, yer kiddin', Vicar,' he said with obvious relief. 'Ye nearly got me there, right enough. For a minute I thought ye were serious. I should ha' known better. You'd never speak to anybody like that. An' ye don't need to worry. There's naebody in the church. But I wanted to show ye somethin'. Can I come in for five minutes?'

The last thing Pippa needed right then was an early morning visitor to the vicarage, particularly one as cheerful as Billy. But there was something about his demeanour that made her think that whatever it was he wanted her to see might just be of more consequence than a discarded polystyrene cup that he'd found under one of the pews. It took a considerable effort of the will for her to ask her guest if he'd like to have breakfast with them. But it was an offer he accepted with such unfeigned appreciation that his gratitude rubbed off on her and she found her spirits begin to lift as the kitchen filled with the aroma of bacon frying.

Joe headed upstairs to check on the children and she and Billy sat down to breakfast together.

'Now,' she said between mouthfuls of bacon butty, 'what is it that's so important that you've got to wake us up on a Saturday morning to tell us about it?'

Billy pulled an envelope from the back pocket of his shorts and pushed it halfway across the table. Pippa, noticing that it had a Glasgow postmark, was about to pick it up, presuming that he meant her to read it. But Billy kept his hand firmly on the envelope.

'Naah, don't read it until ye hear whit I've got to say,' he insisted. 'I need to tell you whit I done.'

Brevity of speech had never been one of Billy's strong points, and his explanation of the events that had preceded the arrival of the letter took several protracted twists and turns before it reached a satisfactory denouement. But after almost ten minutes, during which Pippa initially struggled to curb her impatience, she understood both the importance of what was in the envelope and the reason for his unusually high spirits.

After his flight from the church on the morning of the break-in and his subsequent drinking spree, it had taken Billy some time to get back on an even keel and resume his role as caretaker at St Peter's. His gratitude at the willingness of the vicar and the PCC to keep his job open and trust him again had heightened his sense of shame at his reaction to the sight of Josh Naismith kneeling at the communion rail. It had troubled him to the point where, unbeknown to Pippa or anyone else, he'd plucked up the courage to visit Josh and seek his forgiveness for his behaviour on their first meeting. Josh, who understood his struggles with alcohol, responded positively to his approach, and the two men had actually met several times in the ensuing weeks.

'Ye know, he speaks a lot o' sense, that man,' Billy observed to Pippa. 'See, I've spent maist o' ma life runnin' away from the past. But he talked aboot whit he'd learned – ye cannae put everything right but ye can say sorry and ye can forgive other people.'

And that simple counsel had given Billy the incentive to find out where his ex-wife was now living. He'd written to her, offering his apologies for his drinking and his unfaithfulness, which had been a major factor in the break-up of their marriage. He also told her that he was gainfully employed, attending AA meetings regularly and working hard to maintain his sobriety.

With a look of triumph, he pushed the envelope all the way across the table for Pippa to read.

'This came in the post yesterday. I havnae showed it to anybody else. I wanted you to be the first to read it.'

Pippa opened the envelope, carefully unfolded the letter and read it while Billy looked on.

> Dear Billy,
> Thanks for your letter. It was a surprise to hear from you after all this time, although, funnily enough, I've actually been thinking about you recently and wondering where you were and how you were getting on. I guess we both made

mistakes when we were together and I agree with you that it's time to let bygones be bygones.

I'm not sure if you know, but five years after the divorce went through I married again, a man called Bob McDonald. I don't think you'd know him. He wasn't in our circle of friends back then. He's a good man and it's been a very happy marriage. From what you say, I'm guessing that you're still on your own. I'm glad to know you're managing to stay sober and I hope you're looking after yourself.

It's good to know that you've found regular employment, though I never imagined you working for a church! Not sure what you're old drinking pals would make of that.

The main reason that you've been in my thoughts is that Anna is getting married in August. She still remembers you and talks about you, even though she was so young when you left. She was really pleased when I showed her your letter and she wants to invite you to the wedding. And now that she knows you're staying sober, she'd really like you to give her away. I hope you'll be able to accept.

That's all for now. Let me know what you think about Anna's request. And I hope to see you in August.

Agnes McDonald

Pippa folded the letter up again, slipped it back into the envelope and handed it back to Billy. She was feeling just a little ashamed of her annoyance at his arrival on the doorstep half an hour before.

'Billy, that's lovely. And you will go to Anna's wedding, won't you?'

'Oh, aye,' he responded enthusiastically. 'I widnae miss it. I've no' seen her since she was a kid. Still got a wee photie in ma pocket that I've kept all these years. I cannae go back to the past, but I can dae ma best from here on.'

He stood up, looking happier and more pleased with life than Pippa had ever seen him.

'Well, Vicar, I'll leave ye to enjoy yer Saturday. I've ma work to attend to. Got to make sure the church is ready for tomorrow.'

With that he hurried out of the kitchen, whistling a collection of unrelated notes that made up for what it lacked in any recognisable melody with an undeniable, if untuneful, exuberance.

Pippa was just clearing the mugs and plates from the table and looking forward to the rest of the morning being undisturbed when the doorbell rang again. She took a deep breath and reminded herself to be pleasant to whoever it was this time. To her surprise, the face that greeted her when she opened the door was that of Eddie Shaw. He looked exhausted and his clothes were even more crumpled than usual.

'Eddie,' she exclaimed with genuine concern, 'you look as if you haven't slept all night. Come in.'

He stumbled his way to the kitchen, gasping and wheezing with every step, where he collapsed into a chair and slumped over the table. Pippa suggested that she should call for an ambulance. He shook his head and mouthed that he'd be alright in a moment. It took several minutes before he recovered his breath sufficiently to speak.

'Actually, you're right. I *haven't* slept all night. Too wound up after the debate.'

Pippa filled a glass of water and he drank it slowly as his breathing began to return to a more normal rhythm.

'That was quite an evening. Really got my adrenaline flowing,' he grunted with a half-smile. 'But that wasn't the only thing keeping me awake. And I need to talk to someone about it. Have you got half an hour you can spare me?'

It was already turning out to be a very different kind of day from the one Pippa had anticipated. As someone who was by nature a busy activist rather than an attentive listener, it certainly wasn't the kind of morning she would ever have chosen. But it was becoming clear to her what the task was that was being demanded of her right now.

Joe was just leaving to take the children out for breakfast, having quickly decided on hearing the doorbell for the second time that being Zoe and Harry's dad was a much preferable option to that of playing the role of vicar's assistant on this occasion. Pippa waved her family goodbye and offered up a slightly impatient prayer for extra patience. She settled down to hear what Eddie had to say, thinking to herself just how uneasy she was feeling at the thought of what this man, who was more than old enough to be her father, was about to reveal.

As soon as he started to speak, Pippa could see that he was even more nervous than she was. Eddie had spent his adult life listening to other people talk, reading between the lines of what they said, asking the searching question that would cut to the heart of the matter and expose the truth that needed to be uncovered. It was a role in which he excelled and in which he always exuded confidence. But this was very different and obviously far more difficult for him. As a reporter, he could intimidate the most self-assured individual with his penetrating stare. Now he was struggling to make eye contact as he spoke.

'You've been long enough in Penford to have heard the talk about how I managed to purchase *The Gazette* way back when I was only in my twenties. The rumour that I'd had a big win in some casino is just nonsense. I was a useless gambler. I lost far more than I ever won.

'Then there's always been speculation that my parents, who were both only in their early sixties when they died, must have left me a small fortune. There was no truth in that either. They had a decent standard of living, but they weren't wealthy, and most of what they did have was used up getting me a private education at a posh school. They'd very little money left by the time they died.

'The fact is that I was a disappointment to them when I didn't go on to university after school. And my lifestyle caused them a lot of worry in their last years. I'm not proud of any of that part of my life. The truth about where I got my money from is a whole different story, one that I've never told a soul until now.'

The story that Eddie went on to tell was one for which Pippa was totally unprepared. During his final year at school when he was seventeen, Eddie related, he and a classmate, Tom, were told by a boy in the first form that he'd been molested by Dr Maxwell, the headmaster, a single man with no immediate family. The two boys decided to confront the alleged perpetrator themselves.

'To be honest,' he mused, 'I'm not entirely sure what our motives were and why we didn't report it to the police. Back in those days, of course, there was nothing like the safeguarding policies we have today. Looking back, I think we felt that we imagined ourselves to be some kind of heroes challenging an authority figure. And besides, neither of us particularly liked the man. We thought he was pompous and self-important. I don't know what we expected the outcome would be, but we certainly never anticipated what actually happened.'

What did actually happen was that Dr Maxwell broke down in tears and immediately confessed. He pleaded with the boys to keep his secret. It had never happened before, he assured them, and it definitely wouldn't happen again. If this got out, his reputation would be destroyed, the future of the school would be in jeopardy, and the parents of the boy in question would only be hurt and embarrassed by the resulting publicity.

'Had he stopped there,' Eddie reflected ruefully, 'I think we were ready to accept his explanation and say nothing. That wouldn't have been right, but it wouldn't have been as bad as what did happen.'

Pippa could feel her heart beating faster at the thought of how much worse the story might become. She'd retained enough from her training in pastoral counselling to know that it was important not to register signs of being shocked by whatever she was about to hear. So she consciously took long, slow breaths and waited for Eddie to continue.

'It's hard to believe it from this distance in time, but presumably he thought that we weren't persuaded by his pleas. I can still remember the beads of sweat beginning to run down his face. He was in total panic. Without any warning and to our amazement, he said that he'd got some money put away for his retirement and he'd give Tom and me £15,000 each to keep quiet. We were a couple of teenage boys who couldn't believe our luck. We looked at each other and said we'd take it. And he was as good as his word. Late one evening a couple of weeks later we were summoned to his office when no one else was around and he gave us each an envelope stuffed with cash.'

Now Pippa was racking her brains, furiously trying to think of how to respond meaningfully to such a confession. Her inability to think of anything didn't matter at that moment. For, after a pause to take another sip of water, Eddie continued with his story.

'We'd never set out to blackmail the man. But that's what we did, in effect, by taking his money in return for our silence, though that didn't even occur to me then. I left school and came back north and used the money to fund what was by Penford standards a fairly lavish lifestyle. I'd been home three or four years when I heard from Tom that Dr Maxwell had been charged with the abuse of another pupil and had taken his own life before the case could come to court. I felt really guilty, felt that I had some level of responsibility both for the abuse of the boy and for Maxwell's death.

'I thought about going to the police. I didn't have the courage to do that. But it stopped me in my tracks. Made me think about how pointless and empty my life had become. And that's when I settled down, got married and bought *The Gazette*. The owners at that time were desperate to get rid of it so I got it for a knock-down price. The money I'd got from Maxwell would be worth more than a quarter of a million in today's money. So I could easily afford it.'

He sat back in his chair and shook his head. Pippa gave up all pretence of trying to stay in counselling mode. 'Wow! That's quite a tale,' she said softly. 'But why have you decided to speak about it now? Are you going to do anything about it?'

Eddie put his hands on his knees, closed his lips tightly and breathed noisily through his nose for a second or two. 'When I turned up here on that Saturday morning after Christmas, I thought it was just because I could sniff a good story. Which, of course, it was. But the more I got into it – after I interviewed Frank Cassidy and as I began to know more about what had happened to Josh – it became much bigger than that. It brought back memories of the past and I saw it as an opportunity to go some way to making up for what I'd done.

'I'm not sure how someone like you, Pippa, categorises sins but, as I see it, I've been living most of my life with a *double sin*, if there is such a thing. I covered up for an abuser and put other young boys at risk. But I also abused the abuser by taking his money and allowing him to remain in the situation where a person with his weakness was surrounded by temptation.

'In fact, looking back, I can see that ever since I bought *The Gazette* I've been trying to make up for what I did by throwing myself into my work, by trying to create the best local newspaper that I could, by trying to make Penford a more just town. But last night I realised what I've been avoiding for so long. It's all been built on a lie.'

Eddie was looking and sounding just as tired as when he'd arrived at the door of the vicarage. His voice was hoarse and his breathing was getting heavier as he spoke. But there was, Pippa thought, the faintest glimmer of relief breaking through the gloom of utter weariness that hung over him. He summoned up the energy to finish what he had to say.

'I'm tired, not just because I didn't sleep last night. I'm tired from the constant drain of running a newspaper that claims to deal in truth while I try to hide from a lie that I can never get away from. I'm going home to get some sleep. Then I'm going to tell my story to the police and see where things go from there. I'm not sure how I managed to drive myself here. But I'm not risking driving home again. Would you mind phoning for a taxi, please?'

Just at that moment Joe arrived back with Zoe and Harry. There was no need to call a cab, Pippa assured their visitor, since her husband could immediately be reassigned from his role as childminder to that of taxi driver. She could see that Joe, who'd noticed Eddie's Jaguar parked outside, was somewhat confused by his new assignment. But she gave him the kind of look that carried the unmistakable message that this was not a time for either argument or explanation. Eddie mumbled his thanks and headed slowly to the car with Joe, who was still trying to work out what exactly had transpired while he was out with the kids and why Eddie wasn't driving himself home.

As soon as they'd gone, Pippa made sure that Zoe and Harry were settled in their rooms with enough to do to keep them busy for the next half hour while she made herself a cup of tea and tried to recover from the shock of what her second guest of the morning had told her. She was still pondering what it all meant and where things would go from here when Joe returned from taking Eddie home.

'Well,' he said, looking utterly bemused, 'are you going to tell me what that was all about? Eddie slept all the way home in the car. I walked to his door with him, but even then I couldn't get more than two words out of him. He didn't even mention his beloved Jaguar Mark II.'

Joe's expression changed to one of incredulity as Pippa recounted her conversations of that morning, first with Billy Ross and then with Eddie.

'And this is all the result of that Saturday morning right after Christmas,' he observed with a wry smile when she'd finished her report of the morning's encounters. 'Where's it all going to end? And when are things going to get back to normal?'

'I don't know,' Pippa wondered aloud rather than addressing her husband. 'I've got a feeling that it might be a long time before things return to what used to be normal. Especially if Eddie makes some sort of public confession – which I think he will, from the way he was speaking.'

They might have remained in this state of slightly shocked reverie had not the doorbell rung for a third time that morning.

'Oh no,' Pippa groaned. 'Not another one, please! I'm not sure I can take even one more unexpected revelation today. Your turn to answer the door, Joe. You've had an easy morning compared to mine.'

Joe returned, followed by Sam Andrews, who'd stayed overnight with one of Pippa's parishioners. He looked at them both and started to chuckle. 'Now, I can see from your faces that you two have had an interesting morning. The morning after the night before, if I'm not mistaken.'

It wasn't just the characteristic flat monotone of his voice that gave Pippa the distinct impression that he wasn't surprised to find them looking perplexed and that he probably wouldn't be troubled when he heard what had happened. Her intuition didn't let her down. As she went through the morning's events for a second time, Sam nodded frequently and gave the kind of knowing grunt that she took to mean he was neither shocked nor unduly alarmed by what she was telling him.

'Just the kind of thing we could have expected,' he said. 'Of course, I couldn't have told you exactly what would happen after last night. I'm not clever enough to do that. But I've been around long enough to know that when people have an encounter with someone who's plumbed the depths of what it really means to suffer and who's paid the price of what it really costs to forgive, it almost always has an impact on them. Either they open themselves up to it, or they close themselves to it. So you'll be wise to prepare yourself for the opposite reaction from some folk to what you've had this morning. And keep a check on yourself as well.'

Pippa began to ask Sam to elaborate on his warning, but he stopped her with a shake of his head.

'No, Pippa. You've had to listen to more than enough of my advice. I've actually come just to say goodbye and thank you for allowing me to get alongside you in this situation. Now it's time for me to get out of your way. I promised Bishop Gerald that I'd be available during his sabbatical, and he'll be back in a few weeks. Besides, this is *your* parish and, to put it bluntly, it's *your* problem and your *opportunity*. From all I've seen, you'll be fine from here on in. And you'll know that not far away there's an old man who'll be mentioning you and Joe in his prayers every day for the next little while.'

Pippa felt a lump in her throat and a tear in her eye at his words. She'd grown fond of Sam in the short time she'd known him and she wanted to hug him, but she was fairly sure that he wasn't the kind of man who was given to such uninhibited displays of affection. She was desperately trying to think of some more appropriate way to express her gratitude when the doorbell rang again, and immediately all thoughts of appreciation were quickly displaced by feelings of irritation at the prospect of yet another visitor before lunch.

Sam noticed the exasperated expression on her face and quickly allayed her fears.

'Don't worry,' he chuckled. 'It's not someone else with a tale to tell. That'll be my grandson to drive me back to Manchester. It's time you two were left on your own. I can show myself out.'

He turned and shuffled out of the kitchen. Joe instinctively wanted to do him the courtesy of seeing him to the door, but Pippa signalled to him to allow Sam to leave by himself. He'd said what he needed to say and he'd completed what he'd come to do. There was, she imagined, something of the Old Testament prophet about him. He would turn up, often unannounced, whenever and wherever he was needed. And once his message was delivered and his task was fulfilled, he would leave with an abruptness that indicated neither discourtesy nor impetuosity, but rather the urgency of a man who had to gather his strength for the next summons, whenever it came and wherever it came from. She was grateful that such a man had come to Penford when they needed him.

There were no more callers that morning at St Peter's vicarage. In the afternoon, the four members of the Sheppard family took a walk along the canal side. Harry and Zoe ran and skipped ahead of their parents, who kept them always within their sight and quickly called them back if they strayed too far or ventured too close to the water's edge.

The children had little understanding of what their parents had gone through in recent days and even less interest in their adult conversation. It was enough for them to know that they were loved and safe and that when they grew hungry and tired there would be good food and a warm bed waiting for them at home. Pippa loved to see them like that and, as they walked along hand in hand, she reminded Joe of the prayer she'd written down when Harry was born and that she'd made every day since then for her family.

> May our kids grow up and may we grow old without ever losing our trust in the love that always surrounds us and the home that always awaits us.

It was well into the evening when they arrived home, and Pippa breathed a sigh of relief that no one was waiting for them. But the day held one more surprise. As he fumbled to put his key in the lock, Joe almost tripped over something that had been left in front of the door. He pulled a flashlight from his pocket to see exactly what the object might be. It was an old, wet and worn rucksack. It was filled with stones and an envelope had been clipped to it. Both of the straps had completely frayed, and it took a considerable effort for him to get his arms round it to pick it up and place it just inside the porch.

Pippa and Joe waited until supper was over and the children had been safely settled for the night before they dragged the rucksack into the kitchen. It felt to them both that they were handling a sacred object as they lifted it together onto the table. Joe took the envelope that was attached to it and handed it to his wife, who opened it carefully and reverently. It was from Chief Inspector Mike Barraclough, the police officer she'd met with Eddie Shaw back in January. She read it aloud.

Dear Reverend Sheppard,

Two of my officers attended an incident early this morning where a stolen car had been driven into the Penford Canal. As the vehicle was being pulled out of the canal, by chance the recovery team also dragged up this rucksack. Regrettably the canal is too often used as a convenient place to dump unwanted items, and normally it would have been taken to the nearby refuge disposal facility.

The sergeant on duty, however, has been following your series in *The Gazette* and realised that this is almost certainly the missing rucksack you referred to in the final instalment. He knew of my interest in the story and brought it to my attention.

We've had a quick look and it appears that the age of the rucksack and the fact that it was holding a weight for which it was never designed resulted in the straps simply wearing away and breaking. You mentioned in your article that Josh had a vague memory of the stones 'sinking into deep water and vanishing from sight'. So it would be reasonable to assume that he entered Penford by the side of the canal and that at some point along the path the straps simply gave way, allowing the rucksack to slip from his back and fall into the canal.

We could, of course, have the forensic team examine it for DNA traces that would confirm beyond all doubt that this is indeed Josh Naismith's bag. But somehow I think that would be both unnecessary and inappropriate. It seems to me that this is a story in which faith and imagination are more important than cold logic and hard proof.

Like I said to you when we met some weeks ago, I have a feeling that this whole affair is more likely to be understood from the wider perspective of faith rather than from the narrower focus on facts that characterises my work. And even a cynical career police officer like me wants to believe that when Josh Naismith's burden fell from his back just as he was getting near to his destination, something more than mere chance was at work.

Anyhow, I'm sure you'll know what to do with this much better than I would.

Sincerely,

Mike Barraclough

Chief Inspector

Pippa folded the letter and put it back in the envelope. She watched in silence as Joe slowly lifted the heavy bag from the table and set it down again on the floor. 'Oh, my Lord,' he groaned. 'It must have been a relief when that weight slipped off his back.'

'Oh, my Lord,' Pippa echoed. 'It's always a relief when you can let go of the stuff you've been carrying.'

Long after the children were asleep, they lay in bed chatting about the day that was almost over and about the days that had led up to it since they had first encountered The Intruder in the church.

'It's an odd thing,' Pippa said, snuggling up to her husband, 'but if anyone was to ask me how all this has impacted my faith, I couldn't give them a neat answer. It's challenged everything I believe and strengthened it at the same time. The truth is that when someone like Donnington can do what he did in the name of religion, I honestly wonder if I can believe anything any longer. But when someone like Josh does what he's done, I know that a faith that's built on someone being willing to pay the price of forgiveness is the only thing that's strong enough to get me through life without despairing of it all.'

She waited for a response from Joe, but all she could hear was his steady breathing. She smiled to herself, and within minutes she too was sound asleep.

Fifteen

Last Things

Pippa turned off the A34 and on to the A339 that would take her the last few miles into Basingstoke. It was the Wednesday before Palm Sunday, and only a few days earlier she'd realised that it was almost two years since she'd visited her parents. Of course, there were legitimate reasons for that. Being the mother of two young children and the vicar of a lively congregation amounted to more than a full-time job. And, since they'd retired, her mum and dad took advantage of their free time and her dad's generous pension to enjoy two or three overseas trips every year, which meant that they weren't always at home during the school holidays. They'd been intending to come up to Penford for a week in July, but Mum had had to go into hospital for a few days and their visit had been cancelled at the last minute. Pippa had seen them at a couple of family weddings and the funeral of an elderly aunt. It was just one of those things. You just don't notice how time goes by so quickly.

That's what she'd been telling herself for some time, and none of it was untrue. In recent weeks, however, she'd begun to admit that there was more to it than that.

Whenever she thought about going to see her folks there was always a reluctance that held her back and that she'd tried to pretend wasn't there. She'd kept it buried for a long time and it was now forcing itself to the surface.

The deeper truth was that the relationship of mother and daughter had always been a difficult one. There hadn't been any major teenage rebellion on her part, nothing that amounted in any way to ill-treatment by her mother, no stand-up arguments, no big falling-out with each other that had driven her away from home. Pippa just felt that in her mother's eyes she didn't match up to her sister, Ann. That snatch of conversation she'd overheard when she was fifteen – the one about her being 'just a nice ordinary child' – had stung her more than she knew. She'd told herself that it was nothing more than a casual remark and that it was childish to give it even a moment's thought. But this year, more than any other, as she prepared for Holy Week, she knew that the hurt she carried and the pain she felt had to be acknowledged and forgiven.

So that morning, after the other three members of her family had left for school and despite needing to prepare for one of the most important weeks in the Church calendar, she made up her mind to act. She sent a text message to Joe saying not to worry, there was something she had to do, and she'd explain everything when she got home late in the evening. And now, at half-past two in the afternoon, she was standing on the doorstep of her parents' house with a large and expensive bunch of flowers in her arms. Her mother was amazed to see her when she opened the door.

'Pippa! What on earth are you doing here? Is everything alright?'

'Everything's fine,' Pippa assured her as she handed her the flowers. 'These are for you. Just to say thank you for everything. And to ask your forgiveness for being busier than I should and being a neglectful daughter. Now, are you just going to stand there staring at me? Or can I come in?'

She stayed with her parents until just after six o'clock. They chatted about all kinds of things, pleased just to catch up on each other's news and be in each other's company. Pippa made no specific reference to what had prompted her visit. Some things, she knew from experience, were better not said. And there was no precise formula of words or pattern of action, as far as she was aware, that had to be followed when seeking or offering forgiveness. It would be enough for them to know that she cared sufficiently to make a 400-mile round trip to visit them. And it would be enough for her to know why she'd made the journey and that she'd been received and welcomed.

When it came time to get back in the car and head home, her dad threw his arms around her and said how much they both loved her. Her embrace with her mother still had that slightly awkward feeling that had always characterised any close physical contact between them. But forgiveness, Pippa was learning, was a journey, not just a destination, and she was glad that she'd set out on that road.

It was almost midnight when she arrived home. She'd called Joe around nine o'clock to let him know that she was safe and to tell him not to wait up for her, but he was standing in his pyjamas at the door waiting for her as she parked her car in front of the vicarage. She started to tell him where she'd been, but he held his finger up to her lips and stopped her going any further with her explanation.

'You can tell me about it in the morning,' he whispered as they tiptoed past Harry and Zoe's bedrooms. 'But I think I know you and your mother well enough that I can guess why you had to go all the way to Basingstoke.'

'I was getting worried that you might be annoyed with me for just taking off like that and leaving you to look after the kids,' Pippa said apologetically, as she got into bed.

Joe turned off the bedside light and pulled the duvet over them both. 'Well, maybe I got just a tiny bit irritated, until I thought about it. Then I realised how comforting it is for mere mortals like me to know that even vicars like you don't always find forgiveness easy.'

She knew it was intended as a tongue-in-cheek comment. But it was one she appreciated, and she fell asleep grateful that she'd married a man who knew that members of the clergy are also members of the human race, and not immune from the weaknesses and struggles of the rest of humankind.

The next morning there was a message on Pippa's voicemail from Eddie Shaw asking if she would meet him at *The Gazette* that afternoon. It was nothing she should be worried about, he assured her. But, since it related to the edition of the paper that would appear the following day, it was fairly urgent. Despite his casual tone, she had the distinct impression that he wasn't nearly as relaxed as he was trying to sound. She immediately cancelled the afternoon appointment that was in her calendar, and by two o'clock she was sitting in the editor's office wondering what it was that required her to be there at such short notice.

Eddie had the galley proof of the next day's front page on his desk. He turned it round so that Pippa could read the headline, 'EDDIE SHAW TO LEAVE THE GAZETTE', and came straight to the point.

'Tomorrow's paper will carry the announcement that I'm stepping down as editor in three months, and that I'll be selling *The Gazette* as soon as I can find a suitable buyer who I can trust to look after it and keep it as a going concern.'

This was the last thing that Pippa had expected to hear. 'But, Eddie...' she struggled to find the words. 'Why? *The Gazette*'s been your life.'

'Yes, it has,' he acknowledged. 'Or maybe it'd be more accurate to say that it's been the substitute for my life, an obsession, something to distract me from the niggling guilt of my treatment of Dr Maxwell and my failure to report the abuse that was going on at my old school.'

He turned the page round and stared at it as if the implications of the headline were only just sinking into his mind. 'The irony is that I've built up a reputation for running a newspaper that's fair and fearless in always telling the truth. But the foundation of it all has been my lack of courage to speak up when I should have done, my abuse of a weak and vulnerable man, and money that wasn't rightfully mine. So I'm coming clean and telling the whole story in tomorrow's paper. I've already been to the police and told them everything. I don't know if they'll take any action. It was so long ago and it's not clear if I broke any law. But that doesn't really matter. What we've all been learning in this town is that there's always a price to pay for justice and forgiveness. And the price I need to pay is to step away from this newspaper.'

Pippa instinctively wanted to persuade him to think again. But she could see that he'd made up his mind, and that what he was doing was honest and honourable, the only way he could be free to receive forgiveness and to forgive himself. To divert him from that course would do him a great disservice. She smiled at him before she spoke. 'You know, Eddie, I'm thinking that for a man who's not religious, you understand what my faith is all about better than I often do myself.'

'Now there's a thought,' he quipped. 'Maybe you should buy *The Gazette* and I'll take over your pulpit. Now that *would* be interesting.'

They both laughed at the thought of such a reversal of roles. Then Eddie's expression changed. 'No, I'm a long way from that. But maybe my perspective on things has changed recently. I'd always thought of faith as being about ticking the boxes, accepting the different dogmas, that kind of thing. I've always struggled with that, though I guess you'd say it's pretty important. But all this stuff with Josh has been making me think. I might even turn up to hear what you've got to say one of these days.'

'Now, that would be a very pleasant surprise,' Pippa replied. 'But I'd better go before I get too excited about it. Joe's got an after-school activity so I'm picking up the kids today.'

They walked to the door together and, as he shook Pippa's hand, Eddie's carefully cultivated façade of northern brusqueness disappeared. 'It's been great working with you, Pippa. I'll miss that,' he said with obvious sincerity, before adding, 'and there's something else I ought to tell you. I'm selling my Jaguar. Now, that's the real sacrifice for me.'

'Eddie, you can't do that,' she replied in mock horror. 'The town won't be the same without you and your Jag.'

'No, it's got to go,' he laughed. 'I'm going to auction it to the highest bidder and give the money to some good cause. A different man needs a different car. You'll see. Who would have thought that a break-in at a church I've only been in a handful of times would have that effect on me?'

He held the door open and Pippa stepped on to the street. Everything looked just as it had done when she'd walked into *The Gazette* offices forty minutes ago, but things were changing, she thought to herself. No Eddie Shaw at *The Gazette*. No light blue Jaguar Mark II driving around Penford. What would happen next, she wondered, and how far would the ripples in this pool reach?

On the very day that Pippa was asking herself those questions, a slim, smartly dressed woman, looking a decade younger than her fifty-nine years and with bright eyes that seemed to take in everything at a single glance, was checking in for the London-bound flight at Tacoma International Airport on the west coast of America. Her luggage consisted of one suitcase and a package measuring precisely twenty-three inches by nineteen inches, which had been painstakingly cushioned in bubble wrap and then covered in several layers of protective packing.

The young man at the check-in desk was adamant that the package, like the suitcase, would need to be placed in the hold. But the traveller with whom he was dealing was not to be easily put off either by his insistence on following the standard company policy or by the increasingly vocal annoyance of the passengers waiting immediately behind her in the line. A supervisor was summoned to adjudicate in this dispute who, to the surprise of the more junior member of staff, instantly recognised the owner of the package, exchanged a few friendly words with her and quickly found in her favour. Not only would she grant the required permission but she would also personally accompany their valued customer to the plane and make sure that a safe place was found in the cabin for what she agreed was precious cargo.

The determined passenger with the important package had decided to make the trip to the country of her birth on a sudden impulse only a couple of days earlier. A painter with a taste for unusual stories that might stimulate her thinking and creativity, she would occasionally take half an hour late in the evening to surf the net for anything that caught her attention. That's when she'd come across a report in the online edition of a local newspaper in the north-west of England. Her attention was initially arrested when she recognised the name of the town. It was a place she'd lived in for some years as a child.

Having made that discovery, she'd followed the story with increasing fascination from the initial break-in at an Anglican church and through the four-part series, written by the vicar, chronicling the life of The Intruder. Instead of her customary thirty minutes, she sat at her laptop printing off the documents she was reading and making copious notes until the small hours of the morning. By lunchtime the following day her mind was made up. She would book a seat on the earliest available flight to London and, immediately on arrival, she would travel north bearing a gift.

When the doorbell of St Peter's vicarage rang at ten o'clock on the Saturday morning, Pippa's reaction was less than charitable. Harry and Zoe were having a sleepover at the home of one of their school friends and wouldn't be home until the afternoon, and she'd been looking forward to a quiet few hours before they returned.

'I don't believe it,' she groaned. 'Don't tell me it's going to be another Saturday like last week. Are you expecting anyone, Joe?'

Joe assured her that he'd no idea who the caller might be but that he'd do the gentlemanly thing and see who it was. He returned a minute later accompanied by a woman carrying a package measuring precisely twenty-three inches by nineteen inches. She made an immediate impact on Pippa before she even said a word. There was a quiet assurance about her that was neither aggressive nor pushy but conveyed the impression that she'd learned how to cope with setbacks and wouldn't easily give up once she'd decided to embark on a course of action.

Pippa suddenly realised that she must have been staring at the woman when Joe gave a theatrical cough in an attempt to alert her to the fact that he was waiting to introduce their latest uninvited guest. 'Pippa, this is Julia Schultz,' he said, just a little louder than necessary to make sure he had his wife's attention. 'She arrived in England from America yesterday, she's come straight to Penford to speak to you, and she has something she wants to give you.'

Joe's introduction left Pippa, who was still struggling to come to grips with the situation, nonplussed and still at a loss for words. What's the right thing to say to someone you've never heard of who's just travelled thousands of miles expressly to meet you? Eventually she pulled herself together enough to introduce herself and invite their American visitor to come through from the kitchen into the front room and take a seat. Fortunately Julia Schultz had no difficulty in knowing what to say.

'Reverend Sheppard,' she said, with an accent that still carried traces of her English roots, 'I'm so sorry to turn up unexpectedly like this.' Then she added, with a twinkle in her eye that left Joe and Pippa in no doubt that she'd immediately summed up the situation, 'I'm guessing from what I've been reading and from your reaction that people turning up unannounced has been happening to you rather too much recently. I guess I owe you an explanation.'

'Well, before we go any further,' Joe interjected, 'let me show you some proper Lancashire hospitality. Let me make you some coffee?'

'Thank you, that's kind of you. But if you don't mind, I'd much prefer tea. Seattle, where I live, is great for coffee, but I'd really love a cup of proper English tea. And I hope you won't think me a pushy American, but I just loved your kitchen when I came in. If I'm not mistaken, that's where you do most of your living. Can we drink our tea there, please? It would remind me of my English childhood.'

So it was that Julia Schultz, her parcel carefully propped up by the side of her chair, sitting at the old kitchen table where so many significant conversations had taken place, began to explain the reason for her journey from Seattle to Penford.

'I moved to the States with my mother almost fifty years ago. We settled on the west coast where I met and married Brad Schultz. I'm a widow now, but if I tell you my maiden name you'll probably begin to understand why I've travelled all this way to meet you. I'm Julia Donnington.'

'Herbert Donnington's daughter!' Pippa gasped.

'Yes, I am,' she answered very deliberately. 'I only discovered all that's occurred here since Christmas when I happened to come across the story online just at the beginning of this week. Whether that was sheer chance or whether something led me to it, I can't say. What I do know is that I had to come and talk to you. Are you alright with that? I would understand if you didn't want to speak to me after what you've learned about my father.'

'No, please,' Pippa responded immediately. 'You've come a long way and we certainly want to hear what you've got to say. The truth is that we've learned a lot, not just about your father but also about ourselves through all this. I'm sure it'll be good for us to learn from what you have to tell us.'

Pippa could see from the look of gratitude and relief on Julia Schultz's face that, even for a woman of her strength of character, it had been a difficult decision to turn up unannounced at St Peter's vicarage.

'Thank you for making this a little easier for me,' she smiled. 'I was just a kid when we left Penford, too young to understand what was going on. I'd made friends at school and I was upset at having to move. And I recall sensing, even at that age, that things were very tense between my parents. But it was only much later, when I was an adult, that my mother told me the story. Even then, I'm not sure she told me the whole truth or even admitted it to herself.'

The story that her mother had told her came as no surprise to Joe and Pippa. Herbert Donnington had had a long history of abusive behaviour prior to his arrival in Penford. For most of their married life his wife had refused to acknowledge what was really going on, even though she must have had her suspicions about his relationship with the teenage boys who seemed to spend an inordinate amount of time at their home.

The events at Penford Grammar School, the persistent rumours surrounding the reasons for his sudden resignation and their hurried departure from the town had brought things to a head. Mrs Donnington confronted her husband, who admitted that he 'might have been a little unwise and over-affectionate' towards his pupils. He promised that nothing like that would ever occur again. Within a year of his taking up his new post, however, the same pattern of behaviour had emerged and again he'd been forced to resign. Mrs Donnington had finally had enough. She left her husband, taking her only daughter with her, and moved to live with her brother and his wife in America.

It was a painful and confusing time for their only child, who was distraught at being separated from her father. She never saw him again. Herbert Donnington, despite his conduct towards other people's children, had been in many respects a good parent and there had never been anything inappropriate in his relationship with his daughter. Her mother had prevented any contact between them and it was only when, without her mother's knowledge, she tried to get in touch with him to tell him she was getting married that she learned of his death at the age of sixty-three.

'You can imagine,' Julia concluded, 'how conflicted my feelings towards him are. The more so because my most lasting childhood memories of life in England are of him teaching me to paint. And I've inherited his talent as an artist. It's my passion and my profession. So there's not a day goes by that I don't think of him. I understand enough now to know that what he did was wicked and destructive, that he did terrible damage to people. To those people he must be a monster. But to me, he was just my dad, my flesh and blood.'

Pippa wished that there was an easy solution to the puzzling contradiction that her guest was facing. What *was* Herbert Donnington? A man or a monster? A loving father or a sexual predator? She sought deep within herself for the right words to respond to her guest.

'The truth is,' she said, as gently as she could, 'there's something of the monster in all of us. We help each other and show each other great kindness. And we hurt each other and do each other terrible damage. We're all flawed creatures in whom good and evil coexist and often fuse together. And I've been learning at a deeper level throughout this whole affair what I've always known, though I've often neglected it in the busy routine of running a church. It's what I'm charged to teach from the pulpit and what I'm ordained to present in all the ministries of the church. The only hope for each one of us – the only way we can ever hope to tame the monster – is that we passionately seek forgiveness for the monster in ourselves and we generously offer forgiveness to other people for the monster in them.'

'Seems like you and I are enlisted in the same course,' Julia laughed. 'We're both majoring in forgiveness. For years I couldn't forgive my mother for taking me away from my father. Then, when she told me the reason we'd left England, I couldn't forgive my father. It left me dry and hard and I completely rejected the faith in which I'd been raised. I came close to a complete mental and emotional breakdown on more than one occasion. But that really does bring me to the reason why I'm here.'

'Well, then,' interrupted Pippa, whose earlier uncharitable thoughts had been banished and whose interest had been captivated by their guest, 'let's take a break. It'll soon be midday. You can relax for ten minutes while Joe and I rustle up lunch. You will stay for lunch, won't you? Let's talk while we eat.'

As they ate the simple but satisfying meal of soup and sandwiches, Julia Schultz told her hosts how her journey back to faith had begun when she came into contact with a Greek Orthodox priest.

'Partly it was the liturgy and mysticism of the Orthodox Church that appealed to my artistic sense and drew me in.

But, even more, it was the fact that, whereas I had always viewed religion as being all about guilt and justice, Orthodox teaching tends to use words like sickness and healing. And, for someone who was as spiritually and emotionally unwell as I was, that was just what I needed to hear. But Father Georgoulis became more than a spiritual guide. He also became my artistic mentor. I'd been earning a good living as a portrait painter for some years, but he was a gifted and experienced iconographer working in the Byzantine tradition.

'At first I found his paintings too "other worldly" for my taste. And, I guess, at the back of my mind was the idea that an icon was some kind of idol. But gradually, as I learned more and started to immerse myself in that tradition, I began to see the beauty and to sense the power of these paintings. What I'd just dismissed as idols, to be worshipped in themselves, became sacred objects that inspired my mind and kindled my imagination and helped me to become more aware of the divine. The experience didn't only change me as a person. It changed how I worked as an artist.'

As she spoke, she reached for the package that she'd kept by her side and began to unwrap it slowly and carefully. 'You're probably wondering what I've got here. Let me show it to you. It's the reason why I've made this journey and turned up at your home.'

The conversation that ensued became the loom on which Pippa could at last weave together the disparate threads of all that had happened in the past three months into a pattern that possessed design and even beauty. And, as they talked, she knew exactly where and when the

striking painting that Julia Schultz had just unwrapped
should be unveiled, and how others might be helped to
discern some purpose in these unexpected events.

Epilogue

The Easter Sunday morning service at St Peter's was drawing to a conclusion with the singing of one of Pippa's favourite hymns which spoke of the importance of forgiving. As the rumble of the organ subsided and the last notes died away, Pippa looked around the crowded building with a very particular sense of satisfaction and anticipation. Christmas and Easter always meant a larger than usual congregation, of course. This, however, was the first time she'd ever witnessed standing room only in the old church. Joe had whispered to her just before the service began that they were all there just to hear her sermon. She'd replied that she hoped that was one of their purposes in attending, but she knew there were other reasons why so many were present. Five other reasons, to be precise: two paintings and three people.

The two paintings, each covered in a purple velvet cloth, were set on easels at the front of the church. And facing the paintings were three people who were sat side by side in the front row. One of them, a man no more than five foot six inches tall, but weighing more than twenty stone, had drawn a spontaneous round of good-natured applause on arrival from the congregation who noticed, to their surprise and amusement, that he was wearing new shoes, a new suit and a smart white shirt.

The man sitting on his left, the same man Billy Ross had discovered kneeling at the communion rail on a cold December morning, was noticeably taller and dressed more casually in a cardigan, checked shirt and corduroy trousers. He'd drawn a very different reaction from the congregation when he'd taken his place just before the service began. As he walked up the aisle, people had stood silently in a moving demonstration of respect for someone who was, at one and the same time, a stranger to them but also one of their own whom they felt honoured to have in their midst.

The third member of this trio was an immaculately dressed white-haired woman who had travelled a long way to be present. She had slipped in unrecognised by anyone and unnoticed by almost everyone to take her place.

Pippa pronounced the benediction and invited everyone to resume their seats. She stepped down from the pulpit, stood by the side of the two pictures and addressed the congregation from her carefully prepared notes that she had placed on the lectern in front of her.

'I'm sure that everyone present this morning is aware of what happened in this church a couple of days after Christmas. In a way that none of us could have envisaged that morning, the unexpected arrival of one man has posed questions and raised issues that have challenged and, I believe, even changed many of us in Penford. It is, I think you will agree, particularly appropriate that on this Easter Day we can begin to draw some conclusions and bring some sense of closure to all that has happened. But it's time to introduce to you the three people sitting in front of me.'

She began by thanking Eddie Shaw, much to his embarrassment, for his commitment to truth-telling and wishing him a long and happy retirement. Her comments brought everyone present to their feet as they responded spontaneously to her words with a prolonged standing ovation. It was, they recognised, the end of an era and Penford wouldn't be quite the same without Eddie at the helm of *The Gazette*.

Then Pippa introduced Julia Schultz, saying only that she'd flown from America to be present, before inviting her to address the congregation. If they had no idea when she stood up who this woman was or why she was present, their attention was immediately arrested when she began by telling them she was the daughter of Herbert Donnington. Soon they were hanging on her every word.

'My father's painting, *A Portrait of Pain*, viewed purely as a piece of art is, many experts agree, a work of considerable merit. The suffering my father inflicted on others during its creation, however, makes it questionable as to whether it has any place in a church. I know that some of you even believe that it should be destroyed. And I would have fully understood if that had happened. However, the decision has been made by the Reverend Sheppard and others that it should remain in the church, if only to remind us that the truth of the faith this church declares is that good can conquer evil, love can transform hate, and new life can flourish where there has been death and destruction.

'I am different from my father in so many ways, and I'm sure you can imagine how what I have learned of the hurt he caused to others troubles me as his own flesh and blood. But I have inherited something good from him. I, too, am an artist, and I have flown to England to make a gift to this church. It is a gift that comes with my apologies for the hurt my family has caused this town. And with my thanks for the welcome I have been given and for the respect I have been shown.'

There was complete silence for several seconds after she sat down, and Pippa feared that she might have made a serious misjudgement in inviting her to speak. But then it came, sweeping across the pews – a great, rolling wave of applause that seemed to carry everything before it. And when it reached the front of the church it swept over a white-haired woman who rocked back and forth as she sobbed for a past whose hurts she would never be able to undo and for a parent whose conduct she would never be able to understand. The tall man sitting beside her turned towards her. He offered no words to comfort her. But he took her in his arms and allowed his tears to mingle with hers until the wave had passed and the storm had begun to abate.

When, at Pippa's invitation, Josh Naismith stood to unveil the two pictures, Pippa sensed that they were about to reach the climax of a strange but wonderful drama. One that she was glad was almost over, but one in which she knew she would always be grateful she had been caught up. Like everyone else in the church, her attention was fixed on Josh as he walked towards the first painting and grasped the edge of the velvet cloth that covered it from view.

'We've all seen this picture before. But perhaps everything that's happened will help us all to look at it with new eyes when I unveil it.' He stopped speaking momentarily, as if he was uncertain whether or not he should say what was in his mind. Then he smiled and continued. 'I know that different churches have different opinions on whether or not we should pray for the dead. But I'm going to take the risk. I unveil this painting, *A Portrait of Pain*, with a prayer in my heart. It is a prayer not only for all those who suffered like I did, but also for the man who painted it and inflicted that suffering. I pray that he too might have found peace and forgiveness in the end.'

The silence that fell on the church was broken only by the soft swish of the velvet as it gently slid from the canvas to reveal Herbert Donnington's painting once more. Josh Naismith stood and looked at it with an expression of sadness that Pippa thought would cause her heart to break. Then, slowly, he began to smile again before turning to the second picture that was still draped in the velvet cloth that Pippa had carefully hung over it early that morning.

'I've only met Julia Schultz in the last couple of days,' he said, the sombre tone of his voice giving way to a joyful, almost youthful, lilt. 'But I am so glad to have had the opportunity of making her acquaintance. She is a good woman and an unusually gifted artist. The work you are about to see is in the tradition of Byzantine iconography. It is an ancient style of painting that is intended to create an attitude of worship and adoration in everyone who takes the time to stand before it.

'I did just that for half an hour last night, and I want to say to you, Julia, that you have succeeded in your task. If your father's painting confronts us with the pain and suffering that are part of life, yours offers us the answer to that pain and suffering. You present us, not with a portrait of pain, but with an image of the love that seeks us, heals us from our hurts and ultimately brings us home. It is a great honour for me to unveil your beautiful depiction of *The Good Shepherd*.'

He invited Julia to stand with him. And, as they stood together, he uncovered the icon. The image that was revealed was in sharp contrast to that on the canvas that stood next to it. Set against a background of gold leaf and with the cross behind Him was the figure of Christ, clothed in a wine-coloured inner garment under the luxuriant folds of His blue cloak. His face had an expression of utter stillness and infinite tenderness. And lying over his shoulders, its front legs securely grasped in His right hand and its back legs firmly held in His left, was the sheep that had been lost, its pure white wool standing out vividly against the deep richness of the darker colours and giving it a prominence that seemed almost to equal that of the Good Shepherd Himself.

It was only later, when the congregation filed slowly past the icon at the conclusion of the unveiling ceremony, that many of them noticed a detail that could be seen only by those who came close enough and who took sufficient time to look long and carefully. On the backs of the hands of the Christ, the hands that held the sheep safe, the nail prints could be seen. They were still wounds. They would always be wounds. But they were wounds that had healed.

They were no longer a source of pain, but a sign of hope. Hope that even the lost can be found, the worst of their sins can be forgiven, and the most grievous of their hurts can be healed.

Later that week, Josh Naismith returned to his cottage in Langborne and resumed his life as an artist. He had been in Penford for only three months, but the manner of his coming and the impact of his presence has not been forgotten. Many Penfordians live in expectation that he might one day return, and that expectation seems to help them to live better lives.

Eddie Shaw has settled into happy retirement and is often seen, to the surprise of everyone who has known him over the years, strolling slowly through the town. From time to time he slips into the back of St Peter's after the service has begun and slips out again just before the end. To those who jokingly ask him if he's 'got religion', he says only that he's just trying to be less of a sinner than he used to be.

Pippa Sheppard continues to combine the roles of a loving wife to Joe, a caring mum to Harry and Zoe and a faithful pastor to the congregation at St Peter's. On days when it all gets a little too much for her or she feels she's in danger of getting bogged down in the routine of her life and ministry, she stops and thinks about The Intruder who turned out to be a Pilgrim and then became the Guest who changed everything.

And Billy Ross has now added the position of unofficial guide to his job as caretaker. If you ever visit Penford and make your way to St Peter's, he will proudly lead you to the little side chapel (now renamed The Pilgrim's Chapel) and show you the two paintings that hang side by side – *A Portrait of Pain* and *The Good Shepherd*. He will also point out to you the pile of stones and the battered old rucksack that lie on the floor between the two pictures. He'll quickly explain that, far from being an indication that he's neglecting to keep the place tidy, they have a very special significance. And, if you have an hour to spare and an ear for a broad Glaswegian accent, he might even tell you about the day he found a stranger kneeling at the front of the church.

Also by Chick Yuill

Where can a man find grace when he no longer believes?

Ray Young, an experienced Christian leader, has been married for almost thirty years. But his once vibrant faith, like his marriage, is steadily fading, and relations with his only son, Ollie, a struggling stand-up comedian, are increasingly strained.

Facing a looming crisis of faith, Ray begins an anguished, escapist affair, only for Ollie to discover his father's infidelity. Confronted by his actions, Ray has one chance to rescue the life that is crumbling around him.

But when tragedy strikes, it seems all hope of redemption is gone...

Rooks at Dusk sensitively explores questions of confession and forgiveness in a world where not everything can be mended, but where there is still reason for hope.

Published by Instant Apostle (978-1-909728-65-3).